STREET LIVES
AN OTLEY WRITERS ANTHOLOGY

OTLEY WRITERS

© The copyright remains with the individual authors.

The right to be identified as authors of these works has been asserted by them in accordance with the Copyright, Designs and Patents Act 1988.

All rights reserved. No part of this publication may be reproduced, stored in a retrieval system, or transmitted in any form or by any means, electronic, mechanical, photocopying, recording, or otherwise, without the prior permission of the author.

A CIP catalogue record for this title is available from the British Library.

ISBN – 9781790373628

Wilson & Canning
BOOK DESIGN AND PUBLISHING

Introduction

Otley Writers are a group of authors who write in a wide range of genres from poetry to fiction and memoir to non-fiction.

The group have published previous anthologies of their work: *The Pulse of Everything, The Darkening Season,* and *Goodbye Mr Nash*, a retirement tribute to the poet James Nash who had been the mentor of the group for many years.

Street Lives is the first anthology with a specific theme. Each writer has chosen a property or properties in Asgard Close in the town of Oakley. It is just as well the street and town are fictitious otherwise Asgard Close would be one of the most dangerous places to live in the UK! Behind the doors live the most eccentric people. There are family scandals, murder and mayhem. Neighbours die or disappear or are haunted by ghosts from the past.

AIREBOROUGH Chronicle

Street Lives

Local historian George Broadbent is continuing his series where he looks at the history of streets in our beautiful town of Oakley.

***

Today I am looking at Asgard Close a street one could say, with its rich layers of architecture, is a microcosm of the history of our town. Let me take you on a tour.

As we walk along the High Street towards the town centre you will find Rowan Lodge, a small, quirky building that once guarded the driveway that leads to Oakley Manor. Records show that a fortified manor house stood here in Norman times. The Carnforth family bought the land in 1450 and still live in Oakley Manor today. The farm and cottages were built in 1730 and the existing Manor, designed Sir Gerald Gibbons, in 1796.

The reason why the farm is named after a dwelling place of Norse Gods is lost in the mists of time. It is quite possible that the farm stands on the site of a Viking settlement or building but I am not aware of any evidence to substantiate this. Interestingly, in the Yorkshire Post of 16 February 1866 there is a report of a sinkhole appearing during the construction of the large villa opposite the farm. It was thought to be caused by the collapse of an ancient mining tunnel. As the tunnel appeared to run under Sir Peter Carnforth's land investigation was discouraged. Even today historians and archaeologists are denied access by the Carnforth family to an area that would tell so much about the history of the town.

The Industrial Revolution brought changes to the town. In 1876 Charles Barraclough built a textile mill on land on the High Street. To house the mill workers, land was bought from the then owner of Oakley Manor and rows of terraced houses were constructed. The stone terrace houses that face onto Asgard Close were the last to be built. The lucky occupants would have enjoyed uninterrupted views across the meadows. Perhaps there may have been some privilege attached to the allocation of these particular houses. Larger Victorian villas were built for the management and professional class of the town with accommodation in the attic space for domestic staff.

The Great War saw the removal of the grand entrance gates and the ornamental fencing on top of the low walls, the metal being recycled to make munitions. Sadly the decimation of the local 'Pals' battalions during the Battle of the Somme brought unimaginable sorrow to the area.

The next stage in the evolution of Asgard Close came in the 1980s. With the import of cheaper textiles from abroad Barraclough Mill closed and the terraced houses were bought by private owners and buy-to-let investors. Then, in 1984 a large housing estate was built on the farmland with bungalows facing the terraced houses. Asgard Close as we know it today came into being; the road was surfaced, street lighting installed, and trees planted along the grass verge.

That brings us up to date with Asgard Close. The next threads of this streets historical tapestry will be woven by the people who live there today.

STREET LIVES

ASGARD FARM

12 11
FARM COTTAGES

10

13

MODERN
DETACHED
HOUSES

ASGARD
CLOSE

14

OAKWELL
MANOR

15

9
8A
VICTORIAN
VILLAS
8B

16

MODERN
BUNGALOWS

17

7
6
5
4
3
2
1

O THE WELL

TERRACE
HOUSES

18
19

ROWAN
LODGE

GAIA'S
GARDEN

OAKWELL ARMS

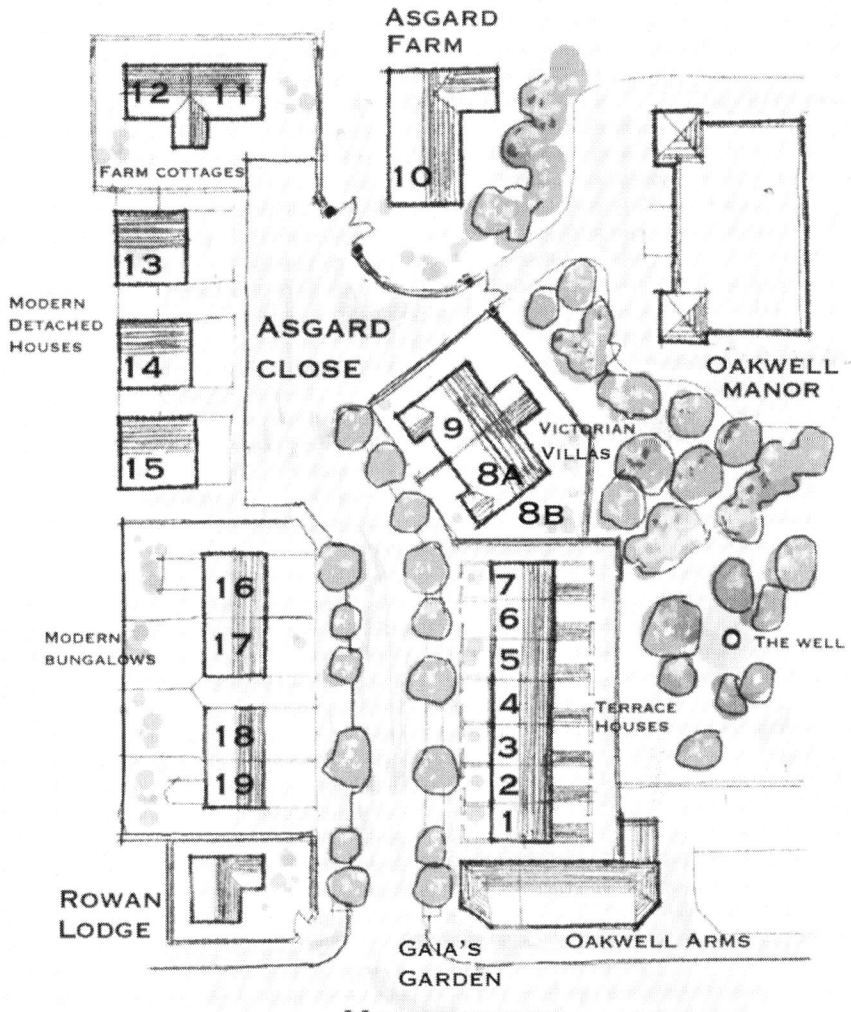

MAIN STREET

'The things that happen to people we never really know. What happens in the houses behind closed doors, what secrets -?'

Harper Lee, To Kill a Mockingbird

Authors by Property

The Oakwell Arms
Suzie and Steve
by
Mari Phillips

Shop
Say It with Flowers
by
Carrie Canning

1 Asgard Close
Empty Houses Talk
by
Pauline Harrowell

2 Asgard Close
Dominic
by
Pamela Line

3 Asgard Close
Amelia Carpenter
By
Alex Williams

4 Asgard Close
The Leavings of War
by
Sandy Wilson

What Lies Under
By
Sandy Wilson

5 Asgard Close
Family Matters
by
Jo Campbell

6 Asgard Close
Pussy's in the Well
by
John Ellis

7 Asgard Close
Tommy's Trench Warfare
by
Christine Nolan

8a Asgard Close
Sweet Peas
by
Cynthia Richardson

8b Asgard Close
Is That a Poem in Your Pocket?
by
Kelly McCarthy

9 Asgard Close
Hairshirt and Locket
by
Pauline Harrowell

Oakwell Manor
All Manor of Things
by
Martin P Fuller

Asgard Farm
Lambing Time
by
Hannah Silcock

Mr Fox
By
Hannah Silcock

11 Asgard Close
From Little Acorns
by
Russell Lloyd

12 Asgard Close
The Enemy Within
by
Carrie Canning

13 Asgard Close
In the Frame
by
Alyson Faye

14 Asgard Close
Alex
by
Jo Campbell

15 Asgard Close
The Dummy in the Corner
by
Cynthia Richardson

16 Asgard Close
An Empty Tin Rattles the Most
by
Serena Russell

17 Asgard Close
Fighting for Life
by
Sandy Wilson

18 Asgard Close
Michelle
by
Alex Williams

19 Asgard Close
Looking After Your Own
by
Polly Smith

Rowan Lodge
When Flowers Talk
by
Carrie Canning

Colonial Gossip
by
Peter Lewis

Street Lives

STREET LIVES

Suzie and Steve

by

Mari Phillips

Suzie sat on the bench in the sharp autumn light. The mottled yellowing leaves gathered in scrunchy piles at her feet and the musty smell seeped into her senses. The sunshine always cheered her when she had a difficult morning, and as mornings went, this was bad. She'd overslept, hangover.com again! She'd had a drink, just the one glass of red wine, to take the edge off the day, then another, until she woke curled up on the scratchy sofa, nursing the empty bottle, her tongue temporarily replaced by sandpaper and a thousand volts zapping her head. She had the fleeting thought that moving in with Steve had been a mistake.

Doreen, her first appointment, was too polite to complain about Suzie's lateness even though she couldn't have breakfast until she'd had her morning dose of insulin from the community nurse. Suzie had struggled to measure it through her puffy eyes and throbbing head and avoided contact with her patient's trusting face.

Suzie sipped her take-away espresso and waited for the caffeine shot to resuscitate her jagged nerves as she planned her afternoon. She wasn't supposed to visit patients in Asgard Close now that she lived there herself, but she had continued to make weekly visits to Miss Fullilove until her recent death, and she had handed over Harry's care to the health visitor. But, because of staff shortages, her manager asked her to continue until a replacement was found. It made for busier days and encroached into her own time. Time she wanted for other things.

She checked her personal phone, scrolling through the messages. Her finger hovered over one titled '*Help Needed*' and she scanned it quickly. It seemed genuine enough: I've been recommended...I'm in such a lot of pain...can you help?' She tapped a response. 'Thanks for your message, will call you later.' She logged the details, then pressed delete.

Her work phone pinged, and she cast her eyes over it before setting off for her afternoon visits, the usual mix of postoperative checks, medications and suppurating ulcers, followed by the unremitting paperwork, now mainly computer entries at the surgery. She also remembered the meeting with her manager; shit, she didn't need that; she already had an official warning for lateness. Suzie recalled that day well: summoned to the office for a meeting to discuss her progress; a euphemism for watch your step, I've got my eye on you. It was just like being in front of the head teacher, but with a guilt trip included ...your patients rely on you...professional standards...blah, blah, blah.

At 5pm, taking care not to be late, Suzie took a deep breath to steady her nerves and knocked on the door.

'Ah come in Nurse Richards,' a voice boomed from beyond. 'Thank you for making time in your busy diary'.

There was a sarcastic edge that Suzie recognised, and she noticed her manager glancing at the clock behind her.

'I'll come straight to the point, I have to tell you that I'm conducting an investigation.'

Suzie felt her mouth dry up and the butterflies on her stomach seemed to be wearing jackboots.

'Of course it may not involve you, but I am speaking to all members of community staff.'

There was a pause and Suzie tried to not to let her anxiety creep into her face.

'There have been a number of deaths recently and whilst not totally unexpected, as these were ill patients, the coroner has drawn our attention to them.'

The manager pushed a piece of paper along the desk towards Suzie. 'Do you recognise any of the names on this list?' she asked.

Suzie scanned the list with feigned professional concern. 'None of these patients were on my case-load,' she answered carefully. 'Would you like to see my diary?'

Suzie rummaged in her bag for her daily notebook and schedule of visits and was thankful she kept the details of her other activities totally separate.

'As I thought. So you haven't visited any of these people?'

'No… no not at all.' Suzie hoped that her manager couldn't see her heart trying to leap out of her chest.

The manager thumbed through the diary and returned it to Suzie; 'Thank you Nurse Richards, if you are sure that you don't know these patients that will be all. I will be in touch again if necessary. She turned to her PC and started tapping the keyboard, indicating that the meeting was over.

At 6pm Suzie slipped in through the back door and shouted, 'Hi Steve, I'm back'. She kicked off her shoes, fumbled her feet into a pair of crocs and made her way to the kitchen.

Steve plonked a glass of wine in front of her. 'How was your day?' he asked.

'Not good', she answered. 'I was late for Doreen, had a stinking headache, spent the morning on catch up and I had to meet the head teacher this afternoon. How about you?'

'All quiet here, trade is slow. If it doesn't pick up soon things might be tricky…' his voice trailed off. 'Sometimes I think there's more action in the Close than here.'

Suzie looked at him closely, but he turned away. Trade wasn't the only thing worrying him, but he didn't like to talk about it.

When Steve disappeared to open up for the evening shift, she headed to the bedroom, shut the door and prepared to respond to her *'Help Needed'* caller. Her call was brief but to the point: a date and time for a visit and confirmation of the address; nothing explicit mentioned over the phone.

Two hours later Suzie popped her head into the oak-panelled bar. It certainly wasn't busy and in the gloom the room appeared larger than usual. There were a couple of unfamiliar faces sitting near the wood-burning stove, which was taking the chill off the October air, and one or two regulars at the counter nursing their pints, lost in their own thoughts. She recognised Frank perched on his stool near the door.

'Evening Frank how are things?'

'So so,' he replied. 'Better than here at any road.'

Suzie nodded in agreement. She remembered that Frank was in the process of clearing out his father's house and worried that even the occasional customers were beginning to notice the dip in trade.

'Is everything a'right our lass? Steve's not lookin' so happy these days,' he mumbled under his breath.

'Yes he's fine,' she lied. There was no need for Frank to know all the details.

'That's good. I'd hate to see the place go downhill like it did with last landlord... went to rack and ruin it did and the beer was rubbish too. Your Steve's really turned this place around.'

Steve pushed another glass of wine towards her. He had his customary small tumbler of beer in his hand, so it was difficult to know exactly how much he was drinking, though he never appeared drunk. As she acknowledged his gesture with a nod, Suzie remembered the first time she met Steve and wondered when everything began to change.

*

It was a night out with her colleagues in some sleazy club in Oakley celebrating someone's promotion; she had been unsuccessful, again, so she was hitting the red wine. She had noticed Steve at the bar. He seemed rather out of place; six foot, fit and dark haired, brooding over a pint and a whisky chaser. She made a point of standing near him as she placed her order and tried her usual chat-up line.

'Hi, what's a nice guy like you doing here alone?'

It didn't work, though at least he looked at her and grunted. She noticed his rather mournful eyes, but they didn't give anything away.

'That's Steve, you won't get 'ought out of him,' the barman replied as he proffered her change. He added. 'He always spends his day off here; you'll find him at the Oakwell Arms the rest of the time.'

Suzie was intrigued; she didn't know the pub, but it was on her patch. A couple of days later, after visiting Harry at number seventeen and George at number nineteen, she decided to stop at the Oakwell before heading home, and there was Steve pulling pints. He recognised her immediately.

'Well hello again - fancy working a few shifts? I could do with some extra help, my bar man just quit.'

Suzie thought it was an unusual chat-up line but emerged some red wine hours later, curiosity and lust coursing through her veins, with plans to meet again the following week. She was more than happy to help out in her spare time and enjoyed pulling a few pints. Steve worked hard to turn around the pub's failing fortunes.

It had taken several weeks and quite a few alcohol fuelled late nights for Suzie to begin to understand Steve's story. He told her about his 12 months' military training at Sandhurst: two overseas tours, then resigning his commission and using his gratuity to set himself up in the trade. The Oakwell Arms had been neglected for years and Steve had transformed it from a dingy junkies' dive to a real ale lovers' pub; the locals flocked back.

Although she had seen Steve's physical scars, the full extent of his Afghan legacy only became clear after a couple of months. Some nights he paced the bedroom unable to sleep and on others she would be woken by his sweaty flailing nightmares, barking orders at imaginary soldiers and then she would find him, at 4am, whisky in hand curled up in a corner of the bar. He gradually told her about the mixture of boredom and stress; the horrors of IEDs; the life changing injuries, surgery and rehab. One day she had walked into the kitchen as he was struggling to open a packet:

'Steve, are you ok? What are you doing?' her eyes widened as she picked up the box and checked the details. 'These aren't your usual meds, where did you get them?'

He turned towards her from the sink, glass in hand and took a gulp of water to delay answering her questions. The words of explanation suddenly morphed into protests,

'I need them...the ones from the doc just don't do anything for me anymore.'

Suzie was speechless – since moving in with him she had discovered that Steve was quieting his emotional demons with alcohol but didn't know he needed extra help for his physical pain.

'How did you get these?' she recognised the odd packaging – it wasn't in English for starters. She tried hard to control her voice.

'Steve, what are these? Tell me for fuck's sake!'

'Fentanyl...' he mumbled, 'I get them online'.

Suzie fingered the packet and avoided his eyes as she took a couple of deep breaths to calm herself. She had discovered that he didn't respond well if she lost her temper. 'OK' she said, 'tell me what's really going on.'

Steve shrugged his shoulders and slumped into the chair. 'The pains in my legs were bad and I couldn't sleep and when I did... the nightmares...' his voice trailed off. '...always the same...faces, blood and limbs tangled up. A mate from Afghan - he told me about this - it's the same stuff some of the medics used out there, but you can't get it from the GP, so I get it off the internet.'

'But how?' Suzie asked. 'You just can't order these like paracetamol?' She knew this wasn't one of the usual drugs used for pain relief.

'It's the dark web,' Steve replied. 'My mate showed me how...and it helps.' He pulled the lap top over and demonstrated how he made the request and explained how the encryption process worked.

'My god,' Suzie said, 'it's another world.'

They had endless discussions, Suzie suggesting he sought help from a different doctor and stop using the Fentanyl, Steve insisted it was the only way he could get any relief, until she was too tired to argue. After that episode he didn't bother hiding it and she realised how easy, but expensive, the whole process was. That sparked the idea for her own business.

*

After her morning visits the next day Suzie took an early lunch break and stopped at a local café for a quick coffee and to use their facilities. She removed the evidence of her usual job: stuffing her ID card into her handbag and swapping her tunic top with the embroidered logo for a more professional looking white shirt and jacket. Fifteen minutes later she was perched on a rather battered Chesterfield and facing a gaunt faced woman.

'How did you find out about me?' she asked. The first visit to a new caller was always a bit tricky.

'I know Jeff, we see each other at the clinic, and he gave me your number.'

Suzie nodded, she preferred word of mouth and Jeff had been a client for a couple of months. The arrangements worked well for him, Suzie visited once a fortnight and delivered a supply of Fentanyl. He didn't have his own computer and wasn't 'IT' savvy, so she supplied the drugs and he paid her in cash. She was careful with the money, it went straight into a separate savings account, though increasingly it was propping up Steve's fragile finances.

'So, Annie,' she said, 'tell me about yourself?'

The stories were always similar; some sort of treatment, not enough pain relief, not coping and often depression. Suzie listened carefully and explained how she could help, finishing up with 'I'd prefer it if you didn't tell your GP about these.'

After about 20 minutes she stood up. 'I'll be back in touch as soon as I can, and I'll need cash. Take care of yourself and remember what I said about keeping this between us.'

Later that evening she looked for the laptop to order supplies for her new client. Steve didn't know about her side-line or how Suzie had watched him accessing the dark web; she was a fast learner. As she removed it from Steve's desk she noticed a couple of official looking envelopes. She extracted the contents carefully; she didn't normally pry but she was getting worried about Steve's behaviour. She gave an involuntary gasp; the situation was even worse than she thought.

When she joined Steve in the bar he appeared tense and was drinking whisky rather than his usual.

'Is everything OK love?' she asked.

'I'm fine. I need to check the beer,' he mumbled and headed for the cellar.

Suzie cast her eyes around; it was like a barn. She knew that he could ill afford to lose customers, but he didn't want to talk about the business, or anything else.

'How about we take some time out tomorrow' she suggested, when he returned to the bar.

'It's my day off and we could at least spend the morning together.'

'Maybe,' he grunted, 'I'll see how I feel.'

'OK' she said trying to keep her voice light. 'But we could have brunch and catch up.'

The next day, Suzie tiptoed out of the bedroom, leaving Steve asleep; after another sleepless night he had finally dozed off at 5am. She made herself a strong coffee and retrieved the letters she had found on Steve's desk. One was from the brewery, a final demand for unpaid bills, and similar from his mortgage lender; even her extra money couldn't help now. As she pondered the problem her work phone buzzed. Shit! She should have turned it off. It wasn't a text but a formal email from her manager. She scanned it quickly: Pending further investigation you are suspended from duty. Please attend a meeting on blah, blah, blah... you may wish to be accompanied by a friend or union representative. That sounded serious, but she deleted it and switched it off; not now, this was her day off!

Steve didn't stir till nearly lunchtime and he wasn't in the mood for brunch. 'Sorry no can do, I've got stuff on. You go without me.'

'Are you sure Steve, I think you could do with a break and we need to talk. I'm worried about you,' she added after a slight pause.

'No, I'm fine, just enjoy your day off. I'll check the stock and then open up. See you later, love you.'

Suzie headed for Oakley. There was no point in arguing with Steve so she hoped that shopping and lunch would distract her and give her time to think. She wouldn't tell him about the email from her boss. Things were going distinctly downhill.

She made a couple of small purchases, a scarf and a pair of ear-rings that caught her eye, but her heart wasn't in it. As she walked back to the pub in the fading light, she stopped for a few moments at her usual bench. Her head throbbed with anxiety, things were getting much too complicated: Steve's drinking, the drugs, his business and now her work. She must talk to him.

The pub was still shut when she arrived; that's odd, she thought, Steve should have opened up by now. She made her way to the backdoor and let herself in and shouted.

'Hey Steve, are you in, is everything ok?'

There was silence and she tasted the acid bile in the back of her mouth; this was all wrong. She checked the bar and the cellar first and then the kitchen and sitting room, but there was no sign of Steve. Upstairs the bathroom door was shut and as she tried to push it open found something was blocking it. She took a deep breath and heaved her shoulder against the wooden panels. As they gave way under her weight and she fell through the doorway she screamed...and her world went black. When she opened her eyes she was slumped on the floor, Frank was standing over her and there were two paramedics squeezed into the tiny bathroom.

'Frank, what are you doing here?' she mumbled.

'I was just passing luv,' he said 'and heard you screaming, thought I'd better see what was going on as the pub was shut. Here, have a sip of this.'

He offered her a small glass of what smelled like brandy and she retched; it never was her drink. He omitted to say he had called the paramedics, though he was pretty sure there was nothing they could do, or that he helped himself to an extra-large measure when he poured hers.

As the paramedics packed their bags, she caught sight of Steve on the bathroom floor, needle still hanging out of his arm; a skeleton of the man she thought she knew. When did it get so bad? Why wouldn't he talk?

'We're sorry for your loss, Ms Richards, there was nothing we could do,' one of them said.

'The police are on their way, they will want to talk to you,' said the other.

'Thanks,' Suzie mumbled automatically. 'Yes, I think they will.' I'm sure they will, she thought to herself.

She stumbled down the stairs, she couldn't feel her arms or legs, and slumped into one of the kitchen chairs. This was the worst day. Moving in with Steve had been a very big mistake!

STREET LIVES

Say It with Flowers

by

Carrie Canning

Many people believe a black hole of nothingness is all that awaits when we die, they're wrong. Communing with a spirit, a ghost, is comforting evidence of another plane of existence. Seeing is believing, I see, I always have, so therefore I believe.

I count myself very lucky to have my little flower shop, so conveniently close to my beautiful cottage, Rowan Lodge and the church, not that I'm religious, it's simply good for business. Thanks to my contact with the spirit world, I've earned myself quite a reputation. My floral displays, bouquets and especially my funeral flowers have that little extra something. Discreet messages of comfort passed on from deceased loved ones. People say, 'How did you know Morgan-Fay?' and I tell them, 'Flowers talk to me, tell me secrets.'

I know some people profess to act as a medium between this world and the spirit world, conjure any spirit they choose and pass messages to loved ones. I have never been so fortunate, the spirits call the shots, they will come to me when they can and if they can. The suddenness of an apparition, of an unexpected, uninvited guest sends a jolt, like electricity, coursing through my veins. Like the time Ernest Buckle visited.

Jean Buckle had been in to the shop to order a floral tribute for her deceased husband Ernest. She was very precise. White Roses, white Calla Lilies, a little green foliage, not too much and a spray not a wreath, nothing morbid. I was getting to work when I sensed someone watching me. Ernest Buckle was standing in the doorway, I felt the familiar hotwire of an adrenalin rush.

'Bloody hell Ernest!' The old man, small and dapper as I remembered him chuckled.

'Sorry lass, I didn't mean to startle you.'

'It's fine Ernest honestly.'

'The flowers, the ones Jean ordered.'

'I'm on with them now Ernest.'

'I know I've been watching, you're very talented Morgan-Fay. The bouquet you made for Jean to celebrate our Golden Wedding was the most beautiful either of us had ever seen.'

'Thank you, that's very kind...'

'I'm here to tell you, Morgan-Fay, Jean ordered these particular flowers for a reason. They're the exact same ones she had in her wedding bouquet.'

'Aw, that's lovely Ernest, did you know Calla Lilies represent beauty and the white Roses, reverence and the hope for a new beginning? I thought that was her message to you.'

The spirit of the old man moved closer.

'I think maybe you're right Morgan-Fay, though I want you to add something to the flowers for me.'

'Oh no Ernest, no way, I can't, Mrs Buckle was very clear.' Ernest smiled.

'I know folk think she's a bit of a tartar, but it was just her way. I need to let her know I'm with her, that I'm watching over her.'

'That's very sweet Ernest but...'

'On our wedding day Jean added a little posy of her own to her bouquet. Some tiny Violets for faithfulness and devotion, Borage for love, Honeysuckle for unbroken bonds, an Oak leaf for strength and Rosemary for remembrance of the day. Please Morgan-Fay, if you would kindly put them in, she'll know it was me, my message.'

'What will I tell her when she asks how I knew?'

'Everyone knows you're eccentric Morgan-Fay, you'll think of something.' Ernest smiled playfully.

'You'll have to tell me again...Ernest...Ernest!' The old man had gone.

As expected, after the funeral Jean Buckle visited the shop. A slight, well-groomed woman. Her face was nothing extraordinary, though her fixed, severe expression had served her well, leaving very few laughter lines to scar her ageing skin.

'Morgan-Fay.'

'Hello Mrs Buckle, how can I help you?' I flicked through the pages of my receipt book, feigning nonchalant interest. The elderly woman wafted towards the counter, her expensive perfume vying with the abundant scent of flowers. Standing directly opposite me, one arm crooked holding a neat navy-blue handbag, she reached out and touched my hand.

'My dear, the posy, in the flowers you did for Ernest, how did you know? Did he tell you about them when he ordered the bouquet for our anniversary?'

'Did I get the little posy right Mrs Buckle?'

'Exactly right dear.'

'I think it's always best to be honest, Mr Buckle didn't tell me when he ordered the bouquet.' Her grip tightened on my hand.

'You see Ernest and I always said, whoever...which one of us...whoever went first would try to let the other know.'

'That's a pact many people make Mrs Buckle.'

'Well then how did you. I'll be honest Morgan-Fay, rumour has it that you commune with..?'

'Let's just say Ernest kept his side of the bargain. He knew you understood the language of flowers, so what better way.'

'Yes I think that would be a perfect Morgan-Fay and thank you my dear, you don't know what this means to me.' Mrs Buckle smiled one of the prettiest smiles I've ever seen.

'Oh before I go.' The old lady fumbled around her handbag taking five pounds from her purse. She folding it neatly before slotting it into the charity box.

'I regularly give to animal charities. Ernest and I always kept cats. We lost our last Queenie two years ago and decided not to get another, our age you see. Now I'm on my own...'

I felt the familiar tingle before hearing Ernest's faint voice. 'Tell her to get one, not a kitten mind, an older cat, one that needs a good home, tell her to call this one Queenie like all the rest.' I glanced around. 'You won't see me Morgan-Fay I'm finding it harder to...' Mr Buckle's voice trailed off.

'Get one Mrs Buckle, maybe not a kitten, an older cat, one that needs a good home, you could call this one Queenie like all the rest.'

'I didn't tell you all our cats were called Queenie dear.'

'Didn't you? I was sure I heard someone say...' Mrs Buckle turned to leave.

STREET LIVES

'You have a very precious gift Morgan-Fay, I can never thank you enough. I think I might give the cat sanctuary a call, seeing Ernest's in agreement.' From that day only necessary pleasantries passed between us. Her stern mask firmly in-situ, Mrs Buckle visited the shop as she always had, every second Friday for fresh cut flowers. In the end I asked, did she get a cat?

'Yes dear, nine years old, sweet little thing, thankfully not much of hunter, clean in her habits and quite a serious nature, though she does have a playful side. Actually we're getting along quite famously, Ernest would have loved her.'

STREET LIVES

Asgard Close

STREET LIVES

Empty Houses Talk

By

Pauline Harrowell

An empty house can tell a story,
if you scrape away the layers,
brush off the dust.
It has invisible archaeology.

You might find where a mother cried
turning her face to the wall,
and the window where a man stared
to glimpse hope's tail-lights fading.

But here are pencil marks to show how children grow
like tree rings, year by year;
there smiling faces drawn on wallpaper,
that earned a telling-off, back then.

Cigarette burns on the windowsill
tell of teenage parties, wild and blithe -
Hendrix on the turntable, free love on the carpet,
gate crashers, that night the police came.

You might discover bathroom smells and sounds:
childhood gurgling, hairspray, Harpic,
but sickness and excess add their tang
with secret sobs behind a banging door.

STREET LIVES

The kitchen, scene of triumphs and disasters;
a perfect soufflé in the striving years,
Smash and Angel Delight when time was tight,
but still, the heart of the place -
windows steaming, tea brewing, washing spinning.
Talk and tears, laughter, love and loss
leave traces for anyone to unearth.

Street Lives

Asgard Close

STREET LIVES

Dominic

by

Pamela Line

'Go out. I'm sick of having you under my feet.' My mother must say that twenty times a day. Where do I go? None of my mates live round here. Everyone in this street is old. All the neighbours in this street are boring. They are either waiting to keel over, ex-convicts or batty. There's a dotty old sod, at number nineteen. His son taps him for cash, spends it down the bookies. Old Mrs Smith, at number sixteen, twitches the curtains all day waiting for the ambulance to come. She calls them every five minutes. Her husband left her for a younger woman, don't blame him, she's a right old bag. At number seventeen, he's a hoarder. He creeps around looking in bins. Went round there to look in the windows. He has stacks of newspapers and magazines piled up; shuffles around patting them as though they're his pets. Mother wants me to go out. What do I do if I go out? Build a tree house? Go scrumping for apples, she says? What's scrumping?

Can't wait to leave home. I'm sixteen this year, then I'm off. I'd rather live in a dog's home than here. My sister, horrible spoilt brat, she's the main reason I want to leave. I hate her. She gets everything she wants. She complains that she is bullied at school, not surprised, she's dead gobby. Dad ignores me, unless it's to tell me off. Mum's too worried looking after other people's kids to bother about me. She says she is interested, but she doesn't understand teenagers. S'pose she was one once, but that was back in the dark ages before they had computers. She used to play with a thing called Game Boy; sounds a bit gay to me. It ran on batteries, ha, ha. Was that because they didn't have electricity?

Not that I'm anti-gay, just not interested. Mothers' asked me if I'm gay. That's because there is a girl at Air Cadets who's asked me if I want to go out with her and I said no; thought that my Dad was supposed to talk to me about these things. He is a twin with two elder brothers. None of them talk to one another. I heard Nannafrog saying to Mum that because there were four boys they were told to shut up and behave. Maybe that's why I don't talk about how I feel; I'm like my Dad. It's like with my mates. They all have girlfriends and talk about what they've done. I don't like it. I hate my sister but if one of them touches her like they touch girls I'll kill them.

We moved in here six months ago. I didn't want to leave the old house, I've always lived there. It was comfortable, not far to walk to rotten school. I hate school; it's boring. It's even worse since my mate Micky died. He was playing football when he died. I don't play football, I can play, but if you go to the school lessons we have to practise. What is the point of that if I can play already? Micky was playing when suddenly he collapsed and died, right there, on the spot. They said that it was a blood clot. I was upset.

Yesterday went in the street to kick a ball about a bit; kicked it into Mrs Smith's garden, at number 16, smashed a garden gnome. I didn't care. It was one of those daft ones with a fishing rod. She'd sat it next to a plastic bucket full of water with the rod dangling in it. Ran in to get the ball, kicked the bucket over. She didn't see me. Probably inside looking through her wedding photographs of when she got married to the pillock that left her, piling on the agony, crying into a lace hankie.

She has a stupid dog. It's a Bitchon Frizzy or summat like that. It barks a lot but it's old and tatty. Was probably asleep on her knee when I went for my ball. Old people are disgusting. The new house, well it isn't a new house, it's a terrace house on three floors. It's not detached like our old one. Mother says that it has, 'more character' and it's, 'in a better area.' She talks rubbish like this most of the time.

'Dominic, come and empty the dishwasher please.'

'It's not my turn, it's hers.'

'Milly has taken the dog for a walk so it's your turn to do something.'

Why do I have to do anything? I didn't ask to be born. Shit better do the dishwasher, or she'll be on about it all day. When I'd finished thought I'd go out before she thought of any other jobs. For once she

STREET LIVES

didn't say, 'When I was a girl we went out in the morning and mother said, I want you back when the street lights come on.'
What did they do all day?

Last night it snowed. I wanted to stay in bed because school was closed. But no, Mum came charging into my room and said that I had to shovel the snow off the pavement all the way to number seven. Why should I? She then went on about how I said that I wanted muscles. I do, I said, but only at the gym; you never spend any money on me.
'Shovelling snow is much better for your muscles than lifting weights at the gym.' I said No! That's when she took my phone away and said that I wasn't getting it back until I had finished clearing the snow, then she stormed off.

God shovelling snow is boring. Got as far as number four when the door opened. There are students living there. They play loud music, but not stuff I like.
'Hi Dominic. Coming to the pub?'
'No, I've got to do this.' They know I'm only 15 and why would I want to go to the pub?
They walked off laughing. It's not fair me having to work, and it's boring, nearly as boring as school.

I could hear them arguing at number five. There was a thumping noise, I heard a woman scream, 'That's it, I'm going home to my mother.'
I carried on shovelling the bloody snow.
The next day, it was still snowing, went to kick the football against the wall. Mum came out to say, 'For goodness sakes, take it somewhere else, you're going to break a window, and clear the paths again.'
It was Saturday so went behind the shop. It was closed, probably for good. He's a right old skinflint; once nicked some sweets, he ran after me, thumped me, made my head bang.
'An' if you tell your Dad I'll do it again, but 'arder.' Nasty sod.
Was kicking the ball hard at the wall when I heard a sneeze. Who was that? Had a look round, saw a foot sticking out from behind a dustbin. It was wearing a sandal. Sandals in February?
'Come out or I'll shoot the ball at you.'

STREET LIVES

Waited a second. A boy, about my age, came out with his hands in the air...what the fuck? He was wearing a dress!

'Do not shoot at me, I no have gun.'

He had a skin like toffee, black curly hair, scared.

'What's your name?' He gave me a blank look.

I pointed at myself, 'Me, Dominic.'

He smiled showing black teeth, pointed at himself and said, 'Me, Aram.'

This was turning into hard work. I stretched out my hand. Hesitantly he came out from behind the bins.

'Are you hungry?' I asked, opening my mouth, rubbing my stomach. He nodded.

'Follow me.'

He held back.

'Come on.' Waved him towards me. He scurried nearer, looking about, frightened.

'Do you understand me?'

'Slowly you speak, please.'

'What you wear under dress?'

'Shirt and how you say? Pants?'

'Take dress off.'

I mimed taking off the dress.

'Why?'

'Just it do, I mean just do it.'

Aram slipped the djebellah over his head, I took it and threw it behind the dustbin. He was shivering. I put my fingers to his lips, whispered 'sh.' Looking left and right, seeing no-one, I took Aram by the hand, slipped out from behind the shop and made my way towards the back door of the house. Opened the door and we crept down the hall.

'Is that you Dominic?' Mother called from the kitchen.

'Yep.'

'Have you finished clearing the snow?'

'Yes.'

'Good. Just making some scones, they'll be ready in ten minutes.'

'Yum, just got to go upstairs for something, back down in a minute.'

The Chronicle slid through the letterbox. The headline read...

STREET LIVES

AIREBOROUGH Chronicle

BOY FLEES FROM IMMIGRANT CENTRE...FEARS FOR HIS SAFETY.

A *fifteen-year-old boy from Libya has absconded from the immigrant centre amid fears that he will try to find his mother. They were separated on landing in Greece. Tragically his mother was drowned, although this wasn't known before he went missing. Due to the inclement weather, the authorities have appealed to the public to contact them if they see anyone answering his description. He is fifteen years old, of slight build, wearing a djebellah and sandals. If you have any information please ring on 07899324491.*

I pulled Aram towards the staircase, pressing my fingers to his lips.
Shit, what a bloody fix. What to do? I couldn't dob him in, couldn't hide him forever.
    I pushed him through the door, closed it. Aram stood in the middle of the room, eyes like saucers.
    'Sit down.'
    He fell onto the bed.
    'All this yours is?'
    'Yes, speak quietly. My sister has ears like a bat. She down there.'
    I pointed to the floor.
    'What is bat?'
    'Never mind.'
    'This palace, my house one room.'
    He stood, walked round touching the desk, the chair, the Xbox, the wardrobe. Then he noticed another door. He opened the door.
    'You have shower, toilet of own, and a window?'
    He touched the Velux. I roughly pulled him away, he cringed.
    'Don't go near the window. If someone sees you...' And pulled a finger across my throat.
    He cowered on the floor.
    'No kill me please.'
    I pulled him up.
    'No, but we must be careful.'

He was shaking, I put my arm on his shoulder.
'No Aram, no kill you.'
Mum shouted, 'Scones ready.'
'I'm going downstairs. Be quiet, won't be long.'
He nodded. I went downstairs to find that the poisonous Milly was already stuffing her face.
'I'm starving, all that shovelling snow. What have you done all day? Nothing as usual?'
Milly poked out her tongue covered in scone and jam.
'Stop bickering kids.'
'Mum he's just put two scones in his pocket, greedy pig.'
'Just in case I get hungry before tea. Shut up.'
'Who was that kid I saw you playing with at the back of the shop?'
'No-one.'
'Right, no-one was wearing a dress thing and you were talking to him.'
There was a knock at the door.
'Who could that be?" and mum went to open the door.
'Good afternoon Madam. We have reason to believe that you have a stranger in the house.'
I froze. Bet it was that weird old bastard at number 17, bet he's a member of the National Front. He must have seen Aram at the window.
'No sorry, there's only us here. Do come in.'
The policeman and his mate came into the kitchen.
'We have a report that someone was seen at the loft window. We have reason to believe that it is a young man who has run away from a detention centre. Do you mind if we have a look around?'
'No, not at all. There is no-one else here except us.'
I whispered, 'Mum, ask them if they have a warrant.'
I'd seen enough police programmes to know that they couldn't search anywhere without a warrant.
Mum laughed.
'Take no notice officer, we have nothing to hide. I'll show you around.'
And they set off down the hall to the sitting room. What to do? There was nothing that I could do, just hope that they would be kind when they found Aram.
Their boots clattered up the stairs.

'Bet you've got him in your room.' Milly was still stuffing her face with scones.

I jumped up and got her head in a headlock. 'One word from you and you're dead.'

'Get stuffed.' she muttered through the crumbs.

They were coming back down the stairs. My heart was in my mouth.

'Thank you Madam. We won't be bothering you again. Probably someone who had seen the news, thought that they were being an upright citizen to report their suspicions. Have a good day.'

'That's OK officer, no harm done. Goodbye.'

What was going on? Why hadn't they found Aram?

'Thanks Mum. What time is tea?' I was itching to get back upstairs.

'Is he under the bed?' asked Milly.

I kicked her under the table; she squeaked.

'Stop squabbling children,' Mum said without looking up.

I dashed upstairs, had a look round, no-one. Whispered, 'Aram, where are you?'

There was a sound in the wardrobe. Aram was curled up underneath a pile of clothes. He cowered like a whipped dog, he was scared.

'Men take me back. Not let them, please.'

I held out my hand. He came out stretching.

'No, I won't let them take you. Here have a scone.'

Aram stuffed it in his mouth. I wasn't going to give him up, but what to do?

If I kept him hidden I could steal lots of food and money, we could run away together, find somewhere to live, in February? Persuade Mum and Dad to let him stay?

I couldn't let him go back to the detention centre. Should I tell him his mother was dead?

'Dom, have you any clean clothes for school tomorrow?' Does she ever give up?

If I dress him in school uniform I could say that he's a mate, bring him back for tea?

'Aram, stay here, don't speak, I won't be long.'

Went down to Milly's bedroom, she was cleaning out her bloody hamster's cage. Brian she calls it! Grabbed the hamster, held it in the air.

'If you scream I'll stamp on it unless you do as I say.'
She made a grab for it, tears rolled down her cheeks.
'What do you want? Mum'll kill you if you hurt Brian.'
'Just listen.'
When I'd finished telling her my plan I popped Brian in my pocket as a hostage, went down to the kitchen.
'Mum what can I do? Empty the dishwasher, do the washing, clean the car?'
Mum looked at me, an amazed look on her face.
'What's all this about? What do you want?'
It was all too much, I cried. I don't remember the last time I cried. It all came out, fell out of me.
'He could be my friend, I haven't got a friend.'
Mum held me, rocked me like a baby.
'Hush, hush, we'll find a way round, fetch him downstairs.'
Bloody Brian squeaked.
'On the way back upstairs, give Milly her hamster.'

By the time Aram and me got back to the kitchen Dad was home. They both welcomed Aram and we sat down to talk.
'You'll have to go back to the centre, don't worry, it won't be for long. I've spoken to immigration. If we vouch for you they will let you come and live here until everything is sorted out. They'll be here shortly.'
'But Dad.'
'Sorry son, there are no 'buts' about it, we have to uphold the law.'

And that is what happened. It took a month, but he's here. He's part of the family. He's taught me a lot. Aram is proud of his new family, so am I. I don't mind emptying the dishwasher and Milly isn't too bad, for a girl.

STREET LIVES

Asgard Close

STREET LIVES

Amelia Carpenter

by

Alex Williams

My branches are dark and drip with sweat. Words swirl on a cheap newspaper and the perfect face of Sabrina Knox looks at me. The photo shows her sickening beauty. She had such an unfair advantage; her extinction was a natural law.

As I study the page, the words come together. The newspaper has received information about her disappearance! It gives the source as Morgan-Fay, who I remember from school.... But she knows nothing, or does she? She says she's a psychic, but I don't buy that. No one else saw what happened? Or did they?

My twigs shake, and I glare at my extremities.

AIREBOROUGH Chronicle

PSYCHIC CLAIMS TO KNOW WHEREABOUTS OF BODY

A 'psychic' who believes she knows the location of the body of a girl missing for 25 years has said police are refusing to act on her information.

Morgan-Fay Jones who claims to possess psychic abilities, says she received a message from beyond the grave revealing the exact whereabouts of the body of Sabrina

Street Lives

> Knox, who went missing on the 7th of June 1993.
> The 15-year-old was last seen walking home from school. Her body has never been found.

I close my eyes and remember how Sabrina grabbed the bag containing my bus pass as I pushed her down the hole. How my bark constricted. How I'd considered going down to retrieve my belongings, but it was so deep I couldn't see the bottom. So instead, I patched up the problem with board, sack and dirt.

The hole was inside an old forgotten folly in the woods around Oakwell Manor. I'd tempted her in with the promise of a cigarette, then pffft, she was gone. The next day, my old padlock secured the folly gate and locked my concerns away with one turn of the key. They never found the body.

Although I had beauty too, Sabrina was the special one, the one who took the boys' hearts. She even caught Andrew's eye. But I wanted Andrew, and, five years after Sabrina's tragic disappearance, he became my husband. It was so sad when he died in a 'riding accident' a few years later. Still, whatever I want I get. It's always been that way. Oh, the power of not caring about people, and the sweet strength it gives me. The advantages are astounding. Over the years, weak, scared animals have peppered my flexible branches and been catapulted off, or kept close, depending on need.

Parasites run up my sides, now they're harder to get rid of than other animals, they cling with tiny claws. Morgan-Fay, ever the crack pot claiming to be psychic. No wonder they're refusing to investigate. But the risk is too high, I need to act.

My solution, for peace of mind, is to go back to the folly, enter the hole and retrieve the bag and bus pass. I need to prepare. Rope ladders, torches, gloves, black clothes. I take a trip to an out-of-town hardware store.

As darkness spreads, I reposition myself deep in the Oakwell Manor wood. The cherished padlock key leaves an imprint in my soft hand as the shadows of solemn trees move through the torchlight. My own darkness weaves amongst them.

STREET LIVES

The bars of the gate, like rows of skinny guards, watch over the folly. I peer between two of them and find the concealed hole still keeps its secrets. There's no one around and I giggle as the fleeing parasites tickle my skin.

The padlock rattles as I shake it. It is different, modern. My key is useless. The hoot of an owl travels through the inky sky and a stricken leaf falls to the ground as I rush back to the car. I dump the bag in the boot and apply a silk blouse, skirt and red lipstick. It's seven o'clock, which is rather late, but never the less I walk up the driveway to Oakwell Manor.

'Hello,' I say, 'I'm from the history society, I want to examine the statue in the folly tomorrow. Could I borrow the key for the padlock?'

'Come in,' he says in a whipped cream voice. I follow him through the hall to a grand drawing room. He rubs his chin and his eyebrows raise. I open my blouse a little at the top. 'Would you like to discuss your needs over a cup of coffee?' he asks.

'I would,' I say, licking my lips.

The soft sofa envelopes my seductive form and we chat at length about the 'history society' and the folly. The coffee and cake are delicious, and he gazes longingly at me. I know what he wants. His eyes linger on my body. This will be easier than I expected.

I am so sleepy.

Asgard Close

STREET LIVES

The Leavings of War

by

Sandy Wilson

Oakley, England 1923

He walked across the room, lifted the lid of the gramophone and fitted a new needle then wound the motor. Sliding a black disc from its card sleeve he turned the surface to the sunlight and inspected it then, satisfied there were no imperfections, laid the record on the green baize-covered turntable. As the record spun, he steadied his shaking hand to place the needle in the groove. Massenet's Thaïs Méditation filled the sunlit room, the andante religioso tempo soaring, yet subdued. He stood by the window for a moment before ascending the narrow stairs to the attic.

The hemp noose already secured around the beam swung a little in the draught from the open skylight. Steadying himself on the chair he hesitated, listening, as the heart-rending strains of the violin melded with the sounds of children at play in the street below. Tears slid down his face and fell to the floor.

As the lifeless body swung above the upturned chair the music died. The gramophone needle hissed aimlessly.

Oakley, England 2016

From the back of the taxi Ben watched buildings flit past the side window; disorderly rows of terraced houses in dull red brickwork or soot blackened stone. He could hear his friends jokes about going to live with the Wildings and to be careful he didn't transform into a White

Walker. It was all far removed from his home in the leafy suburbs of Hampshire.

Thinking of home, his mother came to mind. Ben's choice of Leeds University, a Northern university, had disappointed her. He could hear her voice. 'Why not Royal Holloway or Cambridge?' The social embarrassment! Jude, the son of her best friend had gone up to Cambridge to study medicine. 'Benjamin is studying Modern History at Leeds' wouldn't quite cut it as a conversation gambit in her social circle.

There was a soft squeal of tyres on warm tarmac as the taxi turned into Asgard Close and pulled up outside the house where he would live during his first year at university.

The terrace house was so unlike the bland square boxes where Ben had spent his life as a child. It stood in the middle of a row of terrace houses with a flat facade. Double-glazed windows with white plastic frames had replaced timber sash windows, but the panelled front door was original. The stain glass transom displayed the house number, a green four, entwined with red roses. The soot stained stone walls and steps worn by over a century of shoes and boots spoke to the historian in Ben.

Ben pressed on the bell push and heard the ringing tone deep in the house. He turned to take in the modern bungalows on the other side of the street, let down somewhat by the property opposite which had a decrepit Volvo estate stranded on the overgrown lawn. At the far end of the street he could see a large house and a cluster of cottages that pre-dated the Victorian era terraced houses.

'Hi, you must be Ben?'

Ben turned to see an attractive girl with vivid red shoulder length hair standing in the doorway.

'Process of elimination,' said Amy answering his mild look of surprise with a smile. 'The landlord left a list and you're the last to arrive. I'm Amy.'

'Ah, right? Hello Amy,' said Ben. He dropped his bags at the bottom of the stairs and followed the girl down the narrow passage to the kitchen.

'This is Ben, Josh.'

'Hi Ben,' said Josh smiling as he looked up from his mobile.

There was a thudding noise then a thump as if someone had jumped the last three steps of the stairs, which they had. A thin guy with a thick beard walked in dressed in jeans and a T-shirt screen printed with the name of a band Ben had had never heard of.

'Ethan, Ben. Ben, Ethan.' Flip-flopping her hands Amy made the introductions as Ethan took a chair at the table.

'Coffee everyone? There's beer in the fridge.'

Ben sat down at the table. Looking at the people he would share a house with for almost a year he felt excited, yet nervous.

'Right, we need to set house rules,' said Amy. This was her second year in this house. Last year she shared with three girls. Not setting rules had been a mistake. They had fought like cats. She hoped sharing with three boys would be less fractious. With everything agreed Amy stood up from the table and pinned the list of house rules to the back door.

'Hey, listen, how about we tell each other about ourselves?' said Josh raking his fingers through his long hair. 'As much or as little as you like.'

'Cool,' said Amy smiling. 'I'm Amy Lloyd from Hexham near Newcastle. This is my second year at Uni studying Psychology and second year in this house too. The first year was, like wow! Four girls sharing! Bit of a nightmare! I've a part-time job in the flower shop down the main road. It's owned by the woman who lives in the Lodge at the end of the street. Morgan-Fay's a lovely woman but eccentric! Says she talks to the dead, y'know, when she's making funeral wreaths. Your turn Ben!'

Ben looked around the kitchen. He had been half listening to Amy while he thought how much of his mundane life he should divulge. Should he tell them he had been born on the British military base at Osnabrück in Germany where he spent his childhood? Should he tell them how at six years old he watched through the landing balustrade as his father left, the slamming door still an echo in his mind? Should he risk a mammoth piss take by revealing that due to having an OCD mother who thought eating with one's hands disgusting, he had never eaten pizza?

'Come on Ben, your turn. Spill the beans!'

'Okay. Sorry Amy. Yes, well……. I'm Ben and from Basingstoke in Hampshire. This is my first year at university and I'm studying Modern History...em.... Well it's something I've always been interested in. That's about it.'

'What about you Ethan?'

Ethan looked around at the expectant faces. Tell this lot that your dads banged up for burglary and they'll be putting locks on their bedroom doors, he thought.

'Yeah, right? I'm Ethan from Sheffield. I'm doing Media studies.'

Josh told them he came from Nottingham and that he had always liked designing things. His father was a builder and had encouraged him to become an architect. This was his second year and last year he had lived in Uni Halls. 'I prefer living here. There's a sense of history.'

The three students talked until Amy looked at her watch. 'I'm working at Morgan-Fay's shop this afternoon.'

Ben left the kitchen, gathered his bags together and carried them up the steep, narrow stairs to the attic the only room left when he arrived.

He pushed the door open with his foot and dragged his luggage into the room. He liked the sloping ceilings and the small dormer window. There was a desk standing against the wall at the end of the loft with shelves above.

He sat down at the desk, pulled his laptop from its case and steeled himself for a Skype conversation with his mother. After a few ringtones his mother's face and shoulders appeared on the screen with an array of designer kitchen cabinets in the background. She had been waiting for the call.

'Hello Benjamin. You arrived safely then? I see you're in some sort of attic.'

The stilted conversation dried up with a promise to call again in a few days' time. The journey from London and the effort of talking to his mother had drained Ben. He flopped onto his bed. Looking up through the skylight at the blue sky he thought about his first day of independence. His lonely childhood had given him the ability to live within his own world. When in company he had had to push himself to laugh and converse and enjoy a joke. But, in this house, he felt at ease.

The first week passed in a blur of form filling, finding his way around the maze of corridors to locate rooms and lecture theatres, meeting fellow students and lecturers. Today, Saturday, his first weekend lay in front of him an empty void. Amy had gone somewhere with friends and Josh was on a field trip to do with his course. Ethan was still in bed.

STREET LIVES

He threw back the bedcovers and crossed the room and looked out of the dormer window. The first occupants would have looked out over unspoilt countryside. Ben felt oddly lightheaded. He had the weird feeling he could see the farmland. The green meadows, spattered with yellow buttercup, white daisy and blue cornflower, were intersected by grey dry-stone walls. The pastoral scene in his mind felt familiar. Below him, in the sunlight a girl ran across the street chased by a small black spaniel that danced around her legs. She sat on top of the five-bar gate to the field, looked up and waved her small white hand. Ben's head swam as if he was standing on the deck of a ship in a swell. His legs buckled. He reached forward to grip the window sill with both hands, then sinking to his knees his head fell forward to rest against the wall. Hot tears ran down his face. Ben had no idea how long he had been in that position when the throb of Ethan's 'Grime' music vibrating through the floor boards and his bones seeped into his consciousness. Skepta was singing about guns, swinging his nunchuks and being dissed. As Ben laid his palms flat on the wall to push himself away to stand upright he felt a raised edge on the otherwise smooth wall. A panel of some sort. Under layers of paint that had built up over decades his fingertips detected the shape of screw heads.

Undoing the screws didn't take long. His grandfather had given him a Swiss Army Knife, one of his most treasured, and useful possessions with its cluster of fold out tools. The ancient brass screws had resisted then surrendered with angry squeaks. With the screws removed and lying on the carpet he ran the knife blade around the edge of the panel before levering it away from the wall. He peered into the darkness of the eaves.

He could make out the shape of a box with a man's homburg to one side and on the other a lady's straw hat. The hats were grey with age. Cobwebs like camouflage netting and dust covered everything. The way someone had laid the hats and the box on top of the exposed beams seemed symbolic of a relationship. As if to respect the moment the Hip Hop music stopped, and a door shut with the noise of a gunshot. Ben winced. Ethan had gone out.

Ben laid the box and the hats on his desk and sat down. He picked the homburg up by the rim and turned it around. He had seen black and white pictures of busy street scenes from the early years of the last century. Carts, horse-drawn buses, children looking at the camera lens and men wearing hats like the one he had in his hand. Ben felt a frisson of excitement as he opened the box. It was full of folded letters and, lying underneath, faded photographs.

Ben unfolded the first letter, flattening it out on the table top. Considering its age the paper was surprisingly white, its surface covered with words written in a confident copperplate.

Mrs M Harris
4 Asgard Close
Oakley
Yorkshire
England

28 July 1916

My dearest Maggie

We have completed our training and the battalion is due to leave for the front in the next few days and so the next time I write will be from France. The training has been hard for someone in my sedentary profession, but I have come through it and feel extremely fit.

How is Mr Simmons managing at the school after coming out of retirement? As you have often said he was a good teacher and well liked when you were a child, so I imagine he is coping very well.

I pray that this war will not continue much longer, and I will be back in the classroom and he back in his garden tending his beloved flowers.

How is Ellen? I hope that she has recovered from the bout of chicken pox and is out of bed and up to her usual mischief. Oh, how I miss her! Tell her so. And to take care that Poppy does not get through the gate and into the field! The farmer will be none too pleased, especially if there are sheep………

STREET LIVES

Ben hesitated, stumbled over the words, at the mention of the field gate. He remembered the girl and dog he had seen from his bedroom window.

...........And you, my love? I'm glad to hear you are keeping well and that helping at the school occupies your days. Let us pray that we will not be separated for too long. There are rumours of a grand offensive to push the Hun out of France and Belgium. I am apprehensive but proud that I will play a small part in defeating the German invader. I have composed a short poem expressing these very thoughts.

The Last Full Measure

Towards the field of bloody battle,
We march the long straight road
To answer sabres metallic rattle,
Of a godless foe who would goad.
Peaceful nations to stand and fight
And sacrifice our blood and treasure
For honour, freedom, peace and right,
We will give our last full measure.

Write soon my darling.

With all my love to you and Ellen.

Thomas

Many of the letters were mundane records of uneventful times. Travelling in train carriages, marching through French villages and being transport in omnibuses painted a dull olive green. Then the letters felt weighted by anxiety. The words formed by a shakier hand as if to conceal an unspoken truth. Thomas had arrived at the front.

STREET LIVES

Mrs M Harris
4 Asgard Close
Oakley
Yorkshire
England

22 August 1916

My dearest darling

This is just a short note to let you know we are moving to the front line tonight. By the time you receive this we will have completed our stint and be safely back behind the lines. One is always nervous, but our last spell in the forward trenches was uneventful. So hopefully it will be the same this time...............

As he read Ben felt his eyelids grow heavy and the hand holding the letter fell to his lap. He was floating on a gently undulating ocean, then walking, as if he was wading towards a shoreline. Then the water's drag on his limbs lessened. Shadowy figures around him solidified. Odours laced the air: an acrid stench. As Ben slipped into unconsciousness and stepped into Thomas's world, a large raindrop landed on the glass of the skylight above his head.

    Beneath Ben, in her bedroom on the first floor Amy heard the rumble of the approaching thunderstorm. She threw off the duvet and crossed the room to close the window. Over the rooftops she could see jagged forks of lighting dancing on the horizon illuminating the threatening clouds. Amy closed the curtains, got back into her bed and pulled the duvet over her head. Ever since she could remember, thunder and lightning had frightened her.

    The noise of the advancing storm seeped into Ben's mind and into his dreams. Thunder claps became the sound of exploding shells.

STREET LIVES

The Somme, France. 1916

This bombardment had lasted longer than any Tom had experienced. It had been going on for four hours now without respite. Men hunched forward imagining themselves smaller, reducing their frail bodies in their minds to less than the circumference of their steel helmets. The shells screamed through the air. Violent explosions erupted all around sending tremors through the ground and throwing debris to the sky. Soldiers huddled nearby had their eyes screwed tight, others stared wide eyed into other wide eyes, or stared at nothing at all. Men pressed themselves into the wall of the trench as if they could disappear into the earth, wishing themselves into another place far from this cauldron of hell. Winds swirled and raced along the trench driving dust into open mouths and eyes. Pebbles, earth and debris cascaded on men creating a discordant metallic tinkling on helmets while flickering memories, splinters of their other lives entered heads like small fragments of sharp shrapnel. A steel helmet spun down from the dark heavens hurtled there by a shell erupting further along the trench. The misshapen metal disk struck a helmet next to Tom with a dull clatter, eliciting a curse from the wearer. The watchers wondered at the fate of the owner.

A projectile found its mark. The shell exploded just beyond the parados collapsing a section of the trench. The timbers and sandbags that braced the trench walls and the wattle, the woven stakes and branches, had fallen inward burying several of the men. Tom helped dig soil and drag baulks of timber aside to pull out the living and the dead.

The shelling intensified then stopped. In the silence, officers gave clipped orders and sergeant majors barked instructions. The soldiers mounted the fire steps and prepared to fire.

The machine gun next to Tom began its murderous racket sending an arc of bullets towards the advancing enemy. The first line of Germans where cut down as if a scythe had swung through them, some falling forward, others throwing their arms theatrically in the air. Tom watched as the fallen men were replaced by others stepping and jumping over the dead and wounded. As they reached the barbed wire stretched like a thin serpent across no-man's-land the men in the trench fired their Lee Enfield rifles. It seemed to Tom as if he was at the edge of an ocean. As one grey wave fell to the stony beach there was another behind. Then another.

One of the machine gun crew slid without a sound into the trench, his head a bloody mess. Another machine gunner slumped dead over the gun as the Germans reached the edge of Tom's bay. The sound of gunfire died as desperate hand to hand fighting began as the enemy leaped into the chasm of the trench...........

Oakley, England. 2016

At midnight a clap of thunder crashed above 4 Asgard Close. It was as if the heavens had split. Ben gripped by the terror of his dream fell from his bed dragging the duvet with him and knocking books and his bedside lamp to the floor. He stumbled towards his bedroom door. At that moment a flash of lightning filled the bedroom with a cold blue light driving Ben to the head of the stair.

Amy under her duvet where she had burrowed to hide from an imaginary predator heard a heavy thump on the floorboards above her, then a shout. A door opened and a series of bumps was heard, then silence. She pulled on her dressing gown, padded to her door and opened it a crack. At the bottom of the stairs to the loft she could just make out a pale body in a tight foetal curl.

Amy laid her hand on Ben's back. A sheen of cold sweat covered his trembling body. His eyes stared as if he was in another place.

'Ben!' she said as she draped her dressing gown over his shoulders. 'Ben are you okay?' There was no response.

She banged her fists on Ethan's door. 'Ethan, Ethan....!'

The blue lights of the ambulance glittered on the glossy leaves of the trees and reflected on the wet road. Amy, her sodden red hair like rivulets of blood on her face watched as Morgan-Fay hurried up the street towards her.

'What's happened?' Morgan-Fay asked.

'It's Ben. He fell down the stairs and he's unconscious,' she replied, as the paramedics carried the stretcher through the front door with Josh following them.

'They want to know if Ben's been taking drugs,' said Josh. 'I said no. You don't think so, do you?

'I doubt it. Ethan doesn't think so either and he should know. Ethan says Ben found some letters hidden in his room. They're from a First World War soldier to his wife. He's been reading them all weekend.'

They watched the ambulance drive to the end of the road then listened to the mournful siren as it sped towards the hospital. Morgan-Fay looked towards the house. Framed in the open doorway she could make out a shadow, a ghostly figure of a man. A soldier.

'I think you had better show me these letters, Amy.'

Morgan-Fay asked Amy and Josh to wait in the living room while she sat at the kitchen table reading the letters. She was not alone. The shadowy figure of Tom sat opposite her.

'Tell me Thomas, what do you need me to do?'

'Amy, I must speak to Ben's mother,' said Morgan-Fay. 'It has to be face to face. Have you any idea where she lives.'

'You mean you're going to drive there?'

'Yes. Speaking on the telephone won't do. Won't do at all. There is something in the box she must see.'

'See what?' asked Josh.

'I've no idea, Josh.'

'Well I've an idea! Ben speaks with his mother on Skype, so we can too,' said Amy.

'Em...enlighten me Amy. What is Skype?'

At the hospital, unable to identify any clinical reason for Ben's symptoms the consultant decided the best course of action was to put his patient into an induced coma. Somewhere in his mind Ben felt the prick of the needle and the drug coursing through his veins. Once again, he was at the edge of an ocean the water dragging at his legs as he waded towards shore. The air stank: rotting flesh, human sweat and waste, smoke. It was dark and cold.

The Somme, France 1916

Hunched in the trench Tom hugged his fear tight to his chest as if it were a thick coat in a biting wind. It was that moment between night and day when the stars retreat leaving the planets, a celestial rear-guard in the funereal mauve early morning sky. A memory nibbled away a little of the fear. He was standing with his daughter at her bedroom window, looking out into the night, naming for her Venus, Saturn and Mars.

The thunderous explosions stopped abruptly as the barrage of the enemy defences lifted. In the heavy silence the soldiers got to their feet and a silver hedge of sharp bayonets formed along the dark trench. In their trepidation someone fumbled and dropped their rifle and a nervous officer looked up from his timepiece and shouted at the hapless soldier. Someone nearby had voided their bowels. Then shrill whistles sounded. Men, clumsy in their kit and hampered by their rifles cursed under heavy breaths as they clambered up the crude wooden ladders to swarm into the thin mist that covered the colourless landscape. Tom ran and stumbled with them.

Apart from the officers encouraging shouts and sergeant's curses there was silence. Then just as optimism replaced fear, the chatter of machine guns filled the putrid air.

As Tom ran with his head down he heard the whir and thrum of bullets in the cool air and the meaty thud as they found a random target. A soldier in front spun around, a red mist of blood spraying from his throat. Screams of fear and pain drowned the shouted orders.

An explosion erupted to his right and the concussive force threw him to the convulsing ground. Earth and stones fell like hail and grit bit into his face and dust filled his open mouth. Fighting for breath he turned on his side and looked up. In the drifting fog of smoke and stinking cordite he could see bodies draped on the barbed wire dancing in death as waves of bullets struck and struck again. He watched the grotesque puppetry, his eyes wide with terror.

'Get up you fucker, move!' The Sergeant Major dragged Tom to his feet. 'Kill them Hun cunts!' He could see that those who had survived crossing no-man's-land were pouring into the German trench. Tom followed, sprawling into the bottom of the trench.

'Kamerad! Kamerad!' A German soldier knelt before him waving photographs clutched in his fist. 'Miene Familie!' His face was a mask of terror.

Loud orders were being issued along the length of the captured trench. 'No prisoners. Take no prisoners.' Tom watched as the surrendering Germans were slaughtered in a collective convulsion of violence by those who witnessed friends killed and maimed in the *advance across no-man's-land. 'NO PRISONERS, HARRIS! DO IT, KILL THE FUCKER.' The Sergeant was screaming in Toms ear, 'NO FUCKING PRISONERS!'*

Months of intense training flooded Tom's mind and he bayonetted the German in front of him. Stab, twist, pull. Stab twist pull. Stab, twist, pull. 'Tom! Tom! Stop. He's dead now.' Someone held his arm back. 'He's dead, Tom.' The blood-soaked body slid off the bayonet to slump back against the wall of the trench the lifeless eyes staring at Tom. The photographs released by his lifeless fingers fluttered to the ground as the soldiers, guilt in their eyes, went about the business of arranging the defences to repel a counter attack. In the thick silence that filled the trench Tom bent down and picked up a small square picture. It was of a boy with tousled blond hair smiling at the camera. The son of the man he had murdered, he thought. He put it in his pocket and fell forward, the rim of his helmet cutting into the soft earth of the trench wall. He wept heaving sobs

Oakley, England 2016

The Skype ringing tone stopped, and a face appeared on the-screen.

'Benjamin, this is inconveniently early…..'

'Hi Mrs Brookes, I'm Amy. I'm a housemate of your son, Ben. And this is Morgan-Fay, a friend. We need to talk to you.'

'Why are you using Benjamin's laptop? Has something happened?'

As Amy explained the strange events leading up to Ben's collapse she held up the letters. The open box lay on the desk top beside her.

'So,' said Mrs Brookes looking over the frames of her spectacles. 'These are the letters that you say are causing Benjamin to have these….dreams. Dreams that have caused his admission to hospital. I am worried that drugs are involved.' She had heard of the widespread use of 'weed' amongst students. The odd girl with the red hair and the even odder older woman with dishevelled hair reinforced these thoughts.

'Yes, they were in this box. Ben found it in the attic hidden behind a panel in the wall,' said Morgan-Fay. 'A soldier from the Great War has possessed your son. The soldier's soul is not at peace. Tom, that's the soldier's name asked me to speak with you. To show you the contents of the box.'

'You speak with the dead?' her voice cut through the ether. 'Really, this is becoming more preposterous by the minute!'

Amy held the faded black and white photographs up. 'Please, please look at these photos. You might see something that will help. Help Ben.'

'This is completely ridiculous!' Her eyes darted back and forth across the images on the screen. 'I'm going to get dressed. I'd like you to….Wait! The small square photograph….yes….that one. Hold it still please.'

It was the portrait of the blond-haired child with the mischievous smile. 'mien Gott, mien Gott,' she whispered. 'Felix!'

The dining chair scraped on the tiled floor as she stood up and hurried from the room. Amy and Morgan-Fay looked at each other.

'She's German!'

'Yes.' Morgan-Fay placed her hand over Amy's and smiled reassurance.

Ben's mother's face appeared on the screen, her eyes pools of pain, her lipstick a wound in her ashen face. She held up a photo. It was larger, the image was clearer, the surface smoother. But, it was the same blond-haired child with the mischievous smile.

'The photograph in the box is Felix Roth, my grandfather,' she said. 'How did the photograph come to be in this box?'

'If you could explain who Felix Roth is?' said Morag.

Anna looked out of her kitchen window. A grey squirrel was wrestling with the feeder cage trying to tease peanuts through the mesh. 'I am Anna Roth. Felix Roth was my grandfather. He was not a pleasant man. Some say evil. He polluted my father, and my mother with his Nazi ideology.' Anna hesitated. 'I'm sorry. I am rambling.'

'Take your time,' said Morgan-Fay.

'My great grandfather, Ernst, fought in the Great War. He died during the closing stages of what the British call the Battle of the Somme. Felix, the boy in the picture was his son. He was only five or six years old when his father was killed. Perhaps because of his grief and anger the Nazis' movement attracted him and he joined the Hitler Youth movement. When the Second World War started, he joined the ranks of the SS. Felix had a son, my father.'

Anna put her face in her hands before continuing.

STREET LIVES

'My father survived the war and a War Crimes trial. Later, when I was sixteen he arranged for me to marry a suitable Aryan member of his post war cult. But, I ran away to England and disappeared in London. I met and fell in love with Benjamin's father, a British soldier. Jack Shaw. We moved around various military bases ending up in Osnabrück.'

'In Germany?' said Amy.

'Yes, I was back in Germany, but I was now British for all intents and purposes. As you will now realise my accent is perfect. Except in moments of stress. Sometimes I feel as a spy must do, you know, when they are hiding in a foreign land.'

'So,' said Amy, 'Ben's name isn't Brooke. What happened to his father?'

'He fought in Afghanistan and Iraq. He returned a different person. Not the man I loved. He was violent.'

'PTSD,' Amy said in a soft voice. 'We studied it last year.'

'Yes. We divorced, and I remarried.'

'You must come to Leeds without delay, Mrs Brooke,' said Morgan-Fay.

Amy made the introductions. 'This is Ben's Mum.'

'Right, yeah, Mrs Brookes,' said Ethan. 'The doctors say Ben's good, but they're not sure what's wrong with him.'

'Thank you for being with Benjamin

'No worries, Mrs Brookes. Listen, I've been doing a bit of online research and I came across this picture.' Josh opened the laptop on the kitchen table.

'See, it's the old school building on the main street. It's an Indian restaurant now.' Rows of children smiled at the camera. To the side of his young pupils stood the teacher. A man with a strong face and a dark moustache, his eyes shaded by the rim of a homburg.

'The hat,' whispered Amy. 'That's Thomas.'

'Yes, it is,' confirmed Morgan-Fay. 'Before the war. In happier times.''

'There's something else,' said Josh scrolling to another website. 'This is from the Yorkshire Post. It's dated 12th June 1923. Thomas committed suicide, hung himself.'

Anna broke the silence. 'Well, what do we do now, Morgan-Fay, you are the...em, expert in these matters? I must soon go to Benjamin.'

'Please, Anna. What must be done won't take long.'

They followed Morgan-Fay up the narrow stairs. In the loft a paper lampshade swung gently in the draught from the open sky light. The duvet and books lay scattered on the floor. Anna and the three students turned to look at Morgan-Fay.

'You Anna, must return the box and the hats,' said Morgan-Fay.

'What if anyone else finds the hats and box? Won't they be 'possessed'?'

'No Anna. By replacing the box and the hats Thomas will understand you forgive him.'

'Forgive him for what?'

'Thomas killed your great grandfather. In his eyes he murdered him,' Morgan-Fay explained. 'You see, the Germans, including your great grandfather, were trying to surrender, but the British soldiers were under orders not to take prisoners. It was thought that taking prisoners would hold up the advance. A common practice on both sides, I'm afraid. The death of his father, and the eventual humiliation of a defeated Germany sowed the seeds of Nazi ideology in Felix, your grandfather.'

Anna knelt and placed the box and hats in the recess, then Josh replaced the panel. As he turned the last screw the sun shook itself free from a cloud throwing a flare of light across the floor.

'I want you all to be silent for a moment,' said Morgan-Fay pulling a small note book from her pocket. 'I copied this poem, the last one he sent to his wife from the trenches when he thought he wouldn't survive. I'd like to read it now….'

Remember me

Ask not what happened or how did I die.
It matters not where on this battlefield I lie.
My soul will make the long march home
Along tree-lined roads, across fields' loam
And walk our path through blossom scent
To hold you to me in sorrowful lament

And wipe the warm tears from your face.
For you held me close in this heartless place,
When in trembling terror I wept with fear
As horrors seen peeled back sanity's veneer
Hold in your memory the man you wed,
Not the soldier in this war where virtue fled

Morgan-Fay finished reading the poem, then continued. 'But, Thomas survived the war, only to take his own life, in this very attic. You see, he could no longer bear the guilt. He is here with us now. He wants you, Anna to know how sorry he is that he killed your great grandfather.'

'Of course I forgive him!' Anna whispered. 'Thomas was not a murderer. Such a person could never have written such a beautiful, sorrowful poem.'

The air in the room seemed to dance with an electrical energy and the dust motes floating in the sunlight surged towards the corner. It was as if an invisible object had dissolved leaving a void, a space to be filled. Amy was sure she could hear the distant heart-piercing sound of a violin, and a child's laughter eddying through the open skylight. Tears ran down her face and fell to the floor.

Morgan Faye watched as the ghostly form of Thomas became faint, then vanish. She smiled to herself, pleased that his soul was now at peace and reunited with his beloved Maggie.

Josh's mobile rang. He pulled it out of his pocket. 'Hello. Yeah, that's me……yeah…yeah. Cool! We'll come straight away…' Everyone in the loft looked at Josh. 'That was the hospital. Ben's out of the coma. He's awake and speaking to the nurses.'

Weeping with relief Anna fell into Morgan-Fays arms.

'It is so sad,' Morgan-Fay said. 'We are all the leavings of war. Mothers, fathers, lovers and children. Those left behind, once the politicians and generals have done with our young men.'

STREET LIVES

What Lies Beneath

By

Sandy Wilson

Angela gathered the stems in her left hand as she snipped deftly with scissors she had borrowed from the girl with the red hair. They weren't a bad bunch of kids this year, she thought. Her father's house, Angela's childhood home, had been let to students ever since he had been taken into care. Today Angela had decided to call in and inspect the property on the way to visit her father. Pleased to find everything in good order she had looked out of the kitchen window at the red, white and yellow blooms bright in the sunlight. The girl with the red hair said they were awesome. Angela thought the roses rather old fashioned. Flowers from another time.

She held the blossoms under her father's nose. 'They're from the garden dad. They still grow around the edge of the patio. Remember?'

It was unlikely he would. Geoffrey Simms had been suffering from dementia for over three years. He sat slumped in the high-backed chair his chin rising and falling with the wheezing undulations of his chest.

The fragile fragrance of the roses skirmished with the odours of human waste and decay that pervaded the Sunnyvale Care home. Somewhere a patient cried out, the wail dampened as it travelled along the long carpeted corridors. Jenny squeezed his hand, the skin as thin as paper. Fragments of memory assembled in her mind like a creased picture: her father tying the tall roses to canes while she played with her dolls on the sun warmed paving slabs.

Her father gasped, dragged air into his lungs. 'Your mum......'

'Mum?' Jenny was not sure what shocked her more. Her father talking or her father talking about her mother. She had left their home when Jenny was six years old. Ran off with another man they said. Jenny placed the roses, now arranged in a white vase, on the bedside cabinet. The scent of the roses must have triggered a memory, she thought.

'Dad. What about Mum?' she asked with the care of a poacher tickling a trout. 'Tell me about Mum.'

A brittle silence filled the room. In the corridor: soft footsteps, a trolley rattled past the door. Somewhere a mobile phone trilled bird like.

'Dad, please tell me, tell me about my mum.'

His left eyelid flickered open, and a tear gathered in the corner of the rheumy eye. 'She's buried.'

'Buried? Buried where, Dad?'

'The patio. I buried her under the patio.'

Asgard Close

STREET LIVES

Family Matters

by

Jo Campbell

It was incredible meeting my sister, quite by accident, on that misty day in June.

She hadn't seen me since we were tiny; I wasn't even sure if she remembered. After all, I was never spoken about and I don't think her husband knew of my existence.

Oh well, that could be put right.

She was loading her fancy car when I made my way over and tapped her on the shoulder.

It was just like looking in the mirror.

I told her I'd been watching her for a while (never said how many years). She seemed a little put out at first, but I was always good at playing people, so she soon warmed to me. I think she felt a bit sad, guilty maybe, hearing about the different upbringings we'd had.

She was the lucky one, getting Dad and living on Asgard Close. I got left with the bitch in that shithole of a flat. Nothing like Disney's 'The Parent trap' I can tell you.

We kept our reunion just between us, always meeting somewhere out in the countryside; somewhere quiet, where we could get to know each other well.

Once, I suggested tricking people by swapping lives for a while. She laughed, taking it as a joke.

Perhaps it was. There was no one in my life for her to meet.

Never told her that though.

A year soon passed. I took her a little present on our anniversary meeting.

She didn't get me anything; hadn't realised the significance of the day.

She would.

Embarrassed, she offered me something of hers. I took her jacket. It felt nice.

'Where's your car today?' she asked.

'It was a long walk for you.'

I shrugged and said I didn't mind the walk. My car was in repairs until next week.

She offered to drive me, I asked if I could drive.

She said I wasn't insured. I said it didn't matter.

And it didn't matter.

We were practically the same person anyway. Well at least to the outside world. I'd even had my hair cut the same and been working on those make-up techniques for ages.

It didn't matter when I strangled her.

It didn't matter when I stole her clothes.

It didn't matter when I put her in the boot of the car.

It didn't matter when I took her to the quarry to be covered in pouring concrete.

It didn't matter when I took her husband.

It didn't matter.

STREET LIVES

Asgard Close

STREET LIVES

Pussy's in the Well

by

John Ellis

Deep in Jenny's mind is the unfocussed black shape. Sometimes she clutches at it, but it scuttles away. She wants to see it and yet she doesn't. The feelings that come with the blackness of the thing are too frightening. She buries it deeper and deeper over the years beneath the layers of activity: student life, work, family. She stays tied by this thing to where she was brought up. She can't move away because it isn't right to stray from... what?

It is ten o'clock in the morning of a day in the school summer holidays. There is a knock at the door. Three of her daughter Jane's friends are outside, one on a bike.

'Is Jane coming out?' says a rude girl chewing gum. She has a grubby cowlick hanging over her forehead. The others stare at Jenny. Jenny doesn't like this group; she thinks they might lead Jane astray. But Jane is already there in her old jeans and trainers pushing past her mother.

'Hey! Wait a minute; you haven't asked me.'

Jane looks upwards and sighs.

'Please can I go out,' she mumbles.

'Yes, but watch the traffic, cars come quickly round that...corner.' The little gang have already moved off and don't register Jenny's hesitation. For a fleeting, stomach lurching moment, things fit together in her mind: cars turning fast, girls, bikes; leaving a glimpse. She was a bit younger than them when it happened. She watches the gang disappear round the corner talking and laughing.

*

STREET LIVES

Jenny sometimes gets near to the black thing in a dream which haunts her. She is a small child again and there is a tall man in the kitchen dressed in a black uniform and carrying a helmet. He is asking her mother questions. Has she seen anything unusual? Has she noticed any strangers hanging around in the streets? She can hear voices on a radio he is carrying. He towers above her. She is frightened of him and dreads he is going to ask her things next, but he doesn't. He doesn't even seem to notice her crouching in the corner watching him. Afterwards, her mother looks very serious and tells her that a girl has gone missing. She is crying as she says it is very important that Jenny always stays close to home and doesn't go wandering off. After this Jenny is so scared that she daren't say anything to her mother. Instead she walks away into the hall and falls into a long black shaft, down and down until she wakes up with a jolt sweating and panting.

*

Jenny arrives at the nursery feeling shaky. Her mind is a still dark pool, but turbulent bits of the black thing keep forcing themselves up to the surface. She supervises the children doing some painting and reads a story to a group of toddlers. Then it is time for a sing along. She immerses herself in the nursery rhymes and the tambourine shaking until the leader begins a new song:

> 'Ding Dong bell
> Pussy's in the well'

Something breaks to the surface. She is dizzy and drops the tambourine. She feels she is going into her dream, but she is still awake. She is going to fall into that shaft. Her legs give way and she faints.

*

Her husband Alan sits by her bed and holds her hand.
    'How are you feeling? What happened?'
    'Something's coming back to me a bit at a time.'
    'What sort of thing?'
    'Something nasty from a long time ago.'

STREET LIVES

She can't suppress it any more. She will have to let it come back to her however frightening it is. She thinks about her dream. Was there a girl who went missing? Who was she? She sits on the bed with her lap top and searches through the websites of local papers looking for reports of missing people from the time when she was a little girl. If she could read something, the details might jog her memory.

She can't find anything, but this is her only lead, so she decides to go to the police station and make enquiries. This is scary as she'd long ago identified the figure in her dream as a police officer and after that she'd had a life-long fear of men in uniform.

*

She walks up and down the street past the entrance to the police station for ten minutes before she can bring herself to go in. Eventually she faces a burly sergeant behind a desk who sees her shaking and smiles.

'What can I do for you love?'

She bridles a little at the patronising tone.

'I'm trying to find something out. Can you tell if there were any cases of missing people around here about twenty-five years ago?'

The sergeant smiled again.

'That's a big ask. People are going missing all the time. Most of them turn up again before long.'

'I know it was a girl. You see…' She struggles to continue. She feels stupid. He will think she's a mad woman or wasting his time. 'It's something that happened when I was a child. A policeman came to the house but I've never…'

She stopped. She was shaking again. The sergeant looks concerned.

'Come through here,' he says leading her into an office behind Reception. 'I'll get someone to speak to you.'

He returns to the desk and speaks to someone on the phone. She sits feeling that she's made a big mistake and then a female officer comes in. They go into a little private room and the officer shuts the door. Jenny thinks this must be where they interview suspects.

The officer is very kind. Jenny explains again why she has come 'You see I know something. I've never forgotten it, but it's gone deep inside me and I can't remember the details. I have dreams and stuff. I know a girl went missing. I remember my mother crying.'

'And how old were you when this happened?'

'About six or seven and...' She shakes her head.

'It's OK Take your time.'

'Something happened the other day. My daughter and her friends went out on their bikes.' She stops again. It all feels erratic and disjointed.

'Was it the bikes that reminded you of something?'

'Yes. Something moved in my head. I remembered I was on my bike that day. I cycled somewhere and saw something but...' She tries hard to force the memory to come. She is waving and clutching at it but it's too slippery and hot to grasp. 'And I have this dream about falling into a big hole. I think it's a well.'

She looks at the officers' face. What is she thinking? Maybe that this person needs a psychiatrist not the police.

'Look,' says the officer. 'You're clearly very disturbed by something. I think the best thing is for me to do some research and then contact you again. Where do you live? Do you have a partner?'

Jenny assures her that she has support at home and the officer takes all her details and promises to visit her soon. Jenny leaves the police station feeling relieved but apprehensive. She's unlocked a door which is creaking open. What lies behind is terrifying but wants to come out and she has to let it.

She sits on the sofa all evening drinking wine, watching junk television and not talking to anyone.

'What's wrong with Mum?' asks Jane.

'Nothing, she's just a bit tired tonight. It's bedtime now,' says her father ushering her out of the room.

*

*'Ding dong bell
Pussy's in the well'*

The line from the children's song won't leave Jenny's mind for the next two days. She's in a film which has frozen. Paralysed by the suspense, she can barely function until the police contact her.

STREET LIVES

On the third day, Jane is playing out and Jenny calls in sick to the nursery. At ten o'clock she sees a police car drawing up. She is weak and shaky at the prospect of a person in uniform coming into the house. But it is the nice policewoman she spoke to at the police station. She smiles as Jenny opens the door and invites her into the lounge. Jenny collapses into a chair and the officer sits opposite looking concerned. 'How are you today? You look tense.'

'Yes. Have you found anything?'

'Maybe.' She glances down at the papers she's brought in. 'There was a girl who went missing at about the time you told me about. Her name was Sabrina Knox. Does that name mean anything to you?'

The name pushes the door in Jenny's mind a little further open. She was back in the room with her mum and the police officer. He was saying that name: Sabrina Knox; Sabrina Knox had gone missing.

'She was never found despite big local search and a wide appeal for information.'

'Where did she live?'

'On the other side of town over the river.'

'Have you seen her parents? Did they tell you anything about her?'

'Yes, but most of it is confidential. One interesting thing is that she used to spend time near Asgard Close where you lived. She had some friends near there and the area was searched but without success.'
Friends. Yes. She saw two girls that day, older than her, teenagers maybe.

'The other thing...' The officer stops and looks a little embarrassed.

'I don't know whether this is relevant. We don't normally give much credence to this kind of stuff.' She produced a newspapers from the bottom of the pile of papers. 'This is one of the local rags, 'The Oakley Examiner.' Do you ever read it?'

'No'

'I don't think many people do these days. Mostly full of adverts, they're desperate for local news stories. But just have a look at this.' She opened the paper and pointed to a particular story. 'It's all a bit fanciful: spirits and messages and stuff, but I thought you might be interested and if it was true, it might help you to remember what happened.'

Jenny takes the paper and reads the headline 'Could the Ghost of a WW1 Soldier Hold the Answer to a Missing Girl?' Things lurch in her mind again as she begins to read how Morgan-Fay claims that the ghost of Tom, a soldier killed in the First World War, had told her that the body of her friend Sabrina Knox was down a well in the grounds of Oakley Manor. When she gets to this point, she begins to feel faint again. She puts the paper down and leans back in the chair.

'Are you OK?' says the officer.

'No, can you please get me a glass of water from the kitchen? The glasses are in the top cupboard.'

Water. Well. Oakley Manor. The black shape in her mind changes into a fluttering black curtain which opens and dissolves. She is back at the age of seven and finally she remembers what she saw. The raw feelings which flood in cause her to grip the arms of her chair, but she stays with them and with the sharp and painful memories.

The officer returns to find Jenny white faced and breathing heavily. She hands her the glass of water.

'You look dreadful,' she says. 'Shall I call the doctor?'

'No, I can manage. It's all come back to me at last. This is what happened.

'I got a bike for my birthday when I was seven. It was my first two-wheeler and I soon learned to ride it without the stabilisers. It was a lovely feeling to be able to get so far from our house so quickly and back again; it was a new freedom. I used to ride around the street with my friends who had little bikes, but I also liked to go off and explore. My Mum was OK about it as long as I didn't go too far and kept away from the main roads.'

'But you wanted to go further.'

'Yes. The more she said I couldn't, the more I wanted to and there was one place she particularly said was out of bounds.'

'Oakley Manor?'

'Yes. It's not far from where we lived and when I peeped through the gates it looked interesting; lots of roads and paths to cycle on. But she said it was a place with a bad reputation. There were rumours that nasty things had happened there.'

'Did she say what?'

'No she wouldn't. She just said that I hadn't to go anywhere near those grounds.'

'But you did'

STREET LIVES

Jenny sighs. 'Yes. It was an evening in early summer. None of my friends were around and I got the urge to explore. I cycled up to the gates and they were open. Suddenly I was through them. I said to myself that I would just cycle round quickly and come out again; I was terrified someone would see me and tell Mum. When I got further in I felt excited. I remember I wanted to wee, but I daren't stop.

'The further into the grounds I got, the more dangerous it felt and then my stomach churned because I heard voices. I got off my bike quickly and hid behind a tree. I could hear people arguing. Two girls. Older than me. I couldn't tell what they were saying. Part of me wanted to get back on the bike and pedal as fast as I could back out onto the street, but another part wanted to see what was happening. The voices were coming from a small clump of trees in front of me. I slowly edged towards the trees and up onto a slight banking behind them. I was lying flat and crawling slowly, closer to the trees, closer. And then I could see between them.

I was right. There were two older girls standing by a low stone wall arguing. Then they started to struggle with each, and one pushed the other and she fell backwards and disappeared. I could hear her screaming as she fell.' Jenny puts her hands over her ears. 'It was the worst thing I've ever heard. The scream got fainter as she fell further and further down. I knew it was a well. I'd seen one like it when Dad took me to see a castle. The screaming stopped and the other girl looked down the well. I was petrified. If she found out I was watching she would throw me down there too. I tried not to cry and I edged myself back, crawling towards where my bike was hidden. When I got close, I couldn't stop myself from getting up, running the last bit, hauling my bike out, getting on and pedalling furiously back to the gates. I expected the girl to appear chasing me, but she didn't.

'I cycled back down the driveway and straight out onto the road. I forgot to look for traffic and a car nearly hit me. He swerved and sounded his horn. I didn't stop I just cycled back to our front door and collapsed panting. It was only then I realised that I'd wee'd myself. My knickers were wet through. Mum must have heard me because she opened the door.

'Oh Mum, I'm sorry.' I remember saying. 'I wanted to wee and I've come back to go to the toilet but...' Then I collapsed in tears. Mum saw the wet patch on the back of my shorts and must have thought I was crying because I was embarrassed. She just laughed and told me to come in and get changed.'

The officer looks at Jenny who has gone limp in the chair, drained by the emotional impact of recalling this trauma.

'And you never told her anything about what you'd seen?' she says.

'No. I daren't because I was in a place I shouldn't have been and Mum would have been cross.'

'As you weren't very old I wonder if you also thought that the girl who pushed the other one might somehow get to you if you said anything.'

'Maybe.'

'You were still frightened that she might push you down the well which was why you dreamt about it.'

'Yes,' said Jenny. 'You're right. It was all made worse when the policeman came to the house because I knew what had happened but I daren't say anything.'

'So then you felt even guiltier. It was too painful and so your mind has effectively buried it for all these years.'

Jenny looks at the officer, around the room and then out of the window. The sun is shining onto the garden. She feels a lightness of mind she hasn't felt for years. She is elated. She stands up and laughs.

'That was it. It's all over. I didn't imagine it. It all happened. What will you do now?' she asks, her tone changing as she remembers there is a serious side to this: she had witnessed a murder.

'What you've said supports this newspaper account, so now we must investigate this well, more because of what you've said than stories of ghosts. The body of that poor girl Sabrina Knox was never found so I believe you've probably given us the answer even though testimony from a child so young would be treated with great caution.'

'Yes, I understand,' says Jenny. 'But there is a body in that well. I'm absolutely certain.'

The officer smiles. 'I can see how much of a relief this has been to you. You saw a terrible thing happen, but at least some good has come out of finding out the truth.' She gets up. 'I'll going back to the station. We'll need you to come in to make a full statement when you feel up to it. I'll keep you informed about what we find.'

STREET LIVES

As Jenny shows her out, Jane appears cycling down the street. When she gets to the house Jenny catches hold of her as soon as she gets off the bike and hugs her close.

'Mum? What's wrong?'

'Nothing. I just wanted to give you a hug.' She looks at her daughter. 'There is one thing.'

'What?'

'If anything upsetting or nasty happened to you. You would tell me about it wouldn't you?'

'Yes.'

'Even if you'd done something wrong yourself and you thought I'd be cross?'

'Yes. Why?'

'It's just important that's all.'

Jane goes inside for a glass of water. She drinks it and then goes out, gets on her bike and cycles off again. Jenny watches her go and smiles.

Asgard Close

STREET LIVES

Tommy's Trench Warfare

by

Christine Nolan

In 1980 I was working at the Mount Day Centre. I heard Tommy before I met him. 'Fuck off you bastards!' He bellowed as he shuffled along the corridor outside the bathroom. Tommy had a face like a savoy cabbage. He was 85 years old. He wore his stained archaic Crombie overcoat, tied up with string, like a badge of honour. It hung off his skeletal frame, buried him beneath it. He smelled like a compost heap on a sultry summer's day. Silverfish leaped out of his pockets and sleeves and slithered out of sight under the sink. His acid tongue shot venom, like shots in a fairground.

My first impression of Tommy was of a long-forgotten archive, something hidden at the back of a museum and left to decay; a kindred spirit reaching across the generations, a rebel who took no prisoners, asked no favours. I loved him instantly.

Pam tried unsuccessfully to get him to undress for his bath. Finally in frustration, after he wound her up to the point of no return he left the bathroom, tight lipped, and slammed the door. I saw a glint of victory in Tommy's eyes. Before he said, 'I'm fucking not getting in there. No slip of a girl is going to make me.'

I faced my combatant head on. I said, 'Tommy I enjoyed the show. Now cut the crap and I'll do a deal with you. You don't have to have a bath. I'll fill the sink and help you have a wash-down. I'll turn my back while you wash your privates. How does that suit you?'

He nodded. 'I can see I'll get nowhere with a lass like you,' he said. Then roared with laughter.

I went to get him a clean change of clothes. He let me help him, remove most of his clothes. His gnarled hands were embedded in his filthy finger-less gloves. He cried out in pain, as I gently tried to remove them. Apart from his long john's; and a pair of moth-eaten, grey pinstriped trousers. I had won the battle for this week. So I let it go.

Tommy told me Social Services wanted him to give up his home, the home he had been born in. He said, 'No whipper snapper, is going to put me in a fucking home, to rot'. I asked him If he was thinking of returning next week? Tommy said he would think about it. I detected a gruff 'Thank You' under his breath, before he left.

When Tommy failed to return the following week. I had a chat with Carol, my boss. She told me Tommy was a recluse. He lived at 3 Asgard Close in one of the Victorian terraced houses around the corner from me. I said, 'I'll just go check, he's OK.'

Nothing prepared me for visiting Tommy at home. When he opened the door I stepped into a time capsule. Time was suspended in the 1900's. The rusting vintage gas lamps were still in place. on both sides of the long dark brown Victorian hallway.

I recognised the patterned tiles of an 1930's Minton floor hidden under decades of dust and rubbish . A once beautiful chandelier hung down from the original ceiling rose on thick chains covered in grime, cobwebs and forgetfulness. Faded midnight-blue walls and ceilings were damp and dying of neglect, crumbling just like Tommy.

Metal buckets were strategically placed to catch rain from leaks in the roof. They plopped as we made our way into his billet. The only light in the room came from candles. That created an intimate and eyrie atmosphere in the room. I felt someone had just walked over my grave. As we continued our slow march, around what appeared to be a maze of five-foot-high walls of hundreds of coffee coloured copies of 'The Times' newspaper dating from the last century. I was staring at a precision-made replica of an original World War One trench. A living piece of trench art at its finest.

I was struck dumb. I was amazed at the amount of love, the time and years dedicated by Tommy to make this memorandum. I had a lump in my throat and my eyes filled. I felt all his feelings and his sheer determination to complete such an epic piece of work that would not have been out of place in a war museum.

As we emerged out of the trench I spotted an ornate Adams fireplace at far end of the room. Two rusting old-fashioned candlesticks with handles reminded me of Wee Willy, Winkey climbing up the stairs to bed. In a long-forgotten fairy tale. It was surreal.

A crumbling sepia photograph lay on the rubbish filled floor at Tommy's feet.

When we sat down on a ruby red velvet , old chaise longue, all the stuffing tumbling out of it. He picked up the photo tenderly, a dreamy look in his eyes. Tommy's mind became a living camera which seemed to be capturing every special snapshot of his beloved he held in his heart and soul from a long time ago.

As a solitary tear snaked down his cheek, Tommy told me this sad story. The story of his life.

*

When the Great War broke out Edward Eddington, my childhood friend and I were callow youths aged 19 years old. It was 1914 and we were amongst the first to enlist in the newly formed Leeds Pals Battalion, ready to fight for king and Country. We were affectionately known as 'Kitchener's Army'.

Crowds filled Leeds City Centre, and City Square, packed in like sardines, cheering and waving their Union Jack flags. Shouts of, 'Give 'em Hell, and 'Good luck lads', could be heard as we marched by. One rake even climbed on the statue of the Black of the Prince in his enthusiasm to wave his flag and cheer us on.

The carnival atmosphere continued as we pulled out of Leeds Railway Station, flags flapping, brass band playing. The steam train puffed cotton clouds of steam, it's hooter, howling our departure. We were on our way to the Yorkshire Dales to commence our training for war.

Edward and I joined the rest of the raw recruits in our hut at the training camp at Closterdale. We spent 9 months training, marching up and down the dales, in the freezing pouring rain with heavy backpacks on our backs. We bonded over beer, blisters, and bloodied feet and listening to Sargent Boothroyd's, dulcet, sarcastic tones ringing in our ears, declaring, we were 'a miserable lot'

Edward was the joker in our pack. After a particular, long hard day's marching, with our rucksacks stuck to our backs, he decided to put itching powder in Boothroyd's long johns. The hut door was kicked open, by an irate, Boothroyd with such force it was left hanging on its hinges, as he exploded, red faced into the room; screaming expletives and demanding to know, 'Who put the fucking itching powder, in my long johns?'

He gave us no time to reply, before he tore through our billet upending all our beds and bedding. Hurling all the pristine, polished brass badges and buttons on the floor. On his way out he shouted, 'Clear that bloody lot up you bastards!' We all piled onto Edward.

On our return home in 1916 from the scorching battlefields of Egypt defending the Suez Canal, Edward felt it was a good idea to have some fun. We were on embarkation leave before being shipped out to fight on the Western Front.

Nesta Tilley was performing at Leeds Town Hall. She was part of the low-key propaganda machine, to encourage men to enlist in the army, by singing her latest song 'Good Luck to a Girl Who Loves A Soldier'. Edward as usual had his own unique interpretation of the song. He thought it a splendid way to meet the ladies of Leeds, as all women, would love a man in uniform, he surmised. We were due to attend a ball at Leeds Town Hall in honour of the Leeds Pals regiment. I was not so keen being shy and having two left feet. I could just about shuffle round a dance floor.

Edward was a lady's man who enjoyed variety in his woman. Unlike me. I was a one women man who enjoyed the more literary pursuits of reading poetry, writing and walking in the dales.

The first time I saw my Florence, she was in Edward's arms as they flashed by doing a foxtrot. I noticed the magnificent sight of her burnished copper long hair tumbling from its green satin bow that tried and failed, to hold it back from her beautiful face, so thick a man could have his hands tangled within it. Never wanting to be set free I was captivated. During their second turn around the dance floor our eyes locked. I was staring into a pair of the deepest forest green eyes that matched the colour of her stunning ball gown to perfection. In that moment I was lost.

I was enamoured by her. I knew I had to get to know this enchanting woman dancing in my best friend's arms. So I cut in on Edward and asked his permission to dance with Florence just as the band struck up with Roses of Picardy. This would become our song. Especially the refrain 'There's one rose that dies not in Picardy, this the rose I keep in my heart'. I knew it would be forever.

When the song ended I asked Florence for her dance card and boldly wrote 'Full' in it for the rest of the evening's dances. I had no idea where my audacity came from. Florence did not object.

All my senses were assaulted, by her beauty and the citrus scent of her perfume that lived behind her ears and nestled in the nape of her neck. Holding her in my arms felt divine.

Florence and I shared the same interests, attending concerts, books and walking in the Yorkshire Dales. She was a suffragette, a staunch supporter of the Women's Right's movement. I loved the way her green cat eyes, flashed with anger and a crease appeared on the bridge of her nose when she debated the right of women to get the vote with me. I agreed whole heartedly with her views on women's rights. I had a profound respect for all women. Florence thought Thomas was far too stuffy and thought Tommy suited me better. So from that night 'Tommy' it would be. By the end of that evening, Florence and I were deeply in love.

I told Florence I intended to write to her father, to ask his permission to call on her at home. To let him know my intentions were honourable towards her and to explain my business prospects regarding my boot and shoe factory.

It was a rude awakening, when Edward and I returned from the scorching battlefields of Egypt to the appalling conditions of the Somme. Torrential rain constantly cascaded down on the troops making the trenches into a quagmire. We were standing knee deep in ice cold thick putrid mud that soaked through our tunics chilling us to the bone. Soldiers were known to enter no-man's land and disappear into the mud never to be seen again. Rats had the run of the trenches, stealing our food, spreading disease and causing infected bites. Mustard gas attacks meant instant death to some men from our battalion, killing them by blistering the throat and lungs. Terrible blisters erupted all over their bodies. Those that didn't die, wished they had. The gas crippled their lungs and breathing for life. Lice nibbled us like living meals. They caused intense itching and nearly drove us insane and prevented us from sleeping. We would run the flame of a candle down all the seams *of our uniforms to try to gain some temporary relief from our frenzied scratching of the little buggers. We were living in Dante's inferno. Conditions were about to get much worse. We were soldiers who hired out our spotless hearts and souls, for our country and were paid the King's shilling to fight in our own theatre of war. Traumatised daily we watched our Brother's-In-Arms, blown to bits.*

Our trenches ran red with body parts. Our putties stained with blood and tears. We witnessed, one poor sod from our own battalion who was suffering from nerves. Charged with insubordination and shot by a firing squad, he was 18 years old.

These were conditions we endured for months prior to our move to centre stage where so many men would become sacrificial lambs on a crimson sea of innocence.

We were caught unaware, shelled as we poured over the top towards enemy lines. On that bright, sunny morning before the zero hour of 7.30. All hell broke loose. We fell like bloody packs of dominoes. Wave after wave of us were in direct sights of the Germans bullets wailing in our ears. As we walked on a carpet of red and green of our dead and dying, I saw Edward, my best friend fall face down in the mud in front of me, his head blown apart. I had to step over him. I did not look back as we advanced towards death. I sustained a shrapnel wound in my chest and woke up in hospital. I survived the war physically. Looking back we were mown down in droves, like English country gardens on Sunday afternoon, from the murderous assault of the enemy's accurate artillery fire. We Tommies stumbled on in a trance numb with the pitiful cries of war ringing in our ears. Some soldiers never even got the chance to discharge their rifles.

Later that morning few men made it as far as the German's barbed-wire but no further. Later on the enemy came to clear the bodies off their wire killing any soldiers unfortunately still alive. So many of us were slaughtered on a searing bonfire of battle. The scars of that siege would live on in all of us who bore testament and survived the massacre of the battle.

*

STREET LIVES

We sat in complete silence. I did not want to break the spell. Slowly Tommy began to speak. His face was animated. As he began to tell me the story of Florence his fiancé whom he loved we continued our walk back in time. He handed me the photograph. From what I could see, she was a young, vibrant, beautiful woman, with thick, long, curly hair, a swan like neck, and full bosom. She was dressed in a Victorian ball gown.

He talked on and said he met Florence at a dance, just before he went to war, in France. He had fallen in love with her from the moment he saw her dancing in his best friend Edward's arms. Tommy said they were engaged and due to be married.

His face lit up as he talked about her, and their many trips to Sedbergh, in the Yorkshire Dales, which they both loved, and where they went hiking with their friends. He spoke of the beauty of Howgill Fells and the surrounding countryside. Their favourite walk. was to the top of Winder Fell. He said you could see for miles around.

Tommy continued to reminisce about his love for Florence, her beauty, her kindness and the aroma of her Gabilla perfume, when she entered a room. I sat spellbound listening. I could not interrupt his flow of wonder. He seemed lost in a moment of magic. I didn't want to break his connection to his beloved or bring him back to the harsh reality. He had endured for so long. Tommy returned from the Western Front in 1918.

One week before his wedding day. Florence and Tommy had gone to visit a cousin in Leeds. They were all crossing the road after coming out Roundhay Park when a young child broke free of her governess. She ran in front of Florence, straight onto the main road. Florence ran after the fleeing child and threw the small girl to her side. Florence was crushed beneath the wheels of a runaway horse and carriage. She died instantly.

Tommy's face changed to ashes. He started to howl, a deep primeval sound. I got down on my knees, wrapped my arms tight around him, and began to gentle rock him. I cried silently with him and for him; for his Florence, for the life of love they lost, for his best friend Edward, who never came home, for the innocence of youth, for his wedding trousers he still wore, and for the trench he made that meant so much to him.

STREET LIVES

One week later. Rosie his social worker told me Tommy had died in his sleep at home. I smiled. He had got his wish. He would never rot in 'A fucking old people's home'.

Street Lives

Street Lives

Asgard Close

Sweet Peas

by

Cynthia Richardson

The funeral was going the way of so many funerals these days. The widow and family cried, the priest tried his best to speak well of someone he had never met and others in the congregation were like me there to witness the rite of passage for the deceased from this life to whatever comes next.

I was also there in a semi-official capacity, especially invited, as the dedicated young doctor who had tried under extremely difficult circumstances to save the man now resting in the coffin.

I had been in A and E for six months and was just finishing what seemed like an endless shift when there was an outbreak of motorway madness. As I worked the ever-growing flow of casualties

I recognised him, he was in a bad way with multiple fractures and internal injuries. At first I thought he was unconscious but as I bent over him I could see that although in great pain, he was conscious, and his eyes widened in shock when he recognised me. No one will know how I killed him but in all the managed chaos he slipped away as I apparently worked hard to save him. 'Jack, Jack, can you hear me,' I whispered in his ear. 'Here's some tough love from sweet pea.'

Sweet peas are my favourite flower and especially so when I was a child. My grandfather and father had grown them, and I always like bunches of them in my bedroom. The sight and smell of them helped when my father died when I was nine as they made me feel he was still alive. But he wasn't and my mother remarried a good looking 'life and soul of the party' man called Jack.

Jack always called me Sweetpea and at first I was flattered but when he started visiting me in my bedroom when my Mum was working evenings it became a name I dreaded. 'Oh my lovely Sweetpea what a tease you are,' he would whisper in my ear his breath hot on my cheek. You can't tell anyone what we do, it's our little secret. If you tell your Mum I will have to kill her and then it would be just you and me.' Just thinking about the vile things he said and did even now makes me want to vomit. However they did the trick. I was terrorised into silence.

I was saved from Jack by a scholarship I won to a prestigious boarding school where I thrived and gained the name 'Teflon'. That was because no matter how snobby or condescending some of the other girls were to the scholarship girl I just focussed and excelled at my work driven of course by never wanting to go home again.

The years rolled by and I was running out of holiday projects and other 'no reason to go home' activities when my Mum left Jack after suffering domestic abuse. She went to live with my grandparents, so I started going home for the holidays.

After school I went to University where my focus once again was on gaining the best qualifications I could and after gaining a first-class degree I went on to medical school. In all those years I kept to myself never having any close friends. I could outwardly be very engaging but inside I was dead just like Jack had left me. I never saw or heard from him in all those years until the night he arrived in A and E.

So, here I am at his funeral holding in my hands a large bunch of sweet peas picked from my garden. They bring tears to my eyes as the memories come flooding back. I will put them on his grave along with a little card hidden in the heart of them that says, 'To Jack rot in hell from Sweetpea.'

STREET LIVES

STREET LIVES

ASGARD CLOSE

Street Lives

Is That a Poem in Your Pocket?

By

Kelly McCarthy

Howard hesitantly shuffled into the back room at the 'Curly Merkin' 'Is this the writers club?' he asked, his palms sweaty and his left eye nervously twitching.

The seated semi-circle of women turned to look at him.

'Well we've been called a lot worse!' hooted a hoarse woman with a very low-cut top.

'Are you Howard?' spoke a kindly older lady. Her voice was soothing and in some ways she reminded him of his dear departed Elizabeth, although Elizabeth would never have worn so much make up.

'Yes, I called you from the phone at the social club, your poster was a bit torn, but I managed to make out the word 'writing' and your number, Tracy is it?'

'Trixie to friends love, now take a seat over there by Sugar, we've got a lot to be getting on with'

Trixie? Sugar? Must be pen names thought Howard. These creative types are all a bit...out there!

Howard wasn't comfortable about being out anywhere, he preferred being at home in his Asgard Close apartment, watching T.V, drinking tea and dunking biscuits but he had promised Elizabeth to get out more once she'd gone. 'You used to enjoy writing' she had said 'join a writers club' so here he was, Saturday afternoon in a flea pit of a pub desperately wanting a brew and missing the latest episode of Morse. The things I do for you, he murmured looking up as though Elizabeth was there above him floating about in the cobwebs urging him on.

'Is that a poem in your pocket or are you just pleased to see me?' cackled Sugar, raucous laughter filling the room.

'Um, it is a poem actually' said Howard once the laughter had stopped 'One I wrote to my late wife when we were courting'
'Really, well we love a bit of old-fashioned raciness here don't we girls?'
The 'girls' nodded enthusiastically
Howard listened as each lady took her turn in reading a very short poem. Howard really wasn't up on modern poetry, nothing seemed to rhyme, and some words just didn't even make sense, maybe its Haiku he thought, he had never understood Haiku. He started to glaze over; these ladies were really into their cats. Elizabeth had always wanted a cat, but he had said no, it was the one argument in their 50-year marriage that he had actually won.
'Your turn now, Howard' Sugar was stroking his leg!
Howard blushed, cleared his throat and started to read.

'When Buttercups are covering
Our fingers and our sighs
I will ask you for your hand my sweet
Will you be my forever, my bride?'

It was written as a wholesome poem about sitting in the meadows near his and Elizabeth's childhood homes.
'That's a good start Howard' said Trixie 'and with a few changes, that could be a goer'
Trixie proceeded to replace his words with ones so appalling that Howard felt he had been physically attacked by what he could only describe as filth.
'A goer, a goer for whom?'
Howard rose shakily to his feet and shuffled as fast as he could towards the Exit. Only once the door was safely shut behind him did he stop. He leaned back, trying to catch his breath. A flyer had got stuck to his shoe, he reached down and pulled it off, it was the poster he had read above the phone box only this one was complete.

MAKE MONEY FROM SEXTING
Writing for Pros

Phone Trixie on……

'What the hell is sexting?' Howard asked a man standing having a cig in the lobby.

'You don't want to be thinking about that at your age, do yourself a mischief mate!'

'No, I do not.'

Howard got on the number 69 bus back to Oakley. He looked towards the top deck and sighed 'The things I do for you Elizabeth!'

Asgard Close

STREET LIVES

Hairshirt and Locket

by

Pauline Harrowell

Down the years I wore you, Jean,
now a hairshirt, now a locket;
so practised in the rites of silence
no torture could wrench your name from my lips.
I kept my word.
I am a woman of my word,
and little else, bar memories.

Your hands once burned my skin,
your voice enchanted my ear,
your smell intoxicated,
yet the tang of guilt remains.

We would be together again, you said,
my final destination, my holy grail;
but now I am at the gate
remind me what together means?

Miss Simone Fullilove, from the height of her 95 years, is getting on with the serious business of dying. She would like to hurry the process up, but death sets the rules, takes its own time. There is an obstacle in her path. There is something she must do, something she must say before she can reach the promised land of eternal rest in the benevolent presence of Our Lord and his endless capacity to forgive.
She can hear two female voices united in lovely harmony singing one of the old C of E hymns. *I am already there! Please let it be true* – but it is only Precious and Faith, her two Zimbabwean carers come to visit her.

She summons all her strength, and clutches Faith's sleeve. 'Close the door. I have something to tell you....

One Week Earlier

'*Citron....*' she whispered, drifting out of a deep sleep.

'What did you say Simone?' asked Precious, soapy flannel in hand.

'*Citron* – lemon, I can smell lemons – it reminds me of when I was a little girl in Corsica.'

'It's my favourite lemon soap! You lived in Corsica?'

'Yes, I was born there. My parents ran a lemon plantation. That's why they gave me a French name, it was illegal not to.'

'Did you go to school there?' It was easier to get the nursing chores done if you got a good conversation going, Precious thought, applying the flannel.

'Of course. Everything was in French. That was just the beginning, in a way...'

'How long did you live there? It must have been lovely - all those lemon trees.'

Simone recovered some of her spirit as she reminisced. 'Oh, it was marvellous. I used to run around barefoot all the time, swim, climb trees, all sorts of things. I was about 12 when we left, I think. My parents came back to England. Without me, though. They sent me to boarding school in Switzerland. I think they felt I needed breaking in, like a wild horse.'

Precious bit her tongue, thinking of the child she had had to leave behind. *Why would anybody chose to send their child away? I will never understand some people.*

*

A few days later, Faith, having finished her shift, came to sit with Simone for a while. After all, nobody visited her. Faith picked up an old photograph propped up next to Simone's bed.

'And who is this handsome man? Some film star?'

'Ah, that was my Jean – my one and only. Yes, he was very handsome – much nicer in real life than this picture, though. He had a lovely big French nose.'

Faith burst out laughing. Simone never failed to surprise her. 'So this is the famous French connection, eh? How did you meet him?'

STREET LIVES

Simone closed her eyes. She hadn't spoken to a living soul about this for so long, but maybe now the time was right.

'Would you mind propping me up a little? Thank you, dear. If you have time, I'll tell you about it....'

Simone had come back to London after the death of her parents just before the second world war broke out and moved into their flat in Maida Vale. Being a fluent French speaker she got a job on the international telephone exchange. She enjoyed her life as a girl about town, with an interesting job, and there was no shortage of young male company in smart uniforms. Life was good, albeit getting more dangerous all the time. But nothing prepared her for the day when she was called into the manager's office to find a man in a grey suit waiting to make her a proposition that would change her life forever.

'I never went back to the telephone exchange – they made some sort of excuse. Instead I had to go straight into training for the SOE.'

'SOE? What is that?'

'Special Operations Executive, they were based in Baker Street. We were trained to do undercover work in occupied France, sabotage, espionage, resistance – all that sort of thing.'

Faith's jaw dropped. 'I saw a TV programme about it! You did that?'

'Yes. I was in Paris. That's where I met Jean – he was head of a resistance group.' She fell silent, her eyes closed, exhausted by the effort. She thought *that will do to start with.* 'I think I need a rest now, dear, if you don't mind.'

'You are a remarkable woman, you know that? Go to sleep now Simone, I'll see you tomorrow. God bless you.' Simone smiled, shook her head, patted Faith's hand; sleep mercifully took over.

*

Simone, aware that time was running out, was pleased to see both Faith and Precious in her room the next day. She drew strength from their conversations.

'So you've come to hear the next instalment?'

'If you are happy to tell us, we are very happy to listen,' Precious said, as they settled into the visitors' chairs, faces serious.

'Well, after my training they sent me to Paris with a fake Swiss passport. I think I've still got it somewhere, in the loft maybe. I was told to make contact with a resistance network and relay messages back to

London. They kitted me out with a radio set. Everything had to be encoded, of course.'

'And that is how you met the handsome Jean?'

'Yes. Love at first sight, for both of us...' She looked away, silent for a moment. When she turned back her look was intense.

'You know I signed a form to say I would never tell anyone about all this - Official Secrets Act.'

'Simone, we all have secrets. You can trust us.'

'Yes, I know I can. Well, it doesn't matter anymore, really, not now. They told me people's lives were at stake and that I should never tell, on pain of death – *I gave my word*. And I never did tell.'

Faith changed the subject, quickly. 'So where did you live in Paris?'

'I had a little room in the Rue Richer. In the Jewish quarter, actually. There were plenty of rooms to rent there. I was working as a nanny for a Swiss family, well – that was the cover story. But the Nazis were everywhere, and you certainly couldn't trust your neighbours. I had to be very careful with my transmitter. Fortunately the old man in the room next door was stone deaf and couldn't hear a thing.'

'It must have been so dangerous. If you had got caught....'

'Yes, quite – torture, and off to Ravensbruck. That happened to a lot of us. But when you're young you think it can't happen to you, and it was so exciting, in a way.'

Faith, remembering a brother lost to a resistance movement, and how she'd begged him not to get involved, nodded and looked down.

'How long were you there?' asked Precious.

'About 9 months. Frankly I would have stayed forever, but the inevitable happened. Someone betrayed Jean - this sort of the thing was always happening - and the network collapsed. After that I had to get back to London as quickly as possible. They sent me to Brittany, through another resistance group. It was terrifying. I had to find my way along the coastal path in the middle of the night to a tiny beach – and there were Nazi patrols everywhere – but there it was, a little boat waiting for me.'

'And what about Jean?' Precious leant forward, as Simone's voice was weakening.

'There'd been an ambush. He was .... killed.'

There was a chill in the room. All three women's lips moved in silent prayer.

'Go to sleep, Simone. You must rest. We will talk tomorrow.'
I am nearly done now. One more thing to tell them ....

*

The next day Precious and Faith came to visit Simone on their day off. They decided not to distress her with more talk of Jean, but to find out about her life since the war.

'There is something more she needs to tell us, I am sure of it. But we must make it easy for her,' said Precious.

'What I don't understand, is why no one comes to see her? Where are her family, friends and neighbours?' wondered Faith. 'What is wrong with these people? The people from her church, why don't they come?'

Unbeknown to her, Simone declined all visitors from her local church, apart from the rector who came to the nursing home to give her Holy Communion. And she had outlived her few friends from her time in London. She had long since cut off contact with the few distant relatives that she still had. She had no interest in them, nor they in her. As for the neighbours, she kept herself to herself, and she liked it that way. There was only the appalling Mrs Smith from number 16, with her filthy dog, who wouldn't leave her alone. But no-one in the street knew she was even in the nursing home, let alone where it was – so much the better, she thought. The habit of secrecy died hard.

When the ladies arrived they found the room filled with sunlight, with Simone looking almost translucent, her eyes closed. Precious whispered to Faith: 'We're too late! She has already passed.'
Softly they started singing one of their favourite hymns, but suddenly Faith paused.

'No, Precious – look, she's breathing!' Faith took Simone's hand gently. It was warm.

*

With every day that passed Simone seemed to feel lighter, more distant from her physical self. Apart from the time spent with her beloved carers she either slept or relived her past.

Today, before her visitors arrived, she had been remembering her 80th birthday, when she decided to go back to Paris for the first time since the Liberation. She had certain ghosts to lay. She told no-one about her visit – merely asking Morgan-Faye from Rowan Lodge to look after her two cats Odette and Noor.

The day after she arrived she sat for a while in the sun in the Tuileries gardens indulging in memories (*that's how it felt when he put his arms around me*), before setting off to revisit the site of 75 years of recurring nightmares.

She soon found herself in the street where it happened. A quiet, slightly shabby street – much changed since 1943. There were shops with food in, for a start; and the kosher butcher's shop, boarded up and daubed with graffiti back then, was doing good business. And here was number 17, its large dark green door unchanged. As she looked up to locate the 4th floor window that had once been hers, she noticed something on the building's facade: a square cream plaque inscribed 'in memory of Jean Machard, hero of the Resistance, assassinated here on 3rd June 1943'.

Her heart started beating in a peculiar lumpy fashion, her head swam, and the tears came, for the first time in years. She clutched at the massive handle in the middle of the door but still slumped to her knees. A young man in a sharp suit rushed out of the estate agent's office across the road (which used to be a radical bookshop, she couldn't help remembering).

'Madame! Are you all right? Let me help you...' as he helped her to her feet he noticed the discreet red ribbon of the Legion d'Honneur in her buttonhole. 'I insist, Madame – come and sit in our office, we'll call an ambulance, it's the least we can do!'

Rapidly she came to her senses. 'No, no, Monsieur, it's nothing – just a little too much sun, you're very kind – but really, I'm fine.' Furious for drawing attention to herself (*you broke the first rule*), she hurried away towards the metro, with barely enough time for one last look.

*

Simone awoke from her reverie at Faith's touch. She turned to greet her visitors with a radiant smile, feeling that at last the time had come. 'Well, *mes amies*, are you ready for the final instalment?'

Precious and Faith looked at each other. Precious began with an easy question: 'So you were back in London after the war. When did you move up here to Oakley?'

STREET LIVES

'That was when I retired from the GPO, or BT as it is now. I went back to them when I came back from France, and just stayed on. I was one of their oldest employees.'

'It must have been a big change after London! Did you ever miss the big city?'

Simone's laugh was like the faintest rustling of tissue paper. 'Oh no! it's hard for you young things to imagine, but I'd had enough by then. Too much noise, too much traffic – far too many people. I needed peace and quiet. Just me, my cats – and my memories'.

'There was never anyone else for you? After Jean?' asked Faith. Simone's breathing was as shallow as a sparrows. 'No – I could never - get that close again. He was always with me - *mon Jean*.'

'You will be together in the next world, Simone,' said Faith.

'If a communist atheist can go to heaven....' Simone replied, with a weak smile. In her darker moments she wondered if they would be reunited, and whether that was in fact what she wanted; she was a different person now – the treacherous thought came: *had it all been worthwhile?*

'God will find a way, you can be sure.' Faith reassured her.

*

Now Faith has closed the door, at Simone's bidding. They draw their chairs closer to the bed and take her hands.

I need to confess, and be forgiven, I need to break that vow. There is one way I can make amends.

'They brought Jean to my flat that day, after the ambush– he'd been shot – I had to get him up the stairs, 4 flights of stairs - we had to make no noise... and he was so weak....' Simone stops, her strength ebbing with every phrase.

'He couldn't let himself be captured – he wouldn't give them the satisfaction. He told me what I had to do. He trusted me ... he was dying anyway. We said goodbye – then......'

'You helped him, Simone. It was a Christian thing to do,' whispers Precious.

'I took the pillow – may the Lord forgive me....'

'The Lord will always forgive, Simone' says Faith.

A puff of breath, not so much as a sigh, and it is over. They draw the curtains, share a prayer, and sit in silence for a few minutes. When they get up to leave they notice a brown envelope on the bedside table addressed to the two of them.

*

Postscript

Simone's funeral took place the following week. A few church members attended, as did a smattering of people from the street ('well, it'll look bad if no-one goes...' said Steve from the Oakley Arms). All those who attended, including the vicar, were surprised to find an outside broadcast truck from French television news in the church car park, with a journalist doing a piece to camera; they were even more astounded when the French ambassador's limousine arrived, bearing the Ambassador herself and the French Minister for Veteran Affairs.

Precious and Faith, however, merely exchanged knowing smiles .... One evening a few months later neighbours noticed a small white van parked in the driveway of No. 9. It was dark, so they were unable to see who was carrying boxes and cases into the house.

But the next morning a Zimbabwean flag was displayed in the front window.

Street Lives

Oakwell
Manor

STREET LIVES

All Manor of Things

by

Martin Fuller

The corridors were chattering again, creaking their support, urging him onwards. The manor-house's anticipation caused the lights to flicker and doors to swing on their hinges with throaty croaks.

Paul Carnforth's own excitement was growing too, as it always did when he had a 'guest' in the special place waiting to be joined to the house.

He descended the last few steps to the cellar door using his master key to open the well-oiled lock. Inside were the first in a series of cellar rooms, cluttered with old furniture, boxes full of wonders and suitcases of memories.

He squeezed through narrow spaces in between the stacked junk and memorabilia, weaving his way to the far wall where stood the 'guests' room'. He opened yet another sturdy oak door which moved as silently as the first on its well lubricated hinges.

A set of bright bulbs illuminated the stone arched room. One corner was occupied by a large cabinet and a wheel barrow. In another corner stood a metal framed bed holding a dark stained mattress, on which lay a middle-aged man, chained to the metal framing of the bed with iron shackles on his wrists and ankles.

The sedative Carnforth had given him had worn off and the man's eyes were wide in fear, tears running down his face onto the filthy pillow beneath his head. His mouth was securely gagged, for whilst it was doubtful anyone would hear his cries, Carnforth believed in a 'better safe than sorry' policy.

Carnforth put on his happy face, the one he used to try and calm the 'Melders' as he called them; those special enough to be chosen for the great gift of symbiotic immortality in the joining with the house.

As he approached, the man pulled on his shackles causing his already chaffed wrists and ankles to bleed.

'Now my lucky friend, settle down. No one can hear you and you're hurting yourself.'

Carnforth sat on the mattress and gently stroked the man forehead.

'So, I'm going to take off the gag and you can have a drink of water but if you try and scream I will have to hurt you. Understand?'

The man ceased to struggle and nodded, never taking his tear-soaked eyes off his captor.

'Good boy,' said Carnforth as he removed the gag and lifted the man's head, carefully pouring water from a bottle he had brought into the man's mouth.

'OK,' said Carnforth putting down the water.

'Do you remember me Jakub? You worked in my garden some months ago. Its Jakub ...Nowak yes? Now if I remember correctly, you're Polish, been here over a year and living in that cheap boarding house in town, yes? How sad. Do you understand me Jakub? I hope so because you're being gifted with a chance of a sort of ...well immortality.'

Jakob stared at his captor wondering how to respond to this madman. He did indeed remember Paul Carnforth who'd hired him to work as a gardener and handyman some months ago.

It had seemed just a lucky coincidence when Jakub had met Carnforth last night in the alley by his house. They'd talked, and Carnforth had offered him further work inviting him back to the house to discuss it. Jakub had readily agreed as work had become scarce. They had walked along deserted pathways to Carnforth's house, Oakwell Manor. Carnforth had talked non-stop about the money Jakub could make for the work on the estate. Jakub had been offered supper and the prospect of a sandwich and coffee had been happily accepted. Those were his last clear memories and then...and then... he'd woken up chained in this room.

Carnforth continued. 'Are you listening Jakub. This is the best bit. I think you have a pretty good idea your earthly life is going to end soon, but please understand, there will be no pain ... well very little anyway. You will, in part, live forever. I'm joining you to the house in perpetuity and I want you to appreciate the honour we give you. I and the house.

STREET LIVES

This great manor needs certain aspects of your physical being ... which I will extract. For previous donors, it's been blood, but for those with special abilities we take a little ... more specialised pieces.'

Jakub started to cry out, but Carnforth was too quick, too aware, pushing the gag back into the man's mouth. All Jakub could do was stare in complete terror.

Carnforth stood and walked over to the corner cupboard, opening its doors. He took out a silver dish, which he partly filled with water from the plastic bottle, a tool bag and a large piece of flint. Jakub froze and focused on the flint which he saw had been fashioned into a form of hand axe. Carnforth returned to the bed.

'Do you know this part of the manor house is early Victorian. Other parts are Georgian and some medieval. What a delightful patchwork of British architectural history Jakub. But what people don't understand is that for as long as humankind has endured on this island, there's been a structure, temple, or hut even, on these very grounds. There has always been a special place here. Do you know there are tunnels and chambers running for miles under the house and grounds, carved by early acolytes of those devoted to the Black Stone? Oh, I forget you don't know about the stone. Don't worry. You will be very close to it soon. Very soon and very close. This flint axe, incidentally, is thousands of years old. It will end your distress and start the melding process. The house awaits you Jacob, well parts of you anyway. Prepare Jakub. I promise it will be ...'

The sentence was never completed, although the sentence of death was. Carnforth swung the stone axe down in a practised, forceful movement, crushing Jakub's forehead. Two further precisely aimed blows followed, and Jakub Nowak lay still, his blood adding fresh red wetness to the dark dried mire of the mattress and pillow.

The house was pleased, Carnforth hearing whispering drafts of gratitude blowing along its dusty corridors.

Jakub's talent was discovered by Carnforth when he'd first worked in the gardens two months ago. As Jakob tried taming the overgrown shrubberies, Carnforth noticed he possessed excellent hearing, well able to respond to the offer of coffee being called at the kitchen door. He informed the house which promptly passed on its request for Jacob to be 'melded', his hearing gift to be incorporated into its fabric.

Jakub had been paid off, thus cutting the immediate connection to the house but promised work in the future. Jakub was a loner, a hard worker to be sure, but with few friends in the vicinity. He would not be missed.

Patience and careful observation were virtues Carnforth thought he excelled in. After a calculated period, it had been easy to stage a coincidental meeting with a work hungry Jakub. The drugged coffee had ensured cooperation although getting the unconscious Jakub to the cellar had been a serious test of his dedication and strength. He was fifty-four now and it was only the house's generosity that kept him in good health.

He broke off from his self-congratulating memory and focused on the next phase of the ritual. It always unsettled him, as he was not blood-thirsty by nature and a practicing vegetarian. He removed a saw, chisel and scalpel out of the bag taken from the cupboard.

It started off easily enough. Jacobs outer ears were easy to slice from the head but to get at the inner parts was to be a messy and bloody business. Carnforth was forced to constantly refer to an illustrated book on anatomy he'd laid on Jakub's chest, as the house whispered its own advice and support having witnessed many similar rituals before. After an hour's work the tympanic membranes, cochleas and semicircular canals were in the silver dish beside the mutilated head.

'There's a job well done' muttered Carnforth to himself.

He next chanted the words of extraction in a language long lost to the rest of mankind, to assist in the preservation of the late Mr Nowak's hearing organs.

The house moaned its timbers in ecstatic response.

Using the hack- saw, and scalpel, the body was rendered down into more manageable pieces, before being finally loaded onto the awaiting wheel barrow.

The really unpleasant bit was disposing of the body amongst the series of catacombs and tunnels dug out of the rock over thousands of years. The house told him of the niches in the rock providing homes to rat and beetle, bat and worm. And of course, the many guests who had contributed to the house's wellbeing over the millennia.

The journey into these corridors was disgusting, as despite his best efforts with fly sprays, sticky fly paper and rolled newspapers, the whole of the underground pathways was infested with flies, hatched from the decaying bodies of previous sacrifices. This was to the delight of the battalions of spiders which had invaded the tunnels, growing fat in the dark, their webs hanging like draped curtains along the walls, all heavy with the desiccated bodies of their own flying victims.

Jakub deconstructed body was eventually tipped into a small alcove, resting on a pile of bones from another 'melder'. With a cheery 'ta ta', Carnforth retraced his steps back to the 'guest' room'.

It was as he assessed his final chores that he realized the mattress was thoroughly soaked in blood. He'd been extremely careless and unless he wanted swarms of flies in this room also, he'd better do something.

It was all a learning curve really. In his first few nervous sacrifices for the house, he'd bungled the killings. It upset him he had spoilt the 'melding' by his early incompetence. All that screaming, and writhing was unsettling. The bed and mattress had had its day. He would fit shackles to the wall instead, doing away with the bed altogether. The blood could drain through the old drain grills set in the floor. Yes, a good idea. He would burn the mattress later, dumping the springs and bed frame at the local dump. After all, he was a rate payer and he believed strongly in re-cycling.

He cleaned all his tools and equipment, replacing everything into the cupboard. It paid to look after the 'tools of his trade' and he considered himself a conscientious workman, an artist even. Finally, he could get on with the final parts of the ritual. The house squeaked its impatience, its desperate anticipation, causing fogs of dust to seep from the arched brickwork.

'Be patient please. Patience is good for the mind,' joked Carnforth. The house gave stony silence as its reply.

Collecting the silver dish and its bloody contents, he made his way down, even deeper into the house's lower vaults, entering the holiest room built into the very foundations of Oakwell Manor. Carnforth switched on the single bulb hanging from a rusting hook on the ceiling, its illumination revealing a large circular brick vaulted room. At its centre stood a black stone block, his sacred altar. Here was the heart and mind of the house, the hub of its power and the location of its dark soul.

Street Lives

By the black stone stood a simple wooden table on which a mortar and pestle, a flint knife, paint brush and a bowl of herbs had been laid out.

Carnforth tipped the dish with Jakob's dismantled hearing organs into the small mortar bowl. Various sacred herbs and plants were added. Taking the flint knife from the table, Carnforth cut his hand, allowing his blood to mix with Jakub's body parts. Picking up the mortar he ground the concoction into a paste, adding further minerals and plants. He chanted the old songs of binding and whispered prayers of joining. The true melding of Mr Jakub Norwak's magnificent hearing could commence.

Using the brush, he dipped it in the mortars crimson contents and began painting symbols onto the central black rock. The graffiti were of configurations unknown to human kind and even Carnforth had only a merest inkling of what they really meant. It was he was sure, the language of the demon, speaking of an older, darker powers.

The joining had begun. The symbols now decorated the Black Stone, glistened a dark crimson in the sharp light of the room's single bulb and drank in the bloody offering. Carnforth felt rejuvenation flow into the house's timbers, slate and brickwork. He too benefited from the symbiotic relationship, power oozing into the house's obedient servant. Carnforth now felt he detected the squeaks of the mice in the walls, the swish of spiders spinning their webs, weeds growing in the gutters and worms tunnelling through the garden soil. A soundtrack of life brought on by death.

Oakwell Manor was pleased. Its Edwardian plumbing screamed pleasure and twentieth century wiring buzzed and sparked. Carnforth was overjoyed, rewarded by the house's gratitude and affection. It touched him, filling his heart and what remained of his soul, with loving gratitude. The power of the renewal made him dizzy and he dropped to the rough flagged floor, his body tingling but his hearing sharp.

'Thank you, my house, my master, bless you for your gift. I will give to you again soon. Someone younger next time,' announced Carnforth, his voice raised and a note of hysteria trembling in his voice.

'I noticed a little dry rot on the west wing window frames and the paint peeling. Skin taken from the next 'guest' will improve your appearance.'

The water pipes bubbled an affirmative, and the boiler thumped its approval.

Carnforth climbed the steps, dragging the bloodied mattress with him. It had occurred to him to dump it in the tunnels, but why clutter the already packed corridors. Only the rats would benefit, and an excess of vermin could attract unwanted attention if they ever wandered out into the daylight.

'Stick to the plan Paul, burn the evidence, dispose of the rest at the local tip'.

The mattress ended up on a pile of dried leaves and branches, doused with accelerant and set ablaze. Carnforth watched the pyre, flames eating into the red stained material and warping the rusted springs. He gazed into the flames and reminisced how kind fate had brought him here.

*

Paul Carnforth had inherited Oakwell Manor from his 'mad uncle Harry', some fifteen years ago.

Harry had lived in the property for sixty-six years until he'd been dragged away to the local asylum in the early nineteen nineties, after being found naked in the middle of the main road screaming his house was the Devil, telling him to do 'bad things'. His case was considered hopeless by the doctors and Harry had lived a tranquil, if drug infused existence at a local mental hospital.

Carnforth had never bothered to visit the poor wretch, even though he was his only living relative. However, after being informed he was the sole beneficiary of Harry's will, he had a miraculous change of heart taking an extraordinary interest in his uncle's welfare. He'd often visit him for lengthy periods of time, enduring Uncle Harry's insane ramblings, and occasionally, rather interesting recollections on the unspeakable things the house had asked him to do. His efforts to steer his uncle towards financial matters, mainly his potential inheritance, proved frustrating.

After a year of what Carnforth regarded as interminable visiting, he'd managed to get a rough fiscal picture of his expectations, once 'Mad Harry' kicked the bucket. And the fiscal picture was a true work of art.

The manor house would be his; a faded piece of minor history. It had once boasted a farm, extensive wood and park land with ornamental gardens. Financial difficulties over the generations had led to the farm and most of the land being sold off piece meal. An ugly 1980's estate and patches of large Victorian houses, now occupied the once tranquil meadows at the front of the manor. The house still had large gardens and a small area of woodland, but it was a shade of its former self. There were some stocks and shares which provided a modest income that covered taxes and amenity charges and, excitingly, a large number of gold sovereigns hidden in the cellar, unbeknownst to nosey tax inspectors. Whilst some of the wealth would have to be used to cover death duties, it was still a perfect solution to Carnforth's monetary dilemmas. If only the old lunatic would die and die quickly.

Carnforth was a man in need of cash. He was not a popular man. His parents had died years earlier, probably through heart-break over their only son's behaviour. Work had been difficult. He considered he was too intelligent for most of the jobs he'd had, and his work colleagues were usually moronic bastards. The women he'd worked with regarded him as creepy and the men thought him lazy and arrogant. What fools they were.

His life had become a cycle of new jobs, complaints, transfers, requirements to resign or just being sacked. A sexual assault allegation at his last position had caused him to be unofficially black listed in the town and his prospects were gloomy. Even he had had to admit that he'd been lucky not to be arrested; the frigid bitch who had made the complaint being satisfied with his being fired. He'd endured having to walk from the office, his so-called colleagues laughing at his discomfort. Fate conspired to gift Carnforth a present. Facing the prospect of a very lonely Christmas, he'd been visiting his decaying lunatic uncle. The nurses were under staffed and he was alone for much of the time, eating Harry's Christmas dinner whilst the old man sat in a chair.

Harry had been having a bad day, his medication failing to dampen his deluded state of mind. Half way through a rant about the house's voice being that of Satan, he collapsed onto the tiled floor, with severe chest pains, begging for help. Carnforth, never one to miss an opportunity, had gently closed the door, took a cushion and placed it over his uncle's face, and pressed. The move had been inspired. Carnforth had waited a few minutes ensuring Harry breathed no more before making a tearful plea for medical assistance for his rather dead poor uncle.

The success of his deadly move ensured his inheritance. For the sake of appearance, he attended the meagre funeral, moving into the manor house the same afternoon.

The moment he entered Oakwell's crumbling walls with its peeling paint and woodworm infested timbers, he felt he'd come home. Its 'haunted house' look was magnificent, and it had given him a strange but comforting feeling of purpose and security previously denied him.

*

Carnforth drifted back to the present. The mattress was now a tangled spaghetti of glowing twisted metal springs and burnt fabric. He would allow the ashes to cool before visiting the tip. But first he felt the urge to patrol his little kingdom, ensuring no unwanted visitors trespassed. Whilst most of his previous 'guests' were stored securely in the cellars and its adjoining corridors, one body was not, and he always feared it being discovered rightly believing no one would understand his motives and his sacrifices.

He set off across the gardens, following the woodland path, his thoughts again wandering through memories which had seen him become if not the master of the manor, it's very best friend and partner.

Oakwell Manor had started to whisper to Carnforth as soon as he had taken up residence. It had been a shock of course and he recalled his uncle's insane ramblings about the voice and at first doubted his own sanity. But over time the house had become almost family, telling how important he was, complimenting him on his appearance, personality and achievements. It spoke of the terrible injustices poor Paul had suffered at the hands of fools who had crossed his path. It became his friend, advisor and mentor. Paul Carnforth was soon only too happy to act on behalf of the house, once its needs had been made clear; needs which somehow seemed to parallel his own.

The whispering crept into his dreams not unlike woodworm boring into the timbered woodwork of the house. He was, in truth, flattered by the house's interest, knowing the whole situation was weird but feeling compelled to listen to the house's creaking and groaning conversations. After a year the house told him it was dying. Wood rot, damp, subsidence and general age. It was after all, a very ancient structure.

Carnforth had despaired about losing his bosom friend, but happily it provided a solution. At its very core was the Black Stone. It could take sustenance from human sacrifice and re-grow its aged fabric, only the down and outs or persons of no value of course. Just so long as their blood and flesh were right to renew the structure. Carnforth would be its Grand Priest and Chief Protector, being rewarded with a small share of the dark power, allowing him to live an extended, healthy life. 'Mad Uncle Harry' had betrayed the house, refusing to provide victims, his conscience driving him insane. The result of this was the grand old manor had starved, its own dark soul consuming itself to remain alive. Carnforth would be the manor's saviour. He hadn't resisted long its dark siren call. In truth, the house offered him more than health and extended existence. Something life had denied him; friendship, the price being a total commitment to Oakwell Manor, body and soul.

His first act of loyalty had been to cut his arm, collect his warm blood in a silver dish and paint the Black Stone in red, cryptic symbols, reciting words given to him by the house. It was a poor ceremony with insufficient blood and Carnforth was nervous and hesitant. However, when he journeyed around the house, did not the oak panelling look a little more polished, the stones less cracked and the paint work restored? His wound healed quickly, and he felt upbeat and energised. That was the moment Carnforth decided to kill for the house, joining the elements of his victims to the house's wellbeing. He'd practised and experimented on animals at first. The house was unhappy stating only human sacrifice satisfied its needs, but a benefit was he perfected his 'butchery' skills on the various cats and dogs in his dissections.

His first proper 'kill' was an old tramp he'd found sleeping in the grounds. It had been a steep learning curve. He had tried to drug him with alcohol, but the old sod had drunk all his best brandy and upon being told there was no more the vagrant became angry and violent. The struggle had been bloody, messy and damaging. Furthermore, Carnforth had got fleas from the tramp's infested body. It had all been very distressing to the virgin murderer.

Blood was the principal food for the house at first, taken from several early victims, their bodies drained of their vital fluids and painted onto the Black stone, which soon became a crimson and terracotta coloured block. As the body count increased, the house suggested that the 'guests' should bequeath parts of their body to help it see, hear, touch, taste and speak more clearly.

There followed a string of 'melders' who had eyes re-moved, tongues extracted, and vocal cords cut free, all the bits ending up as wonderful artwork on the stone.

And all through this, the house's soft voice gave ease, guidance, support and advice. He learnt of the house's needs, moods, wants and desires, which eventually mirrored his own. His mind resounded with the long history of the sacred ground on which the manor house stood. It had been no simple parasite living off the flesh of those earlier followers. It had dispensed health and intelligence, safety and direction. The house, the black stone and its guardians were conjoined. Carnforth was part of the legend.

*

It was during one of his first walks around the estate that he'd discovered 'The Temple' hidden in the small two acres of woodland at the edge of the manor grounds. The building had been in a sorry state, its ornamental iron gates rusted and secured by a cheap padlock. It was built in imitation of the 'classical' style, a triangular pediment atop Ionic columns and a domed roof originally topped with shiny lead, alas now robbed of its metal protection. Its interior flooring was of black and white chequerboard tiles, and at its centre a statue of the Green man, ancient god of the Britons. There was a savagery about the marble figure with its wild face surrounded by a leaf mane and dressed in the skin of wolf and bear. It appealed to the aesthetic pagan in Carnforth's heart.

His investigation of the structure had revealed a trap door which led down into a very dark and deep shaft. There had been metal rungs affixed to the shaft's walls, but they were dangerously rusted and decayed, and he decided against further explorations. A trapdoor, camouflaged in the same black and white tiles, had once secured the shaft's entrance. Fallen masonry, disturbed probably when the lead roofing had been stripped away, had shattered its boards. A clumsy attempt had been made to cover the gaping hole with broken planks and sacking.

STREET LIVES

As the 'Temple' didn't receive the benefit of the manor's restorative energy, Carnforth resolved to have it restored by other worldlier means. He employed a talented young lad from the nearby town to repair the trap door. Michael had been his name; a rough diamond who'd been in trouble with the police and was anxious to try and rebuild his life and willing to accept secrecy as part of the deal. A generous payment on completion of the work was a wonderful incentive.

The repairs on the trapdoor had proved excellent. As Michael fell asleep over a drugged coffee in the manor's kitchen, Carnforth experienced a moment's regret about losing such a talented workman. Still, his good eyes and skilled hands would be excellent inclusions for the manor.

A few months later a pair of jobbing workmen named Mulligan and Jones arrived at his door asking for work. Carnforth knew they were rogues of the roughest sort and out to scam him, but the Temple roof needed repair. A deal was struck for an excessive amount of money, far more than the job was worth. Carnforth insisted their work would be inspected before settlement of the bill; bad repair and no cash.

The large amount of money promised, inspired the builders who re-laid the stones and re-leaded the roof. So pleased was Carnforth he promised them a 'bit extra' and they would celebrate over coffee and cake at the mansion. Jones had declined stating he had to clean up. In truth, he found the manor's owner creepy. Only Mulligan came to the manor for refreshment. The promised 'bits' which became extras were Mulligan's femurs and tibiae which were later ground to a fine white paste for decoration on the Black Stone. Returning to the Temple Carnforth repeated his coffee invitation to Jones, but something made Jones suspicious. An argument had developed, causing Carnforth great alarm. In a moment of uncustomary panic, he had struck Jones over the head with a shovel. It had all been very bloody, violent and unpleasant. Even worse was Carnforth heard distant voices in the trees and feared local children, who often trespassed into the garden, may discover his messy work. The body was quickly deposited through the new shiny trapdoor, falling into the darkness and landing with a wet thump at the bottom.

After ensuring the woodland was clear of nosey brats, he'd driven their rusting builders van away from the manor, leaving it in a local car park fully cleansed of incriminating fingerprints. Upon his return to the estate he ensured the 'Temple' gates were sealed with a heavy gauge chain and security padlock and Carnforth intended none would enter its precincts again.

*

His last checks were upon estates, the outer boundary walls and carefully cultivated barriers of bramble which added to the security of the grounds. Only one gap in the manor ground's defences remained. A small hole where it adjoined the edges of the Asgard estate. He must get it repaired, if only he knew of a decent set of builders. He'd even be prepared to pay them and let live. Good workmanship was so hard to get now-a-days.

His tour ended, his thoughts strayed towards a hot shower and a dash of brandy.

I will treat myself. Maybe I can rent a whore and get pissed in town. Life is good, he said to himself. His renewed body was hungry for food and pleasure, even if the house's appetite was sated. At least for now.

*

A month later and the problem of finding a 'melder' with skin suitable for the house's paint and varnish work, was praying greatly on Carnforth's mind. The house was pressing him hard to find a sacrifice. It was becoming hard as the sudden 'disappearances' over the years of had led to increased vigilance amongst the populous. How to get someone to the house was a real problem, especially with everyone having bloody mobile phones. He must avoid any trace of his victims coming to the manor house.

Things had been made worse by the bloody crank psychic in the local paper who claimed she knew where the body of a young girl was; someone who vanished over twenty years ago. As he started to read the article the loud chime of the doorbell announced a visitor. He tried to suppress his annoyance at having his 'me time' interrupted.

Probably some wrinkled old prune looking for charity handouts. Why can't it be some gorgeous young female with luscious layers of soft epidermis, all alone, he thought. The tribute of fine skin promised to the Black Stone reared up again in his mind. If this drought of suitable candidates continued, he may have to decorate the place himself. He shivered at the prospect. The doorbell rang again, and he went into the hallway, opening the door ready to bark a curt dismissal.

On the step stood a gorgeous young woman, her enveloping soft skin radiating its perfection. She was blonde, and very attractive. She had a low-cut blouse, unbuttoned at the top and was only just wearing an extremely short skirt. Her smile was a dazzling white, but it was her smooth, unblemished 'peaches and cream' flesh which mesmerised Carnforth.

She introduced herself as Amelia …something or other. He didn't catch her last name. She smiled, pouted and asked in the sweetest of voices, for the key to the Temple folly. Carnforth invited her in where they sat in the formal front room. She went on about a local historical society, architectural interest, photographs and research. It was hard to concentrate when her fabulous skin shone so brightly. She persistently licked her lips slowly with her tongue making Carnforth wonder if she had herpes. This Amelia appeared to be heaven sent, or perhaps Hell sent would be a better phrase. Still he was cautious.

He forced himself to concentrate as Amelia blathered on, and on about the manor's 'folly'. She hoped he didn't mind, but she'd sneaked into the woods to view it and, finding it locked, she wondered if he would grant access. More incessant talk about culture followed, and the possibility of writing an article. Amelia let slip she accessed the grounds via the tumbled down wall adjoining Asgard Close. She also wanted her explorations to 'be their little secret'. More teeth glowed from her smile as she put a hand upon his lap; a smooth as silk hand, of fresh tight skin in harmony with the soft tissue of her face.

'Have you discussed the matter with anyone or mentioned you were coming here,' ventured Carnforth.

'Oh no, it's too much of a special project to spoil. I thought just you and I would know. Of course, I will go down the shaft and report my findings to you'.

Further information flowed from her lipstick caked mouth about the lack of husband or boyfriend and her parents passing away some years ago and how lonely she was. She was perfect.

'Let me make you some of my special coffee, oh and cake too. We can discuss you having the key and access' said Carnforth.

Amelia smiled, delicate creases moving through the soft facial muscles, the suppleness of that delicate skin. He'd noted the tremors in the orbicularis oris, gentle movement of the masseter muscle. Oh, the fun of peeling the skin from the face and the ample body too. The house would radiate beauty and the prospect of revealing the rest of her skin thrilled him in a strange and somewhat erotic way.

She drank the coffee.

She ate the cake.

She slept.

Forever.

Carnforth gently picked the sleeping body up and made his way to the 'guest room'. It looked like his night would be a long one but satisfying all the same.

*

Carnforth took all that day and the next morning in the flaying of Amelia. He was a conscientious worker and tried to preserve as much of the skin as possible. The sacred silver dish was abandoned in favour of a steel bucket. It was an almost industrial step up from his usual working practices.

He was so wrapped up in his work he never realised the police had knocked at his door on a mission to also obtain the padlock key to the 'folly', albeit without the licking of lips and short skirts. Believing the house deserted' a warrant was eventually obtained. The folly's securing chain was cut, access obtained, the trapdoor discovered. A search team was dispatched into the shaft's darkness and the revelations started. For the police it was like a supermarket B.O.G.O.F deal. Two bodies for the price of one search.

The body of Sabrina Knox was discovered, with little clues to her killer's identity. They couldn't miss a bus pass belonging to a girl called Amelia, an old school rival, still clutched in her skeletal hand.

The body of a man, conveniently still in possession of his wallet and driving licence, was also found nearby, his head showing signs of very blunt force trauma, probably by the bloodstained sharp-edged shovel found at the side of the body. Inside the wallet was a small piece of paper with the words Paul Carnforth, Oakwell Manor.

The shovel was 'fast tracked' for fingerprints which, due to a minor fraud indiscretion by Carnforth some years earlier, meant his prints were on file.

The police called on Mr Carnforth again who, hearing the not so gentle knocking at the door, politely invited a gaggle of detectives and forensic officers in. Even with the imminent prospect of arrest, Carnforth eventually offered the Detective Chief Inspector tea and cake which was strangely declined.

As this D.C. I spoke to him, Carnforth waited for the inevitable as the search took place, which caused quite a sensation when a pale faced policeman reported the bloody, de-skinned body of a female in the cellar and piles of body parts in various states of decay littering the cellar. As he became the centre of attention, Carnforth smiled and shrugged his shoulders.

The house whispered its goodbyes as he was led away amongst a fairground of flashing lights.

Revelations in the press followed as the weeks sped by.

A black painted piece of concrete had been found in Carnforth cellar with bloody symbols painted on it.

Twenty-three bodies, including Amelia, had been found, all in pieces and all exhibiting signs of pieces missing or some form of mutilation. Carnforth was a truly helpful suspect, relating his story of the house talking to him, it's almost infinite age and extensive tunnels. He admitted all the killings, including the builder whose hair he had parted with the shovel and deposited through the temple folly's trapdoor, although he strenuously denied killing the girl Sabrina and was most pleased when the interviewing officers fully accepted his word.

In fact, his implication in her death had never been suspected with all evidence pointing to Carnforth's twenty third victim, Amelia. Police speculated correctly, she had gone to the house to obtain the gate key and use the rock-climbing ropes found in her house in her house, to remove incriminating evidence.

Of the extensive tunnels under the house, there was no trace, just a series of damp and gloomy cellars crammed with cadavers. The whole manor was in a state of semi-ruin, it's supposed replenished magnificence only real in Carnforth's mind.

The corridors were chattering again, creaking their support, urging him onwards in a new crusade. The cell whispered sweet things to Carnforth, who realised his friend had migrated from the manor house to be with him. He sat on his bed listening to the comforting words. The dingy brick corridor's anticipation of what was to come caused the lights to flicker, and steel doors to swing on their hinges with throaty croaks.

It was a pity Her Majesty's prison was showing signs of peeling paint, rusty metal work and cracked tiles. He'd heard even the prison's C.C.T.V and tannoy systems often played up. However, with a lifetime behind bars ahead, he was sure the necessary 'melders' could be found to 'do up the place'. Carnforth smiled and lay on his bed awaiting the prison's instructions.

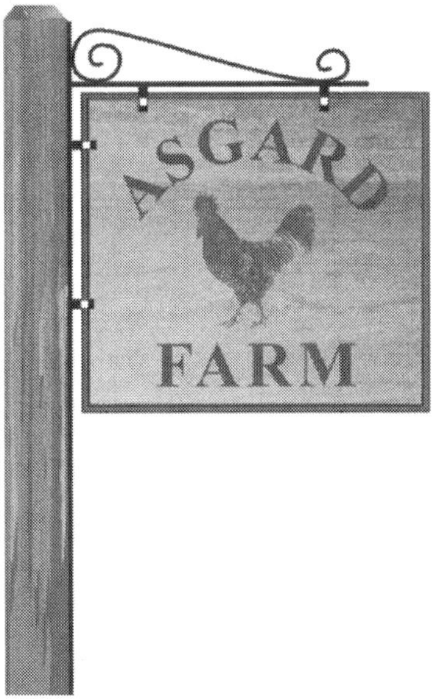
ASGARD
FARM

STREET LIVES

Lambing Time

by

Hannah Silcock

Annie Thrax was short, fat and round, usually seen with her arms folded and wedged between her large sagging bust and protruding stomach. She was 4' 11' tall and proud of it. There was a mass of tightly permed grey hair on her head that no wind condition could move. She was always clean and tidy with her full length paisley patterned apron on. It had a large front pocket where she kept scraps of dried bread to give as a treat to old mother hen, Mrs Clutterbuck, and her flock of 20 hens. Useless the rooster, and he was useless, never having fathered any chicks, knew that the farmer's wife had it in for him and if he got too close he would get a swift kick up the bum!

Her husband, Albert, a tall thin weary man, weighed down by farm responsibilities, wasn't much better and had only managed to father two girls, twins at that. Annie was 47 years old when the twins had eventually arrived; Daisy and Linda, or Loopy Linda as she became known. It had been touch and go whether she would survive the trauma of 3 days in labour. Both girls were born 'breach.' Daisy was born first and stillborn. Linda, being more reluctant to leave the warmth of her mother's womb and follow her sister out into the cold new world, stayed too long and became starved of oxygen. Tragically those extra few minutes of warmth would have lasting effects and gave rise to her nickname, 'Loopy Linda.'

Linda had red hair and pale skin and was covered in freckles of all shapes and sizes. One eye was green and one blue. They seemed to move independently, and Annie found it very hard to know which one to look at. Sometimes the left eye moved up and disappeared under the eye lid leaving a blood veined globe. She had always disliked Linda. Perhaps parts of her daughter reminded her of herself too much, another short round person but clumsy with it and slow to learn. They had never bonded, and Linda always knew she was different and had retreated into her own isolating world.

Annie, not understanding about oxygen asphyxia, blamed Albert for Linda's 'light headedness' and reckoned it had come down from his mother and grandmother. Her marriage to Albert had been arranged by her father, to pay off his gambling debts, and she hadn't met Albert's family until her wedding day. His mother was an 'odd', silly woman who giggled all the time and didn't seem to know what was going on. Grandmother Thrax was another silly giggler and told stories of unseen things that moved about at dusk.

The farm was an eerie place, dating back to the 1730s and, according to the local historian, Mrs Herstory, it was built on a Viking settlement. The locals told tales of ghostly goings on, frightening noises and sometimes even voices in the outbuildings. Old Grandmother Thrax had always kept two large salt pots on the front step and a string of small bells draped across the back door. The bells would tinkle when evil spirits approached, and the salt would absorb their ephemeral bodies.

In early March the Swaledale sheep had been brought down from the fells to the better pasture that was close to the farm, where it was safer to lamb them. Swaledales were a hardy upland breed and survived well on the remote and exposed fells. The Thrax's had five hundred breeding Swales who were good for commercially produced wool and viable mutton that had good flavour and tenderness. In previous years Albert had bred a champion Swale Tup. James 007 read his ear tag and £25,000 read his price tag. He had been sold last Autumn at Hawes Mart to Jack Hope.

On this particular Tuesday morning Albert had checked the ewes, fed the pet lambs, changed the bedding and was wondering about the weather, hoping that rain would hold off for another couple of days. Feeling hungry and drawn by the smell of Annie's cooking he made his way across the stack yard towards the kitchen and lunch. Moss, the sheep dog trailed behind him, hoping for a tasty snack. He had spent a tiring morning pacing up and down watching new born lambs in the pens and hoping one would get close enough to nip.

Their thoughts were suddenly interrupted by the arrival of a battered old land rover and trailer which had rattled down the cobbled

STREET LIVES

lane at some speed and stopped abruptly in the yard, missing Moss by inches. He yelped, leapt back, hackles up and waited his turn to get his own back. Albert turned to see an angry farmer jump out of his truck. He recognised him as Jack Hope.

'Albert Thrax, you are a rogue and a thief, and I should have known better than to buy a tup from you. I'll have none of it, do you hear me? None of it! I should have listened to John Diggle and Thomas Crapp,' bellowed Jack Hope.

'They warned me that buying a tup from you wouldn't go well. Should have listened to them, should have listened...'

'Oh hello Jack. What's that you say? What you going on about?' Albert asked.

'I'll tell you what I am going on about. That BLOODY tup, he's useless.'

Annie appeared from behind the barn door and smiled to herself at the word 'useless'.

'He's useless, not performed, not one ewe in lamb, failed at every attempt.'

Jack knew that James 007 had been hard at it tupping all autumn, so it wasn't for the want of trying. The tup was now well knackered, had suffered serious weight loss and was out of condition. Observing that James had been hard at it, Jack had decided that it would have been an unnecessary expense to scan the ewes for pregnancy too early and now it was too late to use another tup.

'What do you mean 'useless',' spluttered Albert, starting to feel alarmed. Hope stood facing Albert, left hand on his hip, right hand waving about as if conducting.

'I've had vet out. Took three of us to hold him down to collect a semen sample. Then the bugger head butted the vet over the sheep pen gate. £25,000 I paid for him and I want me money back and the vet's bills. That bloody tup, I've fetched him back, you can have him back. I want me money back.' Jack went round to the back of the trailer to open the tail gate and let the tup out.

James 007 knew that something was up as he had been dragged away from a very juicy field of spring grass and was then roughly thrown into the back of the trailer. It all happened so fast that his toe had got caught in the wire mesh and his toe nail had been pulled out.

His head had hit the side corner of the crate at a funny angle and his left eye had burst open. He had spent the last couple of hours thrashing about from side to side trying to see where he was going and understand what was going on. He was frightened and angry and in no mood to be wrestled to the ground again.

James saw his chance to escape to freedom as Hope opened the trailer's tail gate and, without waiting for it to be fully open, he took a leap for freedom. Over the top he jumped, hitting Hope full in the face with his nose. Jack fell backwards and only remembered the pain that followed as a hard kick in the groin rendered him momentarily unconscious. James, bloodied but free, limped off towards the low pasture, happy to be home and in familiar surroundings.

Moss saw his chance for revenge and lunged towards Jack Hope, who was just beginning to come round. He was about to pounce and take a tasty chunk out of Hope's dripping head when he felt his master's hand clasp onto his collar and yank him back. Jack, hearing the dog's incessant barking and seeing him pawing the ground straining to be free, hastened to his feet, still swearing about that bloody useless tup and Albert had better pay up or else.

Albert was flabbergasted and angry and afraid as Jack Hope, being thirty years his junior, was a fit 40-year-old and had something of a reputation as a fighting man. He had come across him in his dog fighting days. He knew he was in a mess but, feeling defensive, he began to hurl abuse back at Hope . He called him a liar and went on about his reputation being ruined.

'That tup was alright with my ewes. Gave a good crop of lambs.'

But he knew that wasn't the truth. James 007 hadn't shown any interest in the ewes and Albert had long suspected that he was gay. Albert had been glad to get rid of him and even gladder with the money he made.

Moss was still snarling and eager for a scrap and as Albert's grip slackened he began to creep stealthily towards Hope. He looked up at his master's face and a knowingness passed between them. The collie stood up, lunged forward growling and went for the intruder.

Hope, who in an instant understood the situation, jumped into his truck, turned the engine on, threw it into gear, pulled the window down and bellowed, 'You haven't heard the last of this, Thrax. I'll have you for this. No farmer around here will buy anything off you again when they hear what I have to say.'

With that he accelerated out of the yard so fast that he hit the calf house door and tore it clean off its hinges, with Moss hard on his heels.

Albert knew he didn't have the money to pay him back. Over the years he had spent a lot of it at no 19 Asgard Close, visiting Vicky, the 'Lady of the night', or in his case the 'Lady of the afternoon'; 4.15 pm on Mondays, Wednesdays and then 3pm on Thursdays in the autumn. He had gambled the rest away on his fighting cockerels and dogs, all of which had failed him, and he hoped Annie wouldn't find out about his little 'sideline' or there would be all hell to pay. He would have to go to that bastard Jameson, the money lender, for another loan.

This lack of money, along with Albert's arthritis and advancing years, had led to the farm buildings being abandoned and left to fall into disrepair. Only one barn was useful and that took the summer's hay crop. Then there was the Low Byre, one Calf House, now without a door, a Tool Shed and the large Sheep Shed that was important and used for lambing each spring. Of course there was Albert's precious dog kennels where he kept his Wire-Haired Fox terriers; Tucker, who liked his food, and Squirt, the less said about him the better. His grandfather William had bred 'Black Jack' and 'Stump,' two of the best fighting dogs in Yorkshire, and Albert aspired to be like him.

Annie knew about his fighting dogs and cockerels. She was also aware that in the early autumn her stash of Guinness went down and, knowing that Albert didn't drink, she suspected it was mixed into that, 'special family recipe,' he fed to them to improve their fighting condition. Old man Thrax had stressed to Albert that this recipe must be kept away from the women in the family. But the women in the family did know and had always known. Annie had never been able to find it and she had looked very, very hard. She wanted this high protein diet for her hens, in the hope that egg production would increase and that they would also get fatter for the pot.

She swore that one night she would forget to lock up his precious cockerels, in the hope that Harry Fox would find them in the dark. 'Special food indeed and them bloody dogs!' She was frightened of his two Wire Haired Fox Terriers. She suspected he took them dog fighting on Thursday nights in the Autumn but never understood why he left in the afternoons? Her suspicions were often alerted when the iodine disappeared from the bathroom cabinet along with her sewing box from the sitting room dresser. She hoped that one of these days he would get his comeuppance.

Annie had employed Dullard, a local farmer's son, from a village over the other side of the fell. She knew nothing about him or his family, but he worked hard. He was a gangly lad with a mop of unruly ginger hair, roughly tied back in a ponytail. There was a permanent silly grin on his face, which reminded her of Albert's mother. Could there be a connection? She was beginning to wonder.

He giggled all the time and hadn't seemed to notice the pain he was in as the skin that Nip had torn off his ankle, in revenge for standing on his tail, was a bloody mess skin and blood congealing on his mucky sock.

'What do you mean you know nought about sheep? You're a farmer's son aren't you?' said Annie

'Aye, well, Mrs Thrax, we only had cattle and pigs but I'm a fast learner. It'll be alright,' Dullard muttered, trying not to sound too lame.

Just her luck; she had employed a 'halfwit.' He would get on well with Linda?

Albert appeared round the Stack Yard wall. 'Six pair of twins, Annie, and another bloody triplet,' he shouted

'Ewe ain't got enough milk for three. We'll have to take little un off. Another bloody pet lamb to bottle feed'.

Annie heard him loud and clear. She was used to his shouting, after all it was all she knew. Her parents had spent their whole lives working in the Lancashire cotton mills, where they had learnt to shout over the noise in the weaving sheds, and both suffered from occupational hearing loss. Sadly for Annie it had its downside as they could both lip read!

She thought she had escaped when she married Albert but, no, he was another shouter, both his parents being hard of hearing. Annie felt she had suffered from earache her entire life.

Fortunately Linda was quiet and walked about in a dreamy state, disconnected from her surroundings. She had no interest in the farm. Her only job was to lock up the hens at night. When she forgot, and she frequently did as her long-term memory was non-existent, Harry fox was straight in and killed enough food for a week.

STREET LIVES

Annie struggled to understand Linda and had grown to dislike her. A dislike that was growing deeper and deeper. She was just a nuisance, always getting in the way and having to be rescued from mishaps. She would be well pleased if Linda didn't exist at all.

As she wandered to the sheep sheds to check the ewes her thoughts were quickly interrupted by Dullard's screams, coming from the Lambing shed.

'Come quick Mrs Thrax, come quick.'

'Why what's going on?' she asked, quickening her pace.

'There's that dog again, the one Mr Thrax took a pot shot at last week,' Dullard exclaimed.

'It's the Cocker Spaniel and he's got Roberta, Mr Thrax's prize ewe, and two others cornered in the far pen.'

Another voice appeared. 'Harvey, Harvey come here, come here.' It was Mrs Sue Smith, the local gossip, from Asgard Close.

'You naughty boy!' she exclaimed.

'Naughty Boy, naughty boy!' screamed Annie in fury. 'Is that it? All you can say?'

Annie looked round and saw Albert running towards her,

'Albert go fetch the 12 bore and don't forget the ammo.'

She turned on Mrs Smith screaming at her, 'What part of the sign on the farm gate can't you understand? It says,

'DOGS WORRYING SHEEP WILL BE SHOT'

'You have been warned before, why won't you listen? Why? It's all out of my hands now. When Albert gets back, God help that dog!'

Roberta had won best Gimmer Hog in 2015, Best Fleeced Sheep in 2016, Best Ewe Suckling Mule Lambs in 2017, all at Otley Show. Then in 2018 she became Overall Champion and was worth a hefty £22,000.
Roberta was now so famous that Albert had soared in the ranks of the Swaledale Sheep Breeders Association and had been elected president for the 2019 – 2020 season.

Harvey continued to growl and bark and ,when he thought no one was looking, made a swift attack on Roberta's milk laden udder, damaging her left teat which now hung in lacerated bits, oozing bloody milk.

All three sheep were terrified, panicking and making ear piercing sounds. One of them jumped over Harvey, giving him a quick well aimed kick that hit him squarely on the side of the head. He staggered backwards, confused, giving a second sheep her chance. She charged, trampled the dog underfoot, knocked Dullard over and raced out of the shed, into the field and freedom. But Roberta was too heavy in lamb to run and jump and unable to follow. Harvey, dazed and shaken, got to his feet, stumbled, regained his composure, saw what he had lost and advanced towards Roberta.

Mrs Smith looked up and saw Albert running back across the yard, carrying the shot gun. She became hysterical at the thought of losing her beloved dog, who was continuing to ignore her.

Dullard, now on his feet, lunged towards Harvey, missed and hit the ground hard, face down in sheep muck and straw.

Annie's heart was pounding. Her face was scarlet and sweat was pouring from both hands.

Albert arrived and loaded the gun.

'I'll kill the bloody dog, once and for all. It's the last time he will worry my sheep.'

Mrs Smith screamed and screamed louder and louder, ' No, No, No, …..'

Albert paused, turned to Mrs Smith, 'Have you any idea what that bloody dog has done, chasing those ewes round and round. Those lambs will be all jumbled up inside their mothers. They won't lamb themselves now. They'll need help and that's bound to be in the middle of the night and that's if they don't abort first. You stupid, stupid woman.'

'Just wait 'til I get my hands on that bloody dog.'

'Harvey, Harvey, come here, come here,' she continued to shout, her voice shaking with fear.

But Harvey was having fun and not listening to any command.

As Albert lifted the gun to his shoulder and took aim, finger on trigger, the dog looked up, saw the gun, knew his time was up and bolted out of the sheep shed and off down the farm track. As Albert swung round to follow the dog, his right foot slipped on some abandoned after birth. He fell sideways and as he did so, the gun went off. BANG!

All became silent. The sheep shed was silent. Albert became aware that he was splattered in blood, lumps of flesh were sticking to his face and jaw. Shocked and stunned, he got to his feet in disbelief at the sight in front of him.

Roberta, his prize ewe was dead, with her unborn twins inside her. The shot had gone straight through her head. Dead in an instant. Albert had an image of pound notes floating away and his life along with them.

A new kind of rage filled his whole being. Picking up the shot gun he turned, with amazing agility for a man of his age, jumped the sheep gate and set off as fast as he could down the farm track after the dog.

It didn't take long to find the culprit. He was lying exhausted in a ditch with a still squealing baby rabbit in his mouth, not yet fully dead. Albert raised his gun, aimed and with a single shot the offender was gone.

Harvey, now in several pieces was not easy to pick up. But his head was still intact and recognisable as,' that bloody dog.' After a short but bloody walk, Albert finally arrived at Mrs Smith's house. He opened the garden gate and dropped the remains of the dog on the door step. He knocked several times on the door and shouted through the letter box that he wanted recompense for his loss. No answer! After several minutes of silence he walked back down the garden path, closed the gate behind him and, with a sadistic smirk on his face, felt it was a job well done. He set off on the walk back to the farm.

As he reached the last gate to the stack yard, he found a dead ewe half impaled on the barbed wire fence. Part of her stomach was open, and a single leg was hanging out. That 'bloody dog' had had the last word after all.

Albert returned to the sheep pen to find that Annie had staggered to her feet and pulled the dead Roberta off Dullard, who had rolled over in the sodden straw and dragged himself up to sit on a bale of steaming mouldy hay.

'You'll have to get the knacker lorry to come and pick her up,' Dullard said in a whisper.

There was a long pause as the Thrax's looked at each other and Albert saw a way to make some money out of this disaster. 'Can't waste good meat. we'll take her to the barn and send for Hatchet the butcher later.'

'Oh! And there's another dead un on yard fence. I'll fetch her,' said Albert

Between them they got the ewes to the barn, hung them up by a back leg, slit their throats and drained the blood into a bucket. It would make good black pudding. Albert removed the livers and Annie took them back to the kitchen for the pot, them being the best part. Albert would leave Roberta to stiffen for a few days before Hatchet the butcher would come and cut her up.

But two sheep were too much for their freezer, so his mind was mulling over the possibility of selling the 'other meat' as Roberta's to Hatchet as prime lamb. There would be a bag that read, 'Roberta's leg' and others that read, 'other leg', 'Roberta's rump', 'other rump', 'Roberta's Chops' and 'other chops'. If they bagged the cuts themselves no one would be any the wiser and it would help to pay off his debts. Of course they would need to be careful to keep 'other meat' for themselves as that would actually be Roberta.

Annie returned to the farmhouse, put the lambs' livers into a large stewing pot and sank into Grandmother's old rocking chair. She pulled her shawl around her and rocked gently back and forth. The Aga cooker was warm and comforting and she briefly nodded off to sleep. She was brought round by the sound of two bleating lambs in the lamb box next to her. They had been born outside in the wet and cold, their mother having died in a ditch. She had tipped herself over and got stuck . On her back, wedged in the ditch, feet in the air, she had soon died. Albert suspected suicide; drowned in her own body fluid.

Her lambs had spent the night under an infra-red heat lamp in the kitchen lamb box, only big enough for two. They weren't expected to survive but they had and somehow the sound of their bleating and their empty little stomachs and need for milk gladdened Annie's heart. She smiled at the new orphans in front of her and got up to make some powdered lamb milk.

The next few days passed in a blur for all of them. Nothing much was said between Annie and Albert, but she did feel an unusual amount of sympathy for his loss. The weather had improved, which meant fewer dead lambs, the sheep had settled down. They were both tired of long days and especially the night shifts.

Linda was no use on the farm, of course, and preferred to spend most of her time either in her room or wandering off for days at a time. She was a thin, awkward, gangly girl who didn't eat much, was malnourished and didn't speak much either. She inhabited a world between worlds and didn't relate to her parents. Linda needed to be alone and didn't care where she was and rarely wanted to return home. She wanted to disappear into her world, away from prying eyes, questions, rules and, worst of all, conversation. Where she went no one knew and no one cared.

On the following Monday's night shift, Albert had a disaster. He lost two large lambs. The ewe had been in labour too long and the lambs had become distressed. One was born dead, strangled by its umbilical cord which was wrapped tightly round its neck. The second lamb had suffocated in its birth sac. She was a big healthy ewe with plenty of milk. He knew he had two spare lambs that he could 'set on' to her. He rushed to the kitchen to collect the two orphans from the lamb box and began his work. With a sharp knife he cut the skin from round the dead lambs' ankles and necks, slit them underneath and proceeded to pull the skin off each lamb. He then rubbed the dead lambs' skins over the two orphans and dressed them in their new coats. These new lambs were put in front of the ewe who sniffed and sniffed them.

Fortunately she soon accepted the new orphans and their adopted coats were removed and after a few days they were safe enough to go outside with the others. Albert had a sense of satisfaction that this had worked. As he watched this happy little family run and jump together on the fresh morning grass, he remembered how transient it all was. They would have four or five months together before they would be separated for ever, she to breed again and the lambs to be sold to Hatchet the butcher. Spring Lamb! But that was farming.

Lamb losses were about the same as usual. They now had six pet lambs to feed. Two of them were from triplets, the small ones taken off because the mother didn't have enough milk for three. One had been rejected and the other three were orphans. There were also two other orphans, both very small and weak. The lamb box in the kitchen was full and they needed warming up, so Annie put them in the Aga oven where it was warm and dry, having first turfed out the farm cat from his favourite resting place. The oven door was left open and Snap the dog was left in charge to make sure that ,when they came round, he would bark. Snap loved this job and had become an expert over the years. He wasn't so much guarding them as watching his lunch.

That afternoon Linda had just got up and, half asleep, breezed into the kitchen. As she made her way to the Aga cooker to warm her hands she tripped over Snap, who growled and snarled at her. She jumped back in alarm and as she did, so her right hand hit the oven door and it closed with a sharp click. Slam. The faint sound of the bleating lambs was now inaudible. Snap looked confused and wondered where lunch had gone.

Meanwhile, Annie was in the sheep shed having a particularly tough time trying to lamb a large ewe, who was carrying two lambs that had got their feet tangled together and were stuck. She had managed to wrestle the ewe to the ground and stuck her right arm inside her back end and was now feeling for legs. The plan was to find which leg belonged to which lamb and then pull them out one by one. Lambs are born front feet first with their head nestled closely in between them. After what seemed a long time, the first lamb came out, was given a quick hard slap on the back and dragged round for the ewe to lick and bond with. Then the second lamb, with its feet pulled into place, experienced he same procedure.

These had been big lambs and Annie's arms ached. She sat down on the straw next to them and felt a sense of achievement. Hands resting on knees, she looked down at her left hand, paused then screamed. 'AGH.' 'NO NO NO.' She saw that her wedding ring was missing. In an instant she knew it had come off inside the sheep. She couldn't believe it. In all that pulling and pushing of feet it had worked its way off. Not wanting to believe it, she quickly checked both lambs, frantically searched the straw and examined the afterbirth.

There was nothing for it but to go back in and feel around. In what seemed like an age of rooting about her fingers eventually wrestled a small metal object into her hand. 'Found it!' There she sat ,relieved, covered in afterbirth and blood, and she stank.

'Is everything alright?' Albert had arrived. Looking at Annie he surmised what had happened and felt relieved that he could now confess that that was how he had lost his wedding ring years ago but had been too embarrassed to tell her. They both sat on the sodden straw and laughed.

Together they checked the other sheep for new arrivals and walked back to the farmhouse for lunch and a quick 40 winks. Approaching the kitchen door Annie's nose picked up an unfamiliar smell, something unpleasant. As she opened the door she recognised the smell of burning flesh. Her eyes immediately flew to the closed door on the Aga cooker. Screaming, she ran, pulled open the oven door and there in front of her was the sorry sight of two half cooked baby lambs curled up together for comfort. They had suffocated in the dry heat, being unable to breath.

Both Annie and Albert were enraged, shouting at each other. 'Who shut the oven door?'

'Who, Who, Who?'

'Who did it? '

'Who has baked these new borns alive? '

Annie's eyes then fell on the shadow of Linda in the corner. She was hiding behind the bookcase. Their eyes met.

'I didn't know they were in there, she wailed, although she did have a faint recollection of bleating lambs and falling over the dog.

'You didn't know, you stupid halfwit. It should have been you in that oven not them!'

Annie kicked the dog out of the way, grabbed the kitchen broom and proceeded to chase Linda round and round the kitchen table, whacking her as often as she could.

Linda, for once in her life, tried to defend herself.

'It's not my fault. I didn't put them in there.'

'Oh it's my fault is it?' 'Well I'll show you, young lady, whose fault it is, you stupid. stupid girl. If you had any brain at all you would have seen that the lamb box was full, and Snap was on guard. What did you think he was guarding?'

Snap, on hearing his name, sat up and tried to extract lunch from the open oven door.

Annie swung the broom round for the umpteenth time and this time she caught Linda squarely on the side of her head, sending her crashing to the ground and hitting her head on the sharp corner of the table as she fell.

Within seconds her red hair was covered in blood that began to trickle slowly down the side of her face, soaking her freshly ironed white blouse, as it made its way down to her right leg and was absorbed into the kitchen rug. She lay there in a pool of blood on the dirty kitchen floor.

For a few seconds there was an eerie silence only broken by the sound of Snap dragging his lunch out of the oven and Albert giving him a quick whack with his cap.

Annie, dazed and still holding the broom, stood over Linda wondering what she had done to deserve such a hare-brained girl. She was surprised that she felt no emotion but checked that she was still alive and went outside to calm down. Snap, seeing his opportunity, sneaked back into the kitchen and stared at the oven door, hoping to have lunch without being noticed.

Albert helped Linda to her feet, carried her to the bedroom and laid her on the bed. There didn't seem to be any serious damage. He cleaned the blood off her face as best he could. She came round, smiled at her father and then began to giggle and giggle. Albert, exasperated and tired, went downstairs and collapsed into his armchair. He held his head in his hands and just wanted it all to go away, for Linda to go away.

His wish was granted sooner than he expected because two days later Linda disappeared. A few of her things were missing, the wardrobe was half empty, as were the shoe and boot cupboards downstairs and the bathroom cabinet had been raided. When Annie realised that 'Muffin,' her favourite teddy, had gone, she knew that Linda was not coming back. She sat on her bed and looked round and felt nothing. It was over, they were both free of each other.

In the following weeks days tumbled into each other and life settled back into a normal routine. Only a few ewes were left to lamb now. Most of the heavy work was over. Shepherding the ewes and lambs and feeding the ewes sheep nuts to keep their milk production up was the hardest part of the day.

By now it was late May and Annie and Albert sat together on the porch talking about the events of the last few weeks. Dullard had returned to his family over the fell.

It had been one of the toughest lambing times she could remember. Albert sighed, put his hand in his pocket looking for his pipe tobacco and brought out a handful of rubber castration rings. He smiled and Annie was pleased he had found them because last year they had fallen out of his pocket in the washing machine and blocked the drain, much to the amusement of the local plumber, Mr W. C. Tapp.

Albert's hands were still stained with various colours of marker spray. It was always annoying when the ewe moved just as he was about to spray a number five on and it turned out to be a six, or a one turned out to be a seven. Ewes and lambs were all numbered, so he knew who belonged to who.

Annie, rested and calm, was suddenly engulfed in a sea of emotion towards Albert and felt the need to be kind to him. She brought him a bucket of hot salty water and washed his stained hands. Then his feet and ankles were in the bucket, soaking, resting and healing. His ankles were sore from lambs insisting on running figures of eight round them and ewes had the ability to tip freshly filled buckets of water over his feet. Most of his days were spent squelching around in soggy, smelly socks. Annie fussing over him and his feet being washed and dried and having warm dry socks on made him feel good. She raised her head and smiled and something unspoken passed between them, a sense that things would be okay. They still had each other, the farm and their sheep, life would go on. The wheel of the year turns, and they would turn with it.

STREET LIVES

Mr Fox

by

Hannah Silcock

One late September afternoon Mr Fox emerged from his earth, stretched his old weary grandfather limbs, sniffed the air and thought about last night's adventure.

Although it had been a successful night's hunting, he, a veteran of more than 150 chicken house raids, had slept fitfully. There had been troubling images of men with dogs, wire snares, leg traps and humans shouting.

He remembered hiding in the thicket of brambles and nettles, waiting for darkness to fall so he could extract supper from the hen house. Then there had been images of the farmer walking into his woods carrying a bag of large clanking things. Alarmed, heart pounding, he had frozen hardly daring to breath.

After a while, peace had returned to the wood and he waited and waited. As it grew darker he saw that the farmer's girl, 'Loopy Linda,' hadn't closed the hen house door. Tonight he would eat well. As he crept towards the open door the moon, conveniently for him, cast a shadow in such a way that he could see where the hens were sitting. He paused and made a quick decision as to which perch to attack first. Then he was in. Feathers began flying, hens everywhere, lots of screeching, screaming and clawing. He had grabbed two by the neck, a quick snap and that was it. Others were trampled underfoot and suffocated each other. One died as he dragged her backwards out of the hen house door. She had become stuck and, with all his pulling, her left leg had ripped off and she had died of shock and he had been left with a mouthful of bum feathers up his nose.

He knew he had to be quick. He could hear feet racing towards him and the farmer, Albert Thrax, and his wife, Annie, were shouting. All the commotion had woken them up. He had managed to drag two of his kill away and decided to return for the others the next night.

He shivered with the memory of it all. But he was now fully awake, his stomach felt heavy but happy.

He sniffed the air and sensed that all was not well, something in his world had changed. His well-worn track smelled as it always did, yet ,as he made his way deeper into the wood, the bramble patch carried a less familiar scent, alerting him to beware.

As he trotted further along, stopping only for a tasty early treat of black brambles, something ahead of him moved quickly and darted into the bramble thicket; perhaps a shrew, a bank vole or a tasty big fat mouse.

Without thinking, he plunged forward into the tangled bramble thicket and, in an instant, got caught in its woody stems. Pulling and tugging made little difference but the stem around his neck was getting tighter with each movement.

Then the realisation dawned, that he wasn't caught in a bramble stem but a nasty wire snare.

'So that's what the farmer had been setting last night.'

The snare was now gripping tightly round his neck. Instinct told him to free himself, but his brain said, ' be quiet, be still, don't struggle'.

The instinct to survive took over and he struggled even harder to free himself.

Thrashing his body back and forth, tossing it in every possible direction, he none the less became more and more wrapped up in thorny bramble stems.

Front feet, when not pounding on the soft earth, were furiously tearing up the ground, entrenching him further into a deep soggy pool of slippery mud and blood. Each movement tightened the snare around his neck just that little bit more.

After many hours of struggling, he paused out of sheer exhaustion and became still. In the stillness he realised that the hot warm sensation on his beautiful red chest and front legs was blood, his blood, pouring faster and faster from his broken neck. The snare wire had now pierced his skin and his neck artery and was rubbing on his vertebrae.

The pain was unbearable. Each breath was more difficult. Choking and gasping was all he could do, eyes bulging, vision becoming blurred.

He began to have a sensation of floating. His thoughts turned to home and to his long-lost family. Was he dreaming? Where was he?

He became aware that the pain in his feet was subsiding. Breathing was easier. His neck felt free. His body, relaxed and heavy, settled gracefully down onto the bramble patch. He was gone. The last breath had left his body and he was free. Free from pain.

In death he had found freedom; freedom from being chased, hunted, persecuted and starved. As his weary old grandfather body lay on the soft bramble bushes, his soul made its journey back to the land of his ancestors in the Otherworld.

STREET LIVES

Asgard Close

From Little Acorns

by

Russell Lloyd

I lie, that is the truth. It was a child's way. It began with Jackanory. It made me realise what people liked didn't have to be real. It pixelated the rest of my life a shade of untruth even I couldn't always see – 'I'm fine'; 'we must do this again'; 'pleased to meet you'; 'no, it's OK really, I don't mind', so forth and so on were the words I came to lie.

Back then Jackanory was my time, my bastion away from truth, reality, and a world I already knew wasn't mine. Fifteen minutes that seemed to pass and be finished faster than I liked and sooner than I wanted and then I'd be back seated cross-legged my hands clutching the soles of my Clark's Juniors looking up at a mahogonyesque brown box TV with an oval screen no bigger than a dinner plate, in the family home. Family house, I mean, I should say. Home implies something we never had. Family, bah – strangers with the same name. The only other strangers were feelings. We didn't do feelings. My Dad was ice and Mother was fire. But there I go again, lies. Because we had to do feelings; her feelings, her anger, her tantrums, her 'I'm leaving you all'. Over time, when minutes could seem like years and years flickered by in recollection like minutes, I'd stopped asking or pleading or clinging above her knees with little hands punched into 'don't go' fists full of skirt. Soon, but not quickly enough, I didn't care if she did and then was sorry she didn't.

My Dad, as good sometimes with words as he was with emotions, would blurt out 'Don't be such a big girl's blouse,' or such like to my sister or me when our tears wouldn't be dammed. 'We'll be OK,' he'd say. We never were, or would be, because she always came back.

My Dad, well, we never really did know what he felt, my sister and I. But mostly he looked like he was waiting to say 'Well, I did my best' or other stuff he thought ought to be heard. Who could blame him, we hadn't but then we didn't need to? She was good at that, blaming.

It wasn't all bad – see, there I go again! At Christmas we got presents that cost a lot but not in time or effort...the latest gizmo, the next craze, so forth. We'd all say words we didn't mean to people we didn't care for about things that weren't love. The best gifts we never got were the ones we couldn't see like love, security, trust, honesty and on and on.

There were family outings and some of the places were OK, but it was always the wrong family, wrist flicking watches, glad to return; didn't matter we didn't want to be there so long as we could retreat back into our rooms, separate and apart like.

'...so what's your story?' She'd been saying other words first but that was all I caught through the musak as the memories subsided and the bar filled my gaze. Shame, I was supposed to be listening; it was my job right now. She was thirty-nine – I was guessing she'd been that way for years. Groucho Marx eyebrows, Thunderbird eyes, and tentacle eyelashes all atop clothes that seemed to be mostly permatan and flesh. I wasn't complaining; how she looked made me glad I'd got her here, Friday evening in Korks' Wine Bar.

She was waiting for me, for an answer, for details that connected hers with my story, but I hadn't heard her talk and didn't need to listen. I knew her way better than she did. Another reason to choose her. She'd helped with the selection with her words 'men are all the same'. I'd agreed which was, of course, reassuring. I wasn't like them. I was different. Different good, she thought, and different new, I knew.

I talked some words I wasn't thinking. But before the smile they slid on her face sidled away, I said 'Actually, I only live five minutes round the corner.' We talked how noisy it was there, par for the course, etc, so on. You get the picture, so did she but, naturally, it was as fake as I could make it be.

Outside, our bonhomie parted a darkness the street lights only infringed, and we arrived. I keyed the door wide and she sway-hipped her path to the lounge, swivelled her pert behind and smoothed her skirt, what there was of it, softly on to the sofa. Lucky sofa, I thought.

'What can I get you?'
'G and T.'

'Does that need ice?' I asked. It did.
'Lemon?' Another yes.
'Rohypnol?' She laughed, I laughed but only she meant it. They always laughed at this stage.
We toasted each other.
'Did you know this place has a basement?' I said, as if just making conversation.
'No, really?'
'I've had it done out as an extra special bedroom.'
'Hmm, maybe I could see it,' she said which was par for,' I'm not sure I know what I'm letting myself in for.'
'I'm not sure you're not sure, 'I said. Her tongue ballooned one cheek outwards, blatantly coy.
I moved the rug, pulled on the D ring in the floor, and raised the cellar flap up. We went down the stone steps. My breath shortened, my blood hurtled round me, my loins swollen, tacky. She seemed to sense it too, but it wouldn't make a difference.
'Oh, it's lovely, all this pink...'
'...cerise,' I corrected, 'and the four poster and drapes are all red imported velvet.' Red's such a stain friendly colour.
She turned towards me, 'This'll be my first time with...'I knew what she meant. I reached round behind me.
'...my first time with a...'She was choking on the word.
I hurried on, my hands at the back of me unzipping my dress and shrugging it forward down from my shoulders, stepping back out of it in my full first date thong and bustier.
'Oh, you're beautiful.' I was, part of nature's camouflage. On her neck, all orchid pale, a small pulse wriggled to the surface, as if escaping. I leant forward and her neck filled my hands. Her eyes pleaded words my fingers snared from her throat. And sooner than I liked and shorter than I wanted, it and she were done. She'd been right, nearly, her first time with a woman had become her last.
I loosed my hands and the floor wore her like a silent brooch. Dark hair atumble, her middle age her last age, lithe and fiery once, now dead and gone just like...In the red suffused dimness she was the image of my Mother.
I made the call.
Two rings and he answered.

'She's ready.' I was expected. He knew what I meant. No friend of mine, this man but he liked women, anybody really just so long as they were still and warm, still.

'Five minutes, I'll be there.' Click, the phone was dead too.

I never asked him any questions about what he did here. I had all the answers, they were in his notes in his file in the draw of cases closed. Wah-wah, the ring tone blared. Him again, perhaps? But no...it was a woman's voice I didn't yet know.

'Is that Dr Verity Cullingworth, Otley Psych Centre?'

I said all the things this woman wanted me to say.

She was just like the one at my feet – wore a life that didn't fit and ran from feelings she couldn't stand off somewhere better that never was. Fuelled by misery and compelled by treacherous hope she'd circled life's roundabout for an exit that wasn't there. She had the photos to prove it in a box under her bed – her faded ex's on the front in colour and the small print on the back in her precise hand, only its ink was indelible, that told dates and places but nothing about despair. Lacquered by life, her face was brittle, a mask that caged the past, smiling on the outside and screaming on the inside. Unavoidably single, lonely in a crowd, the outsider looking in, and family-free. She was successfully unhappy, embalmed in a busy numbness being kind to everyone but herself. She had everything but nothing was how it felt. She wouldn't be missed, and she knew it, which was sad. And I knew it now, which was worse. We, she and I and the ever so many before, were the same, co-suffers in an ordeal only death could end. I was glad to help; it was my duty, I felt.

'Well,' I said, 'I don't charge for my first session. Working from home it's more secure – I'm sure you understand – if we meet somewhere comfortable, safe where I can assess your needs. Somewhere local works best...'. We talked more, it was going well. She knew how to find Korks'.

'I'll call you back,' I said into the echo of the doorbell. It was the man. He was a butcher, by trade, I mean.

I unleashed the front door. 'You know where you're going,' I said into the hallway.

He hardly looked at me, I was too alive. I watched his back disappear down the steps and he turned for a moment, his face flaring something upward towards me, feral and unquenchable. It was a look that suited him and me.

But he had his uses. Tidying up afterwards was hard for petite me but easier for him. The best butcher in Otley, they said. I had to take their word for it, never could stomach one of his pies or sausages.

I palmed the phone from my pocket.

'Yes, I'm sorry we got interrupted there….thank you. Please do call me Verity And let me assure you, I'm going to know just how you feel. Believe me, it's true what I said…you won't have to be miserable much longer.'

Asgard Close

STREET LIVES

The Enemy Within

by

Carrie Canning

The affair with my ladies began as a dalliance, a flirtatious fancy. Sadly enticement has taken a stronger hold, one that could very well spell my downfall.

My neck was stiff from a night in the chair, my mouth so dry my tongue felt like cracked earth. I stumbled to the kitchen, grabbing the table for support. It was then to my horror I saw it, the cellar door, yawning wide. The key never leaves my person, yet there it was, proud in the lock.

'Who's there?' Show yourselves! Damn you! Heard the old Major's a bit of a crack shot eh? Taken many a pheasant down at 60 yards.'

Checking for signs of forced entry and finding nothing untoward, I concluded the blighters must have scarpered. I precariously made my way down the stone steps, smooth from the many pilgrimages to this, my inner sanctum. Each tentative footstep evoked a recollection of the night before, each one telling of the debauchery that lay ahead.

The usually cool dank cellar was a wretched sight. The air, drenched with the unmistakeable blowsy aroma of one of my less robust girls, smashed to her demise on the cold stone slabs. The floor had thirstily soaked up most of the puddle, leaving just her gluey, Claret remains, littered with dark shards that crunched beneath my feet. Yesterday morning my ladies had been safe, undisturbed, cocooned, in blankets of thick grey web, flourishing to fruition amidst the cool gaps in the stone. What lumbering fool would bother them when they were resting so peacefully?

The drawing room was airless, choking within the claustrophobic smog of cigar smoke. I threw open the curtains and windows. The sun pierced through, dust particles dancing as the harsh reality of a very toxic love affair became clear.

My finest cut crystal goblet was teeming with rancid Montecristo stubs, suffocating in a volcano of ash. A handsome Edwardian decanter and two empty bottles, strewn, in an ungainly fashion on the floor. Rummaging among the slouching cushions of my aging High Back for spectacles, I huffed on the cloudy lenses erasing sticky finger prints with the crumpled sleeve of my old smoking jacket.

The labels told a sorry tale. Not recalling the pleasures of my *'Chateau Lavielle Rouge,'* I could just about make my peace with, but my darling *'Ridge Monte Bello!'* The precious creature was unripe, racy, lacking finesse and needing at least three more years to develop. Now she was the innocent victim of a reckless stupor and her well rounded elegance would never be enjoyed.

Distraction arrived via the ridiculous post lad, bellowing senselessly. His mucky fingers protruding through the letter box, ham-fisted pounding on the door marking time with the thumping in my head.

'What the devil do you think you're doing? What do you want, damn you?'

'Delivery for Major Bullen.'

An all too familiar sight gaped at me from the hall mirror. A burgundy tinged perma-smile garnished an unwieldy moustache. Topped off by insubordinate strands of fading hair, hanging lank, above blood lined eyes, and yet another cravat, stained beyond redemption.

'Leave it at the door, I'm indisposed.'

'Can't Major, I need a signature. If you remember the drill, I push it through, then you sign, and I get it back.'

'Well get on with it then, what are you waiting for?'

Manoeuvre completed, I ensured through the slimmest gap the young idiot was well out of sight. My spirits lifted when I discovered the parcel to be a wooden casket from *'Quaffers'* containing my allocated wine of the month. Though how many times must I assert to that damned company. *'Discretion if you please! Wrap in brown paper!'*

STREET LIVES

Ah! A Beaujolais, hmmm, a bit young, light bodied, not really one for the cellar. I supposed if I were to decant now, the little madam will have just enough time to breathe raising her bosom perfectly to accompany me in a light luncheon. This naughty young lady will be enticing me to join her by let's say, 11am. A tad early, though I think close enough to the yardarm to be deemed civilized. A collation of cold cuts, bread and cheeses would partner her perfectly. In fact, I concluded I was rather peckish so I should perform my ablutions and opt for an early lunch. Though I would never name it 'brunch,' I refuse to consider the word, a most vulgar vernacular, typical of the damned Yanks, decimating the Queen's English.

In light of the insalubrious state of the cellar I vowed to be more respectful of my ladies and cut back on the old cigars too. In my defence, I concluded my downfall the previous evening to be entirely the fault of a rather alluring, velvety, Bordeaux. Full bodied, with quite a grip. Then, I am well aware that visiting the wine cellar whilst at the mercy of my ladies, had never ended well and really should cease forthwith

I concluded I will select my girls before noon in future, when I'm less fingers and thumbs. I would decant them slowly and take my pleasure reverently.

After a luncheon in the company of my latest filly, I carried a bucket of hot soapy water, down to the cellar, to make good the damage. Whilst there, I decided on a rather fine boned Chablis, thinking her hint of youthful bitterness just perfect for a touch of light afternoon amusement. For this evening, a pertinent, more intimate, little burgundy would provide my entertainment.

Today I will celebrate the fact that, my darling *'Chateau Latour,'* has survived my latest transgression. She is, after all, one of the few left in the world and worth a fortune.

Is it any surprise that I protect my beauties, keep them safely under lock and key? If only it were as easy to shield them from the enemy within.

Asgard Close

STREET LIVES

In the Frame

by

Alyson Faye

He'd been trapped inside the painting, suffocated by oils, for half a century. He knew May sensed him and his anger, which was growing steadily and leaking over the edges of the gilt frame into the parlour. His favourite room, where he and May had laughed, danced, kissed and fought until that last Christmas. . . Here memories bled into viscous paint swirls and it was hard to recall what had happened. Except May was out there - alive, albeit now an old woman and he wasn't. He was trapped, flattened and raging. He peeked out from their bedroom and watched the young woman settle on the sofa to drink tea with May. Youth, ah sweet youth! He could smell her. She might be his way out.

*

Ellie smiled at Grandma May, as she sipped the weak Earl Grey. She didn't like to tell Grandma she preferred Yorkshire builders', just like Dad. *Small deceptions didn't matter,* she told herself.

Ellie glanced at the easel, propped in its usual place in the bay window, supporting May's current work in progress. Her house, Number 13, Asgard Close, was May's favourite subject. She painted it repeatedly in all seasons, from every angle. May did portraits too, but oddly none of her late husband, Grandpa William; long gone, but never spoken of.

Despite this lacuna in the family history, the front room was preserved as if William had just stepped outside. His slippers resided under his armchair, his pipe and baccy rested on the walnut sideboard and his whiskey decanter gleamed from regular elbow-busting polishes. Ellie didn't pry. It wasn't her business.

STREET LIVES

Ellie's favourite painting hung above the mantel; an oil, executed in minute detail, depicting all the interiors of number 13, like a doll's house, but with one wall removed. Every stick of furniture was duplicated, so too every pattern on the wallpaper. Glossy and luscious in texture, it dangled out of Ellie's reach for years, until she grew tall enough to touch its curly-wurly gilt frame.

That particular October day, when dusk tapped early at the windows and May closed the heavy velvet drapes by 3.30pm, Ellie pointed at the painting.

'Granny May, is that a face? See - there - in the bedroom? Top right?' She leapt up. In that moment the face or perhaps it was only a smudge, disappeared. Ellie paused, nonplussed. 'It was there. I'm sure it was.'

May's reaction surprised Ellie; the old woman retracted her head, tortoise like, defensive and wary. 'What? Don't be foolish child.'

When May left the room to put the kettle on – again, Ellie, her curiosity piqued, stood on tip toe and peered at the painting. The patio doors were depicted as thrown open. Though Ellie was certain they were usually closed. Or were they?

The lights in the parlour dimmed, dipped and flickered - on and off, three times. In the brief flashes Ellie glimpsed a shadow in the painting creep down the main stairs, into the hallway and reach beyond the frame. A thin wisp of smoky darkness hovered, Ellie stretched out her finger to touch the . . .

'Stop peering at that daub, child.' May's sharp tones made Ellie jump and drop her hand. 'You didn't touch it, did you?' May added. Ellie shook her head, wondering what May had seen, but not daring to ask.

The weeks flew by in the lead up to Christmas. Ellie, busy with work, friends and parties, didn't visit May as often, so it was a shock when her Dad warned her May's health was failing.

'Like a bird now she is, tiny and frail; pecking at food. She's got something to give you though, lass.'

Ellie was taken aback by how dilapidated Grandma May had become; her cardigan buttons and wig were askew, but May's smile was as warm as ever. Perched on the familiar easel, in the front room, stood a brown-wrapped rectangular shaped package with an accompanying empty space above the mantel.

'For you, Ellie. You'll know what to do with it. I trust you to do the right thing.' The old woman seemed anxious. Ellie wanted to reassure her, so she nodded. May muttered, 'You give them power when you paint them . . .I should have stopped but I couldn't. This house is unlucky.'

It was to be the last time Ellie drank weak Earl Grey with her Grandma, for May passed on just two weeks later. The subsequent clear out of her house produced a surprise. It was Ellie who unearthed the folder full of faded, foxed newspaper clippings.

'Dad, didn't you say Grandpa walked out on you and May? When you were a baby?'

'Yeah, that's right, love. Why?'

Ellie felt her stomach lurch. 'You'd better read this then.'

Several newspaper clippings from January 1966 ran with the story of *'Local man . . . missing after 3 weeks.'* *'Not seen since November 1965, William Phelps. . .'* *'Has anyone seen this man?* (A fuzzy black and white photo). Then - *'Presumed dead.'* The mark of officialdom, the death certificate, dated seven years later.

Ellie squeezed her dad's calloused hand. 'It's OK love, I never knew him. May raised me. Still it's a mystery . . .'

Ellie hung the oil in her apartment, where it took over the walls. Everyone commented on it; Ellie however had to live with it. For most of that first year of their shared habitation nothing happened, until October, with its briefer days and longer nights, rolled around.

Coming home from work, Ellie switched on her desk lamp and noticed a face-shaped smudge staring at her from the master bedroom or on another evening in the kitchen or standing in the hallway. The impression grew stronger as the weeks passed - of someone watching her, but from within the gilt frame.

The features of the face grew more defined too. Ellie bought a magnifying glass. Yes - it was a man's face, with tufty dark hair, an open-mouthed expression as if he was shouting, (this development rattled her), hot flushed cheeks and a stain flowering on his shirt front, which began as a pink daisy and transformed into an ugly crimson geranium. It was the face from the newspaper. It was William Phelps.

'Granddad? Is that you?' Ellie whispered. In the magnifying glass she saw the man's face react to her words. 'You can hear me?' She felt sick at this realisation.

STREET LIVES

As October morphed into November, Ellie took to keeping all the lights switched on, hoping to blast the dark oil painting into submission. Finally, she resorted to draping a sheet over the canvas.

Christmas Eve was her last day at work, so Ellie stayed on for a few drinks, reluctant to return to her apartment. The figure was there all the time now, sometimes leaning out of the frame, beckoning her; his face eager and greedy.

Opening her apartment door, Ellie noticed the painting lying face down on the carpet. Cello-taped to the back was a small lavender coloured envelope, covered in May's copperplate handwriting. Ellie opened it, with a glass of red wine at her side for courage, but she left the painting lying blind. Just in case.

'This is the last letter I will write, dearest Ellie. My darling granddaughter. I think by now you will have guessed my secret. It is hard for the dead to tell lies. You will know your Granddad went missing . . . have you guessed the rest? It was Christmas Eve, he was so drunk, and I was three months pregnant. It was an accident I promise. . . he got as far as the patio doors….before he ….' Ellie gulped the wine down in one go. 'He never left though. The house kept him here and somehow - I kept his spirit alive in the painting. He wouldn't let me give away his possessions. Be careful Ellie, he wants to escape. His power grows as my health fails. . . It is up to you now.'

Ellie's eyes lifted. She gaped at the slow, lazy trickle of cerise paint escaping from beneath the painting, oozing towards her, reaching for her toes. Rivers of vermilion and magenta paint poured forth, swamping her pale carpet, spilling onto the balcony. The painting began to lift off the floor. A long skinny hand crawled from beneath the frame, its fingers questing and clawing. Ellie cried out and the hand froze, then turned towards her. Another skeletal hand crept out, flexing long bony digits with black nails attached. *How long before the body climbed out?*

Wine befuddled, Ellie was slow to move, but the sight of the creeping fingers with their hairy wrists, replete with raised bulging blue veins, forced her to her feet. Looking round, she grabbed the first object which came to hand - a pearl handled letter opener – a gift from May for her 18th birthday. She thrust its blade deep into one questing hand. Paint poured forth, black and viscous, whilst the fingers curled up and scrabbled at the air. One elongated finger scraped her bare ankle, from where tiny droplets of her own vermilion blood erupted.

'Ow! You bastard!'

Frantic, panicked, she stabbed repeatedly, skewering one of the hands to her once luxurious, vanilla carpet, rather like a bizarre BBQ offering. The fingers went into a spasm, scrabbled, a blackened nail dropped off, finally the appendage stopped moving.

Ellie collapsed onto her leather sofa. Sweating and panting; she watched the rivers of paint seep down into the floors. Later that night in bed, Ellie tossed, embalming herself in her fluffy duvet, scratching her ankle in her sleep and bleeding blackly onto her bedding. In her dreams she screamed in silence, trapped within a frame; a living work of art.

Morning came, then the next - but for Ellie it was endless night.

Asgard Close

Alex

by

Jo Campbell

Drawing deeply on his cigarette Alex propped himself up with his elbow on the worn pillow of his childhood bed.

He didn't think she'd changed the sheets since he was last in them four years back. Maybe she'd claim sentiment, wanting to preserve it just as it was but he knew she was just a lazy, dirty bitch too pissed or high to give it a second thought.

Alex stubbed out his cigarette in the saucer and swung his legs over the side of the bed.

He stood and pulled back the thin curtain hanging precariously on a few hooks above the window which overlooked Asgard street. The street where he'd mown that bastard down.

Fucking careless that, but he had it coming. Snooping, questioning Mam, confusing her. Report me, would you? Try it now fucker from six feet under.

Alex served four years of his sentence. Death by dangerous driving. Remembering his trial, he had been so convincing; remorseful even.

'He stepped out of nowhere, I was looking at my radio, just a split second not watching my speed I looked up and hit him.' Cue sad face, sobs blah blah blah.

Prison served him well. A good gym and so many tutors all wanting to help him. Poor misunderstood Alex, drug addict Mother, errant Father, petty crime, bad company and now this dreadful accident. He came out educated and not just academically.

The sound of vomiting jolted Alex from his thoughts. He stepped out onto the landing.

'Look at the state of you.' He said to his Mum, head over the toilet bowl.

You're a fucking disgrace. That nighty's covered in shite as well. Clean yourself up. I'm off out.'

'Alex, love..' she slurred at him, but he was gone.

He swaggered down the street, headed for town, fancying a couple of pints.

*

The Burton Arms was busy with the usual daylight dodgers. Some of the clientele managed to raise their head to greet Alex with a gurn but Alex had no interest. It was the Landlord, Billy he had come to see.

'Pint Billy.'

'Alex. Good to see you fella. You got my message then?'

'I did. What's his game?'

Billy lowered his voice. 'Not here mate. Back room. Let me call Tina down.'

With Tina firmly ensconced behind the bar Alex followed Billy to the back, pint in hand.

Billy cleared the chipped Formica table of its pile of bills and papers and banged an ashtray in the centre. The two men dragged a couple of chairs into place across the hard linoleum tiles and lit cigarettes.

'He wants revenge Alex. Pure and simple mate. Keeps goin' on about what he'll do when you're out.'

'Oh yeah?' Alex leaned forward, blowing enough smoke to make Billy's eyes water. ' And what exactly is he gonna do?'

Billy moved back, laughed nervously.

'Nowt probably. You know what he's like. All talk I reckon.'

'Is that right?'

'Alex, mate. I'm just the messenger, kept my ear to the ground for you. Thought you should know what he's said, you know, in case..'

'In case what Billy?

Alex moved his face close to Billy's.

What could that bastard possibly do to me?'

That laugh again, less convincing this time. Intimidated, Billy swallowed, blinked and paled a little.

'Relax Billy. I know you're looking out for me but without anything concrete your information's not much fucking use now is it?'

Leaning in closer, Alex put his hands-on Billy's forearms, just tight enough to pinch. Billy could feel the heat from the lit cigarette end through his shirt.

'What I need from you Billy is facts. Facts. Got it? You're here at night, I'm on fucking curfew for another week so I need you to do this for me. Right?'

'Of course, Alex. Sorry mate. I get it.'

Alex relaxed, sat back and stubbed out his cigarette.

'Look, sorry Man I just get this rage you know? It's frustrating I'm being watched and it's like they're the good guys. They don't get it. I'm the innocent one here. This stuff I do.. I wouldn't do it if they didn't push. But they keep pushing, asking for it.'

'Alex mate, I know. Leave it with me, I'll dig around a little,'

'Cheers pal. Listen I've gotta go, ring us later yeah?'

'Go out the yard way Alex, I'll get back in the bar.'

Yanking his hood over his head and checking the time Alex headed down the High street; but rather than turning towards home he headed round the side of the shop towards the back of the terraced houses, where he settled behind a low wall and waited.

He didn't have to wait long before he heard the familiar clack of steel boot caps on cobbles.

Uncle Terry.

Alex's whole face tightened. How he hated Uncle Terry; him and that bastard cousin he'd gone to prison for. Both supplied the drugs that were slowly killing his Mum. Not that Alex had time for her either, but they were always round the house, drink, drugs, storing stuff, sending Alex out to steal when he was small, to collect 'insurance' money or batter the clients on their behalf when he got older. And for what. He never saw a penny out of it and the house was an absolute dump.

One down Terry, one to go.

Terry looked tired. Much older than last time Alex saw him. The thought that this was most likely due to Terry mourning the loss of his son never entered Alex's mind.

He stood, instinctively to confront Terry but with no clear plan.

Back off Alex, wrong time.

Terry unlocked his door, kicking post out of the way.

Good. Thought Alex. *No one else living there.* He checked his watch and made a move for home; careful to take a detour via the corner shop and chippy. It was always worth having your journey tracked on CCTV a little.

The house was empty when Alex got home. Never a good sign when his Mum was out in the evening, still he could do nothing now it was almost seven and at least he wouldn't be the one cleaning up after her tonight.

Dropping back into his chair, Alex opened a can and started to eat his fish and chips. He flicked the remote on the alternative SKY box for the Sports channel waiting for kick off. As ever, his thoughts drifted back to Uncle Terry. Alex could feel the rage surge from the pit of his stomach through his entire body.

It was half-time in the match and Alex checked his phone.

Nothing!

Not a word from Billy.

For fuck's sake Billy, what is the point of you?

He thought about ringing, but instinct told him to be patient. Instinct was right. As soon as the second half started his phone beeped.

It was a video, Alex's Mum slumped across the legs of a local scrote with Terry laughing beside them.

Alex felt the familiar eruption of rage inside his gut. He acknowledged the text with a thumb emoji and slammed the handset down.

Twisting his ankle around he slid a small metal pick inside the loose tag which opened so he could free himself.

Cheers Jordan he thought raising his can in a toast. *Always handy to know your security team.*

Leaving the tag safely on the sofa in front of the television, Alex unlocked the cellar door. He took out a pair of boots, one size too large, oversized black padded coat and gloves from a plastic sack.

Locking the cellar up he left the house, hood up and walked with a heavy stride.

From behind a bus shelter Alex watched Terry, the scrote and his barely upright mother leave the pub.

Merging with the shadows he followed them to Terry's house and hid himself behind the back wall.

Raising himself onto his haunches Alex peered through the window where he watched in despair as his Mum was helped to Terry's treasure chest of drugs. Slumped in an armchair next to Scrote she tapped away for a vein, then sunk into oblivion across his chest.

Roughly he shoved her away to join Terry at a table, leaving her head hanging backwards over the arm of the chair.

Like a sack of shit. Alex burned inside.

He couldn't hear them speak but clearly a deal of sorts was being discussed.

Terry stood, strode towards the window, Alex dropped out of sight; Terry stopped and unlocked a drawer, removing something before turning back to Scrote at the table.

Alex, slowly rose from hiding and tried to get a better look.

He saw Terry slap a pile of twenty-pound notes on the table. Scrote reached out but Terry put his hand firmly on the cash and drew it back. In his other hand he held a gun. He slid the gun across the table.

'Fuck!' mouthed Alex, stretching forward.

Terry then produced a photograph placing it face down. Scrote turned it over and, clearly shocked, quickly rose from his chair. He looked towards Alex's mother, still out of it then back at the photograph.

'Shit Terry. You serious?'

'I don't have time to fuck about. I need him gone' Terry said leaning in closely.

'D'you want it or not?'

Alex leaned his ear to the door by the window.

Give us a fucking name.

The door creaked as he fell against it.

'Shit!'

Alex fled from yard, back to the alley where he saw lights appear as the door to Terry's house opened. He dragged his hood over his head and turned for home to Asgard close.

Clearly someone had severely crossed Terry, a severe beating was his usual punishment, Alex knew, he had delivered enough for him in the past, but never been asked to kill before.

Could just be used as a warning. He thought, but, knew this was unlikely given the huge stack of cash up for grabs.

He wouldn't fucking dare intend it for me. He hasn't got the balls!
Alex was unconvinced though.
He might not, but I don't know about Scrote. Not encountered him before.

He needed to do some digging. Billy needed to pull his finger out. Alex slipped the tag back around his ankle before going to bed. He slept lightly, baseball bat and favourite knife beside him.

*

The damp Autumn morning brought watery beige light through Alex's window. The white street lights were still lit as he dressed.

He took his clothes and loaded the washing machine. A strong coffee and a couple of cigarettes served as breakfast. the drone of the washer the only sound. Alex twirled the knife around his fingers as he sat in contemplation at the kitchen table.

He was out of the house, out of the cul de sac and down Town Street, arriving at Billy's pub just as the street lights switched off.

Battering at the door he alerted Tina at the upstairs window who told him quite clearly to 'Fuck off.'

Billy was next, gently moving Tina, still cursing, away back into the bedroom. He signalled a disgruntled greeting, dragged on a pair of boxers, inside-out, and unlocked the door, Alex was through before Billy had chance to move, the heavy entrance door swinging violently slammed into Billy's foot, shattering two of his toes.

Ignoring Billy's pain, Alex grabbed him by the throat, shoved him back against the door, banging his head.

'Shut the fuck up you shit weasel.' He hissed, spit spraying Billy's terrified face.

'I want to know what you know. You can either tell me or I'll beat it out of you, then her.'

He nodded over towards Tina, hovering at the bar, phone in hand.

'Go upstairs Tina, Alex leave her, I..'

'Sit the fuck down Tina. You're going nowhere.'

Obediently Tina sat, all the sass drained from her.

Alex released his grip on Billy, dumped him beside Tina, and pulled up a chair for himself, reversing it so he leant forwards over the chair back.

Lighting a cigarette, squinting, he hissed 'Talk.'

'Look Alex, I've said nothing but only because you'd go ape. They've been supplying your Mum, just to goad you into going after them, get you sent back down. You know she won't turn it down and if she doesn't get it from them, she'll get it elsewhere, by whatever means, you know?'

'Not the drugs Billy, but I will put a stop to it, you're right. I'm on about the gun.'

'Gun? Don't know 'owt about any gun.'

Alex looked at Tina, who looked as blank as Billy.

He stood up, loomed over Billy, flicking ash. Billy flinched

'Alex, mate, I would tell you if I knew about the gun, I just didn't know how to let you know about your Mum. I've tried to stop that myself.'

Alex placed his hand on Billy's shoulder.

'I believe you, but I need to know what the plans with the gun Billy are, get chatting to that scrote Terry knocks about with.'

'Nik?'

'Don't know his name, tall, skinny head, greasy pocked face?'

'That's him. Usually with Terry but I know him Alex, leave it with me. It's serious yeah?'

'I'll call you later.'

Alex left, the bar doors swinging in his wake.

'Bastard.' Tina said.

'Leave it Tina, he's a mate, just a bit of a mess right now. He'll sort it. Let's stay on the right fucking side of him eh?'

'I'll help for your sake Billy, but I want him out of our lives. It was easier when he was in the nick.'

Wiping away an angry tear, Tina began setting up the bar.

'Leave it Teen. It's too early yet'

'I need to do something Terry. I can't sit around worrying.'

'Suit yourself. I'm off for a cig.'

Tina busied herself cursing Alex and Billy under her breath. Lunchtime trade was slow. Tina was flicking through her phone, leaning on the bar when Nik walked in. Her stomach lurched, Billy was in the cellar, so she had to serve him hoping her face gave nothing away.

'Stella.'

Handing him the bottle, Tina asked 'Do you want a glass?'

'When do I have a glass?'

'I know.. just making conversation Nik. It's been so quiet it's driving me crackers.'

Leaning closer to him she added. 'Only old Jeff and his mate over there, they've been nursing that bitter all lunchtime, both deaf as a post as well.'

Nik relaxed a little and positioned himself at the bar. Grinning to reveal a mouthful of missing and rotten teeth he turned his attention to Tina.

'You have my undivided attention Love. '

Careful not to inhale Nik's bin-scrap breath, Tina began chatting. Three Stella's in, she ventured

'Thought your mate would've joined you by now. Y'know? Terry?' Nik's brow furrowed, he took a swig of lager;

'Nah, not today.'

'Oh, He, err.. busy then?'

'Yeah, he'll have something on.'

'What's he up to then?' Tina laughed, nervously. 'or can't you say?'

'What the *fuck's* it got to do with you?' spit sprayed across the bar. Tina withdrew,

Stuff this, I don't need this shit, not for that prick Alex.' She thought.

'Sorry. Not prying Nik; just used to seeing you together in here. Have another on me.'

Nik drained his bottle, the scowl faded.

'Go on then. You've twisted my arm.'

Billy emerged, glassy-eyed, from the cellar.'

'*Brilliant*'

'State of you Billy!' Tina said.

Nik laughed, Billy grinned, and Tina took the opportunity to flounce off, throwing a bar towel on her way.'

'Your bird promised me a beer.'

'Oh yeah? '

'Yeah. Unless you've 'owt better.'

Billy shrugged, passed Nik his beer.

'Not with Terry today then Nik?'

'Don't you bloody start. I've had all that from your Missus. We're not joined. I'm off for a piss.'

STREET LIVES

He swaggered through the toilet door some minutes later, his eyes beginning to roll.

Shit. Thought Billy. *I'll not get any info' out of him now. He's proper faced out.*

Nik swiped his beer and plonked himself down in the corner; leaned back and closed his eyes.

Tina came back downstairs. Looked at Nik, then Billy. She nodded towards the bar surface. Nik had left his phone, Billy swiftly pocketed it and headed to the Gents.

The phone was locked. Billy stared at the screen, touching the button now and again wondering what the code was, but too anxious to try any numbers.

He put it on the basin side and leaned forward, head over the bowl, when the phone pinged and briefly lit up.

Across the screen a partial message appeared, the sender was Terry.

Billy took in the limited information.

7.00 at hers, any time after, listen for ...

Hers? Who's that?

Billy pushed frantically at the phone screen to reveal more of the message, to no avail.

He turned to leave the toilets and collided with the door.

'Fuck. Second time in one day!'

'Ha, sorry mate, I.. what you doing with my phone?'

'Oh, it's yours? I.. err.. just found it on the floor in here.'

Nik snatched the phone from Billy, illuminated the screen, tapped in his pin and accessed the message.

His face paled, he swayed a little to the left. Locking the phone and running fingers through his hair he swallowed.

'Am I alright for a brew Tommy? Summat to eat as well if you've got. I need to clear my head.'

'I'll sort you something. You alright?'

'Yeah yeah, just didn't plan on doing much but, err, need to see our lass later. Can't turn up pissed.'

'Ha, no mate. She'll need you sober. I'll go get you that food. Pie and chips alright?'

Nik, nodded, tapping a reply on his phone. Tommy couldn't see what that reply was.'

STREET LIVES

Tina was just outside the toilet door. Tommy grabbed her by the arm and hurried her over the room.

'He's got a message Teen. Something tonight, it's from Terry. Couldn't see it all but I think, well I think they're going to hurt Cheryl.'

'Alex's mum?'

Billy nodded. 'I'll crack on with his pie and chips out back and ring Alex. Can you sort Nik some strong coffee? Keep him occupied.'

Tina nodded. Billy hesitated, kissed her then went through behind the bar; set the oven and fryer going and turned on the radio to muffle the sounds travelling through to the from. He then made a call to Alex, alerting him to what had gone on and the partial message he'd seen on Nik's phone.

Alex listened in silence.

'Alex? We thought it might mean your Mum.'

Still silence.

'You there? Mate, I said we thought it might..'

'I heard. Leave it with me. Oh, take a piss in his drink from me.'

The phone line went dead.

*

Alex plugged his ears with earphones, turned up the volume on his iPod and sat on the edge of his bed; staring. His eyes betrayed no emotion, but the fight was within him.

Lighting the last cigarette in his pack he replayed the night that brought him to this point. The reason he was jailed. As Radiohead wailed Karma Police through his ear he smiled, eyes darkening.

'Now your turn.' He said to himself.

'Mam, I'm off for some cigs. D'you want owt?'

'Get us some voddy there's a good lad.'

He slammed the door behind him.

*

'Bloody hell, this coffee's like treacle Tina.'

'It'll do the job so shut up moaning. Look, your dinner's here now.'

Billy plonked a huge plate of pie and chips down on the bar.

'Here, and a pint of apple juice for you. Best to drink lots if you're to sober up.'

'Cheers Billy. On the house?'
Billy smirked.
'Oh aye. On the house. Enjoy.'
Nik dived into his food like he hadn't eaten in days. He grabbed the juice to wash it down, took a couple of large gulps then plonked it on the bar in disgust.
'Jesus Billy! What' is that shit?'.'
'It's organic mate. Full of herbs and stuff. Good for you, it'll proper sort you out.'
'Yeah?'
'Yeah.'
Nik took a sniff, filled his mouth with food and gulped down the liquid. He shuddered.
'Think I'll stick to Tina's coffee.'

*

Alex dropped one earphone out inside his hood. His head was down, seemingly engrossed in his music, unaware of others; but his senses were on high alert. The adrenaline in his body was making him jittery and he knew he would have to calm that down to think straight.

He fancied a drink but couldn't go to the Burton, so Alex swung by the Oakwell arms. He hadn't been there in years. Not since Susie, but that was past and another story. Besides, what choice did he have?
Alex ordered, and headed towards his usual seat by the window. Old habit, he turned and moved, to the opposite end of the room. He needed to clear his head, not dig out memory clutter.

Relaxed now Alex quietly left the Pub for the shop, leaving shortly after with cigarettes, a pasty and his mum's vodka. He couldn't resist a smirk as he walked past Heaven's gate funeral parlour. He liked to keep them in trade, support local business and all that. The momentary lapse in concentration caused Alex to miss the figure behind him, who quickly managed to clink away behind the buildings.

Back at home Cheryl was waiting in remarkably high spirits.
'Bloody hell Mam, you've been busy with the Rimmel. What's going on?'
'I'm expecting company son, you'll behave, won't you? It's your Uncle Terry and err, his friend. She blushed.

Pass us that voddy over. I'm parched.'

'Fuck's sake Mam. Can't you just go out? You know I've got my curfew.'

Cheryl didn't reply.

'Mam? Are you fucking listening?'

'Sorry son, lend us a fag, will you?'

He didn't. Instead Alex went upstairs and sat on the top step, lit a cigarette for himself, took off his coat and put Radiohead back on his iPod.

Either of them lays a finger on her, I'll fucking do 'em.

Elbows propped on knees; he was ready.

*

Curfew time passed. Alex heard Terry downstairs.

Just fucking walk in why don't you.

Turning the volume down to hear what was going on, he left the track 'Climbing up the walls' on a loop. It suited his mood.

Terry had brought drink. Cheryl was already half-cut.

'Nik'll bring something stronger. Don't worry. I'll stick this lot in the kitchen.'

Out of sight Terry texted from his phone.

*

Tina and Billy were keeping a close watch on Nik who kept checking his phone. It flashed a message and Tina was quick to respond. She grabbed the phone

'I'm going to ring the number. Pretend you're playing away.' She laughed waving the phone about, slowly enough to read the text on screen, fast enough to look as if she was messing about.

'Give it back you daft bitch. '

'Alright misery guts. Just playing. Is she waiting?'

Nik didn't reply. He deleted the message.

'I'm off. '

'Ok. Have fun.'

Tina turned to Billy as soon as Nik had gone.

'It's not Cheryl they want. It's Alex.'

'What?'
'I saw the text.' **Bastard's in. He's all yours.**' Has to be him.'
'Watch the bar Teen, I'll ring him.'
Alex did not pick up. Billy sent a text, no response to that either. He began to panic. It wouldn't take Nik too long to get there.
'Tina, I'll have to go round. There's no answer.'
'No Billy, it's not your fight. You've done enough.'
She was right. What else could he do.
'I'll try ringing again.'

*

Alex had seen the message, he'd reply later. Right now, he had unsettled business.

Terry had put the TV on loudly, was strutting around the room, on edge.

Alex abandoned his iPod in favour of a bowie knife and using the noise to his advantage, descended the stairs into the hall.

The front door was still open, Alex's eyes followed Terry's movements.

He took his chance as Terry turned his back. Lunging he grappled his Uncle to the ground. Terry was slow but not weak. He threw Alex back and staggered half to his feet. Alex went again, knife in hand. His Mum stared and began to wail.

Terry stumbled through the door into Asgard close.
Where the fuck was Nik?'
As if reading his thoughts Alex said
'Doesn't look like he's coming. Just you and me.'
He stabbed the knife towards Terry, slashing his stomach, then his arm.

Terry went down, checking his wounds and shuffling backwards across the road.

Grabbing him by the collar Alex hauled his Uncle towards the edge of the pavement and slammed his face into the concrete breaking his teeth.

As Terry lay with his damaged jaw against the curb, Alex raised his foot above Terry's head.

Street Lives

Curtains and blinds twitched in the nearby windows, but only Cheryl ran onto the street.

As Alex was about to bring his boot crashing down onto Terry's skull Cheryl screamed.

'NO. Stop! He's your Dad! '

Alex turned towards his Mum. She screamed again.

A single shot rang out.

Alex spun around with the force, then fell to his knees.

Distant sirens matched the wails coming from his Mum.

Street Lives

Asgard Close

STREET LIVES

The Dummy in the Corner

by

Cynthia Richardson

This is the story of Mr Binns who lives at 5 Asgard Close and his doll Emma, the Dummy in the corner.

Cash was scarce and in desperation he turned to 'alternative sources of funding.' They were patiently waiting for him like the Morey Eel waits in its cave to lunge out and grasp its prey. He wasn't the first and he wouldn't be the last young entrepreneur they had dealings with.

A discreet production line was set up and the young entrepreneur was happy with his good fortune until he realised that his invention wasn't being promoted to the medical profession as he intended.

Unfortunately he started digging into the business ethics of his backers and asked too many questions. His death was instantaneous the police told his family, a hit and run driver who left his crumpled and mangled body in the road outside his home.

The production line carried on manufacturing what looked like sex dolls. They hung in line each attached by a calliper at the back of their necks so the silicone they were made off could dry and waiting to be finished to 'buyer's specification'. However these dolls had unique qualities having been developed to be used to train medical students. If cut they would bleed realistic synthetic blood and if touched roughly would scream and whimper as if they were alive.

Mr Binns saw the advert on the dark web 'dolls with all the feelings of humans customised to 'buyer's specification'. What he especially liked was the bit about them bleeding and screaming as Mr Binns was a murderer in waiting. He ordered a doll that looked just like Emma one of his neighbours who was a pretty young women who wore glasses and her dark hair in a soft bob. She worked at the local library and Mr Binns spent a lot of his time there looking at her from behind the shelving units. When he got home from these viewings he would always go into his 'special room' put soft gloves on and get out his surgical knives and instruments and watched the gleaming of the lights on them. They were his pets and he sighed with pleasure as he stroked and polished them.

The urge to use his pets on Emma was overwhelming but Mr Binns was frustrated because he couldn't find a way to get Emma incapacitated in his plastic sheeting lined special room. Sometimes his frustration got so bad he thought about sullying his pets on the old interfering windbag Sue Smith who with her dog Harvey seemed to be always wanting to get into his house for a 'cup of tea and a chat'. However when the doll Emma arrived she was all that he had hoped for and he dressed her just like her namesake and sat her in a chair in the corner of his special room. He would work up to the major knife work on the dummy in the corner, as he thought of her, thus attaining maximum pleasure.

As a prelude he kicked and stabbed the doll as he walked by leaving her with bleeding cuts all over and he revelled in the screams that were the outcome of his brutality. A week of this behaviour went by and Mr Binns was happy, but he didn't know how long he would be able to stop himself from his big finale. Soon the time arrived, and he brought out all this 'pets' they were all gleaming and ready to go. He was so busy with his preparations that he didn't see the doll Emma's eyes light up and her lifeless limbs become active.

What Mr Binns didn't know was that there was another unique invention inside the doll that allowed her to be remotely controlled. An operator could get the doll to come to life and through her eyes record everything that was occurring just as she had been doing since Mr Binns had taken delivery of her.

Fussing over the preparations for his big finale Mr Binns was taken by surprise when a smooth arm with bleeding cuts pushed him out of the way and took hold of one of the knives and stabbed him in his shoulder. He screamed and tried to run away but the doll was stronger than he was, and she soon overpowered him and threw him on to his finale table where she used the restraints on him. Mr Binns was helpless.

As he lay there screaming and bleeding, the doll paused so that the scene was captured in full and customers could get their bids in before the entertainment began.

The company on the dark web were very thrifty, more bang for their buck, and were live streaming the scene from Mr Binn's special room to patrons who had paid well to see their meat freshly slaughtered. When all monies had been collected and cards swiped, the doll Emma efficiently butchered Mr Binns taking her time, so the paying audience got value for money at his torture.

When it had all ended a clean-up crew turned up at Mr Binn's house in a nondescript van. Once inside they put on overalls and masks and all the prime cuts were hygienically packaged for discreet delivery the other offal was put into a container as even this had been sold on. The doll Emma was deactivated and sat in her usual chair in the corner of the special room. It would be too costly to recondition her after all she had been ordered to buyer's specification, but the camera and other mechanisms were removed from inside her.

The police eventually broke into Mr Binns house, alerted by a neighbour Mrs Sue Smith and the milkman. All they found was Emma the dummy in the corner. A thorough search was conducted, and the Scene of Crime Officers were there for weeks as Mrs Smith reported to anyone who would listen to her. Of Mr Binn's there was no trace. Everything seemed in place including the gleaming knives and instruments, but of course the plastic sheeting was missing from the 'special room'. The clean-up crew were very efficient.

Asgard Close

STREET LIVES

An Empty Tin Rattles the Most

by

Serena Russell

Her thread in the tapestry of Life had been caught by the sharp hook of calamity and everything had unravelled. No amount of stitching or mending could ever repair the damage.

As the black hours descended and with the prospect of yet another terror fuelled night ahead of her, Sue Smith sat at the kitchen table. Harvey was fast asleep in his basket.

Tears started to her eyes, filled with the familiar sting of self-pity. She fingered the copy of the Decree Absolute in front of her. Forty years of marriage, of caring, devotion and worshipping John; how could he walk out so abruptly, so callously, leaving her for a younger, prettier woman.

Painful memories glared out of every shadow, exacerbating the nightmare that was her life. Fear twisted her fevered mind into a tangled torment that she could not unravel. She was unable to admit her complete dependence on John for everything; how useless, terrified and incapable she was on her own.

She would go to any lengths to manipulate and cling on to him. She needed to keep playing the helpless victim, in order that he would feel guilty and obliged to help her. With calculated scheming, she was keeping the new woman on side, pretending to be her friend. She could not risk losing John for good.

The blanket of darkness offered no comfort. There was nothing to do, no activity that would still her racing mind. The half-finished jigsaw puzzle neatly set out on the tray had already been discarded.

She picked up a gossip magazine from the pile and flicked through it. A moment later it hit the floor with the smack of her exasperation.

Frightened, shivering, blotted out in the darkness that showed no mercy, Sue sat stock still. No escape, no choice but to endure the suffocating silence of the night and the dread in her heart. She was desperate for the dawn, for some respite from the turmoil.

Sue reached for the phone.

'Mum, do you realize what time it is? Its four am!' Jennifer sounded annoyed.

'I can't sleep, and I've had a funny turn. My heart is pounding, and my chest feels tight. I can't breathe.'

'Mum, the doctor explained all this to you. It's just another of your panic attacks. Take some deep breaths and calm down. Make yourself a hot drink and go back to bed. It's just anxiety.'

Sue gripped the phone tighter.

'Jenny, I can't do this. I want John and I to be together again. I want my old life back. I want the last seven years to have never happened. I want to go back to my lovely home. I want him to still love me the way I still love him.'

Sue sobbed hysterically. Jennifer took a deep breath.

'Mum, we've been over this a million times. You have to accept the fact that Dad isn't coming back. Now please go to bed and try to sleep. We are all exhausted. You are going to have to stop ringing in the middle of the night. We have work and school in the morning. It can't go on like this!'

The phone went dead.

Harvey stirred slightly in his bed. She would walk him extra early in the morning. He would like that. There was something happening across the road at number fourteen. She was determined to find out what. An early prying expedition may prove fruitful.

A hot drink in her hand and, with Perry Como playing softly in the background, Sue returned to the kitchen table and succumbed to the recurring torment of bleak aloneness.

It was eight am and she was already on the phone.

'Mabel, its Sue. I have discovered what's going on across the road. Come round for tea this afternoon about three and I will fill you in on all the details. You won't believe it!'

Harvey barked a warning. The letter box flap clicked shut. A white envelope, hand written and addressed, was lying on the mat. It looked normal enough. An invitation perhaps.

STREET LIVES

KARMA
Tell me not of others woes
Of their misery and calamity.
Only the callous hearted relish the throes of heartbreak and anguish.
Malicious malevolence's with vicious viper's tongue
Restrain your malignant mouth from foul utterances.
It's evil work is never done.
A spiteful Soul is it that takes vampiric delight
In gossiping and stirring late into the night.
Be careful what you say,
For what you now forgo, may visit you another day.
Reflect on the power of each word,
For there is not one which goes unheard.
So close your lips old motor mouth.
Shut tight your peeking eyes.
Cut off your poking nose.
Recall your harpy spies.
Else Life will deliver you a devastating unwanted surprise.
And no one will heed the pitiful mouthing
Of your desperate and terrified cries.

Scrawled along the bottom of the page were the words

Stop your gossiping or the dog gets it.

Sue felt the panic rising. Who would do such a thing? Harvey wasn't safe; she wasn't safe; she had an enemy. Someone in the neighbourhood hated her, wanted her gone.

She felt a sudden pain in her chest and momentarily lost her balance. She sat down on the floor next to Harvey, clutched him to her and wept in despair.

Her flimsy hold on reality was beginning to crumble.

Outside, on the Close, people were carrying on as usual, oblivious and utterly indifferent as to her plight. Inside her four small walls, Sue Smith was floundering.

Her coping mechanisms of the past two years, all her ways of attempting to assuage the constant undercurrent of unease, were failing her.

The endless, pointless busyness, gossiping about the neighbours, offloading her own troubles onto anyone who could bear to listen and dragging the dog round the streets compulsively. Nothing was working. The inner agony was undefeatable.

The black mesh inside her head was becoming thicker, darker. It was squeezing her brain into submission. The only way she could relieve the pressure was to talk. Sue stood up. She needed to find someone, anyone.

Harvey yapped. The phone rang. She glanced at the display.

'Harvey, its Daddy.'

'Sue, I need to see you. Is it ok if I come round? It's important.'

'Of course. I'll put the kettle on. See you soon.'

Sue hurried into the kitchen. John loved freshly brewed coffee. She set out her best china cups and saucers next to the tin of biscuits.

'Harvey, Daddy's coming to see us. Let's go and watch out of the front window.'

The dog responded with a sharp bark.

'Don't cry. Everything is going to be alright now. Daddy's on his way.'

Sue could feel the black mesh loosening its grip.

They were both waiting for him at the gate as his Mercedes swung into the Close.

'What's so important that you need to see me?' Sue asked. 'It's not your normal day for walking Harvey.'

'Come inside Sue and sit down.'

They sat together at the table. Harvey curled up at John's feet. Sue gazed at his tanned face and sparkling brown eyes. He looked well, happy, relaxed. She handed him a cup of coffee just the way he liked it and offered the biscuit tin.

'I'm sorry. It's almost empty. I haven't been to the shops.'

'That's no problem. Thanks. I like the chocolate ones.' John helped himself to the two remaining biscuits.

'So what is it you want to tell me?'

John hesitated. Sue could hear the deep intake of breath.

'There are two things. Firstly, Caroline and I are getting married.'

She froze. 'No, no, no….' she was screaming inside. Don't let him see, don't let him see.

She managed a falsely bright smile.

'Oh I see. Have you set a date?'

Hold it together Sue until he's gone.

John continued. 'In a couple of months, probably around my birthday. There is something else. We have put the house on the market. We are moving away from Oakley. Caroline has fallen in love with a cottage in Wallington. Our offer on the property was accepted yesterday.'

Sue stared at him, her mind frantically computing the implications.

'But that's twenty miles away.'

'Yes, I know. It will mean that I won't be able to come and walk Harvey and I'm afraid you are going to have to find someone else to pop in and do your odd jobs.'

John got to his feet.

'Thanks for the coffee. Sorry for clearing you out of biscuits. Got to go. Caroline and I are off to the Lakes for the weekend.'

'Have a good time' Sue murmured weakly, her head spinning. She could feel the panic rising and the black mesh closing in again. As John's Mercedes pulled away, Sue let out a long, wailing scream.

Next door old Harry heard the commotion.

'Bloody woman. Why doesn't she ever shut up? Noise, noise, noise, noise, noise! All day, every day! And stop that sodding dog barking!' he bellowed.

Minutes later, he saw Sue Smith and the dog walking hurriedly past his house in the direction of Asgard Farm. The woman looked dishevelled and demented, a strange glazed over expression on her face. The dog was still barking.

The window cleaners at number seventeen heard the barking getting louder and louder as Sue approached. She looked into the garden. 'He hates ladders' she shouted, pointing at Harvey. 'He's marrying her. He's going to have two wives. And he's moving away!'

The window cleaners stared blankly as she took off again, dragging Harvey in the direction of the farm.

'Who was that crazy woman?'

'You know…… she's the bonkers old bitch from number seventeen. She's really lost the plot this time!'

'No wonder he went off with someone else. The guy had a lucky escape!'

They both laughed and went back to their work.

Sue Smith opened the farm gate and headed down the footpath skirting the field. She stopped to let Harvey off his lead. Suddenly she bent over in pain.

'My arm...it hurts!' She struggled to catch her breath. 'Must be another panic attack. I better find Harvey and go home.'

She followed the sound of screaming coming from the lambing shed.

'Harvey, Harvey, where are you?' She called again.

'Harvey, come to mummy.'

She could hear him barking inside the shed.

She called out 'Harvey, Harvey, come here, come here.'

Inside Mrs Thrax, Annie and Dullard were watching anxiously. Harvey had three ewes cornered in the far pen.

'You naughty boy!' Sue exclaimed.

'Naughty boy, naughty boy!' screamed Annie in fury. 'Is that it? All you can say?'

Annie looked round. 'Albert, go fetch the twelve bore and don't forget the ammo.'

She turned on Sue Smith, screaming at her 'what part of the sign on the farm gate can't you understand? It says dogs worrying sheep will be shot! You have been warned before!'

Sue was hysterical. Harvey continued to bark and bark at the terrified sheep and was not responding to Sue's efforts to stop him. Dullard yelled at her.

'Have you any idea what that bloody dog has done, chasing those sheep round and round. Those lambs will be all jumbled up inside their mothers. They won't lamb themselves now. They'll need help and that's bound to be in the middle of the night and that's if they don't abort first. You stupid, stupid woman!'

Annie was shaking with rage and screaming at Sue.' Just wait until I get my hands on that bloody dog!'

Sue, her voice quivering with fear, shouted again 'Harvey, come here!'

The dog ignored her, as it always did. He was having too much fun. It was mayhem. Harvey kept on barking. It was then that she saw Albert carrying a gun. The farmer thrust the loaded gun into his wife's hands.'

I'll kill that bloody dog now, once and for all. It's the last time he will worry my sheep.'

Sue shouted even louder 'no, no, no. Please, please don't kill him.'

The dog looked up, saw the gun and bolted at speed out of the shed. It ran off down the farm track, Sue running behind. 'Harvey come back. Stop!'

The dog ignored her and disappeared over the fields. 'This isn't happening' she thought. 'I can't lose him too. I can't.'

He was the only one she had left, her friend, her child, her everything. He was the only thing she had left to care for, the focus of all her attention and devotion. Without Harvey who would she fuss over, obsess and worry about. Who would she talk to, be with, mother, smother, pamper? And, most of all, without him, there would be no reason for John to call round. Her mind was spinning out of control. Without Harvey, she would be forced to face the harsh reality that she was completely and utterly alone and this fact she could not contemplate. The dog was the barrier that kept reality at bay. He was her only protection from the truth.

Sue ran back down the Close and into the house. She reached for her phone. John needed to know. He would know what to do. John would come and find the dog. John would rescue Harvey. Her precious bundle would be safe again! She would be able to go on pretending that the things which had happened had not happened. As long as Harvey was alive she could continue living in the illusion.

Back on the farm, Albert had the dog in his sights. With a single shot the offender was despatched. The shot had penetrated the dog's heart and Harvey's remains were spilling over the heather in a bloody mess.

Albert picked up what was left of the dog and headed back over the fells in the direction of the Close. Opening the gate to number seventeen, Albert walked up the path and carelessly dumped Harvey's remains on the doorstep. 'A job well done' he thought.

'Pick up, for God's sake pick up!' John wasn't answering his phone.

Fifty miles away the Mercedes was speeding towards the Lake District. John's phone rang.

'Turn it off will you darling.'

Caroline reached for the phone. 'It's Sue. Maybe we should answer it.'

'No,' he replied. 'Turn it off. She's on her own now.'

Back in the house Sue grabbed their wedding photograph and, clutching it tightly to her chest, returned to the kitchen table. She gazed at their faces. They looked so young, so happy.

Her sentimental smile slowly changed, chameleon like, into a snarl of vicious spite. She flung the photograph down in a venomous fit of rage. Years of suppressed anger was finally erupting, surfacing, scaring her with its raw intensity, with a fury she didn't know she possessed.

In a final act of defiance, she removed her wedding ring, dropped it into the empty biscuit tin and slammed the lid. Sue heard the rattling sound as the ring rolled and settled inside. For a few brief, lucid moments and, at long last, she had finally accepted the truth.

It was then that she became aware of a beam of golden light gently encompassing her body, radiating out in all directions, illuminating the kitchen with its shimmering beauty.

Inside her was a feeling like a dam had burst in her mind, allowing every memory to flow out. She was seeing and experiencing every event of her life. It was like watching a movie, scenes of her life flitting past at a tremendous speed.

Standing in front of her was a Being of Light, holding out its arms. Sue felt an emanation of pure Love pouring from the Angel. She instantly became everyone she had ever come into contact with, feeling their emotions, thinking their thoughts, living their experiences, learning their motives.

Then she relived every detail of every second of her life, every emotion and every thought, simultaneously.

The Being of Light was speaking to her. She knew that it was impossible to lie to herself or to others or to the Light. In the Light, there was no place for secrets to hide.

The Being revealed that there were no mistakes, only experiences from which to grow and learn. Suddenly she understood that Life was important, because how she had lived her life determined how far she could go into the Light.

She saw quite clearly how and why she was the way she was in life, and that all the negative experiences were to allow her a greater understanding about herself. As the Light began to fade, the Angel said, 'I will be with you when the time comes.'

As Sue opened her eyes she was back in the nightmare.

STREET LIVES

She heard the gate close outside. She ran to the front door. Maybe, just maybe, someone had found Harvey. She flung open the door. No one. And then she saw him.

'No, no, no! Not my darling boy!'

The dog was lying lifeless on the doorstep. She could see the gaping hole in his chest where the gun shot had blasted him at close quarters. A wave of nausea hit her stomach.

Sue scooped up his bloodied carcass and set it down on the grass, murmuring softly 'Oh Harvey, Harvey, please wake up, please.' She knelt beside him and, lifting his head onto her lap, began rocking him tenderly. It wasn't happening, it wasn't happening! 'It's alright my darling, I'm here.'

The dull ache in her chest suddenly exploded into a searing hot pain that shot down her left arm. Sue gasped as a veil of agony descended. She could feel her black mesh returning, circling, closing in for the kill.

Tears pouring down her face, she bent down and kissed Harvey goodbye, as the darkness enveloped her. Sue surrendered to the blackness and let go.

Mabel, arriving just before three o'clock for her appointment to gossip, found Sue crouched down on the grass, as if she were shielding something, her face twisted sideways in a grimace, tear stained and dirty. She wasn't moving.

'Sue, Sue are you alright?'

No response. Mabel gently touched Sue on the shoulder. The body shifted slightly, and Mabel caught sight of Harvey's bloodied remains. 'Oh my God Sue, no!'

Mabel ran into the house and raised the alarm. 'Please come quickly. Something terrible has happened to my friend. She's in the garden. I think she's dead!'

Inside, on the kitchen table, the Decree Absolute and the hate mail poem lay weighted down by the biscuit tin. Next to them, were two empty china cups, the coffee dregs now dried and cracking in the bottom of each. Ripped into shreds, the wedding photograph, together with its shattered frame and sharp fragments of glass, lay strewn across the floor.

It was only later, when Jennifer moved the biscuit tin, that they discovered the wedding ring.

Outside, Morgan Fay was making her way along the Close, as the Police car arrived at number seventeen. Looking into the garden, she saw their bodies lying entwined on the grass. Lifting her gaze to a height some fifteen feet in the air above them, she smiled. 'Goodbye Sue.' she whispered.

Old Harry was watching from his window, as Sue slumped forwards over the dog. 'Good riddance.' he garumphed. 'Maybe now we'll all get some peace and quiet!'

From out of nowhere some words floated into his head. 'An empty tin rattles the most!'

STREET LIVES

Asgard Close

STREET LIVES

Fighting for Life

by

Sandy Wilson

Frank was leaning against the wall enjoying the cool Spring sunshine as a dull grey Honda Accord pulled up at the side of the road, the front near side tyres scuffing the curb. The out of tune engine gave a death rattle before dying and silence descended on Asgard Street, only to be broken by the screech of the driver's door opening.

'Got a car then? Your mum mentioned you'd passed your test.'

'Yeah. What do you think?'

'What about? Your driving or the car?'

The teenager pulled a 'very funny' face.

'Anyway, good of you to come Jenny,' said Frank as he gave his niece a hug.

'It's no problem, I've plenty time, uncle Frank,' said Jenny. 'I've packed in Uni. Mum not told you?'

'No. She didn't.'

'I'm surprised. She went mental!'

They stood at the gate in mutual silence. Frank reluctant to pry, and Jenny relieved not to be interrogated about her university problems. His sister had been overjoyed when Jenny had been accepted by Birmingham University. Frank and his sister Rosemary had not been encouraged to go to university. Not pushed by their abusive father and compliant mother to aim high.

'Hello Frank!'

Frank turned. The next-door neighbour was walking down the drive she shared with his dad. She wasn't wearing her 'very funny face'.

'Hi Michelle.'

'Please tell me it's true.'

'What's true?'

'Sue Smith, y'know the nosey cow that lives in 17? She says your dad's moving out.'

'Yeah, he is Michelle. The house has been sold.'

'I won't pretend I'm not thrilled to bits. I've been planning to murder him and bury the body under the patio at the back. In fact, I was just going to leave him in the jungle.'

'You should have let me know. I'd have helped you dig the hole.'

'I'm guessing you're Rosemary's daughter. I can see the likeness.'

'Yes, Jenny's Harry's eldest granddaughter.'

'Hi Jenny. Your mum, Frank and me were kids together.'

'So, where do we start?' asked Jenny surveying the garden, taking in the overgrown hedge, the unruly grass and rebellious plants that appeared to be devouring a rusty bicycle and the dormant Volvo with deflated tyres. Day of the Triffids, she thought. There was a defeated air about the place.

'I'll get someone to sort this out, it's the inside I need help with,' said Frank. 'I've not been here since the beginning of last year just after he had that stroke. I only came to sort out a disabled ramp when your grandfather started to use a wheelchair to get about. I just met the joiner outside; didn't go inside. Michelle had a go at me then about the mess; Can't blame her. God know what we'll find inside.'

Jenny knew not to ask why her uncle, or for that matter her mother didn't visited her grandfather, she knew not to tread where the ice was thin.

Frank had arranged for the health visitor to leave the door on the latch when she left earlier that morning. Since his father had had the stroke a care worker would call, get him out of bed and give him some breakfast then check on him at night. He'd been managing on his own, didn't always need the wheelchair in the house. But, after the second stroke the social services had pleaded for Frank to arrange residential

STREET LIVES

care. It was all getting too much for the visiting care workers. He was a very difficult patient, they said. Frank couldn't disagree.

'Dad!' He called as he opened the door. 'It's me, Frank.'

He stared in disbelief at the corridor. It was a miniature canyon with a pathway meandering through cliffs of newspapers and magazines. On one side, on top, a Micky Mouse phone looked down on the intruders.

'Jeez!' said Jenny, looking over her uncle's shoulder.

A single, naked bulb swung slowly in the sudden breeze from the open door. 'Dad it's me, Frank.'

There was no answer. Pushed gently from behind by Jenny, Frank led the way into the house; led the expedition into his long-lost childhood home.

They found him in the lounge in a chair positioned in the bay window surrounded by more rubbish. He was asleep, quietly mumbling, twitching; dreaming.

Frank shook him by his bony shoulder. 'Dad, it's Frank.'

His father started awake, turned and looked at his son without giving any sign of recognition. 'Who's she?' he said with rude abruptness, looking at Jenny.

''She' is your granddaughter. Rosemary's daughter. Jenny has come to help, help me sort things out.'

'Haven't seen her in years. How old are you then, girl?'

'Eighteen, Granddad.'

'Right, dad. We're here to sort out things you want to keep, pack whatever it is in boxes. I've got a couple of men coming later in the week to fill a skip with all the other stuff. Then we'll take you across to Holmewood. You alright with that.'

'You bloody know I'm not. I told you.' His dad said belligerently. 'I don't want to live in a home. Just bugger off! I'm fine here.'

'Well, since your last stroke there isn't any option. You're in no state to look after yourself.'

Frank caught Jenny's eye and nodded his head towards the door. 'We'll get on, dad. I'll make you a cup of tea.'

Outside the room, standing in the paper ravine they agreed a plan of action. Jenny said she would tidy the kitchen, make tea for her grandfather, then gather things together that she would recognise as valuable; her grandmother's jewellery, ornaments, that sort of thing. Frank would sort out clothes to pack for the trip to the care home and anything else he could identify as personal amongst the detritus of his father's life.

'We'll put all the stuff we're taking to the home in the kitchen, so your grandad can look through it all,' suggested Frank. Might make the old bastard feel involved, he thought.

'I'll see you later then,' said Jenny, adding, 'hopefully!' with a smile as Frank set off into the depths of the bungalow.

He turned into the main bedroom, another repository for magazines and newsprint. There was barely enough room to walk round the bed. With a resigned sigh he started to empty the clothes into two large suitcases that he had set on the bed. Looking up, he could see a cardboard box wedged between the ceiling and the top of the wardrobe. Frank carried a chair through from the dining room to stand on. As he eased the box from the grip of the ceiling, the box opened, and a red boxing glove fell to the floor landing with a dull thud like soft punch.

He looked down at it and wondered; only briefly, there was a whole house to clear. It had been difficult to persuade his father to move, to sell up. Persuading his dad to allow his house to be...what did the neat estate agent in the shiny suit and shoes call it. Decluttered? Frank didn't think the word declutter remotely encompassed what had to be done. Televisions, transistor radios and microwaves of indeterminate age formed a ziggurat pyramid in the centre of the lounge, a monument to obsolete technology. Every space was crammed with useless junk, no doubt concealing wildlife; insects and rodents. Only the most minimal space had only been left. Space for a threadbare velour upholstered chair in the lounge, a clear, well, almost clear, worktop in the kitchen, a bed with a pathway to allow access and, in the bathroom barely enough space to manoeuvre. Thank God it was a bungalow, thought Frank, contemplating the task before him.

At least the agent had a developer interested in buying at a reasonable price. Reasonable, considering the work that would have to be done. In the state it was in it would be a hard sell otherwise and the money was needed to bankroll his dad's care. At the interview with the care home manager Frank had skimmed over the hoarding issue. Living closer he would be able to keep an eye on him, watch out for any signs, keep on top of his dad's bizarre obsession and keep his room tidy. Not something Frank looked forward to. From hardly seeing his father he was going to have regular contact. No, not something to look forward to at all. He would have to introduce him to Susan and the kids, grandchildren he had never met. Never asked about. Dan and Megan. With packing finished he went in search of Jennie.

'Where's your grandad?'

'He had the tea I made him, didn't thank me then said he was going to lie down.' Frank found his father lying in his bed, a Pharaoh in his tomb, surrounded by worthless treasures. He cleared a pile of Sunday supplements off a chair, moved it nearer to the bed and sat down.

'Why on earth do you keep all these magazines dad?' said Frank. 'In fact, what is the point of it all?'

'Never you mind,' he said. 'Mind your own fucking business.'

'Well, it's my business now.' said Frank, 'The skip'll be arriving soon, and the men. We'll have everything cleared out by about four o'clock, then you and me, we can get off. You okay with that?'

No answer. A tap dripped somewhere in the house.

'Listen I know you're not happy with all this dad, but it's got to happen. There's no way you can live here on your own after that last stroke. So don't argue.'

Silence.

'Okay, suit yourself, just don't get in the way, just get up get dressed and don't interfere,' he said, thinking, some father you've been, you sulking, ungrateful old git. Frank stood up, shook his head in frustration and closing the door left the bedroom, left his father lying silently in his bed, surrounded by his clutter, suffocating in his thoughts, past memories playing out in his head.

.... door swings open. Slam! Banging, hits a locker, a tidal wave of noise floods in, mingles with the smells, odours: a waft of piss, sweat, rubber, leather, and fear. Door slams shut, shuts out the noise. In the muffled silence Tom wraps my hands, an Egyptian priest carefully binding a mummy. Then pushes on the red gloves, tells me: focus, focus, focus.....

Gathering the old newspapers, catalogues, obsolete radios and other pointless detritus of his dad's life, he thought of his fractious relationship with his father. For that matter, his father's fractious relationship with the whole family: his mother, his sister. All of them had suffered, been at the receiving end of whatever was bugging him. There always seemed to be a bitterness, anger hidden just beneath his thin shell. He'd always been a bit odd, but then after mum died ten years ago this hoarding business started. What was that all about? Frank recalled reading somewhere, in a magazine or book, that hoarding was the symptom of an emotional trauma. Pictures flickered in his mind, a thread of memories of happy times: playing football in the park, a dog called Poppy, sandcastles and screeching gulls. Laughter. But somewhere, at some point it all changed. The happy times had stopped, abruptly, like the end of a feel-good film. Well, he thought with a heavy heart, I can't change the past.

With the skip full' he sat in the front garden with Jennie on two plastic chairs discoloured with a decade of exposure to the sun.

Jenny was smoking. 'Want one?' she said offering the packet to her uncle.

'No thanks. Stopped years ago, you should too.'

A blackbird concealed in the beech tree sang and discordant music spilled from an open window of one of the terraced houses. Frank looked startled.

'Grime music. It looks like students live there.'

'Grime music?' Frank sounded like Peter Kaye talking about garlic bread.

'Yeah, latest thing in music.' Appropriate enough considering her grandfather's house she thought.

'He wasn't always like this, your grandfather.' Frank saw ghosts from his past. 'I can remember when I was five, maybe six years old, playing football here in the back garden. He would pretend that he'd fouled me and give me a penalty. Then fumble the ball so I'd score. Mum would call us in for tea and he would carry me over his shoulder into to the kitchen. He would be roaring with laughter.'

'So what happened?'

'Something did. But no one said what. Even your grandmother never said.'

'Well, I need to go,' said Jenny crushing the stub of her cigarette under the sole of the foot.' I'll just push off. He won't notice I've gone.'

'No, sadly he won't. He's never seen your cousins,' said Frank.

Frank went through to the lounge where his dad now sat in his wheelchair in the bay window, caged in the bars of sunlight that slid through the slats of the Venetian blinds. He felt only loathing as he watched his father twitching and muttering as if in dream.

…….walking, legs weak, red gloves heavy at the extremity of my trembling arms. Walking through a tunnel of sound: music, metallic tinny, animals howling, a primeval baying. A tunnel of smells, odours: aftershave, cheap scent, cigarettes. Climb through the ropes into the ring, hands helping, pulling. Focus, focus, focus……

'I've put all the stuff you might want to keep on the table in the kitchen,' said Frank, 'Come on, I'll help you.'

Startled out of his reverie, he turned to look at his son, a look absent of any affection.

'Don't bloody bother, I'll get there under my own steam. I'm not a spastic.'

'Okay, okay!' Cantankerous old bastard!

Frank made two mugs of tea in the now, decluttered, minimalist kitchen then sat with his father at the Formica table. Both men silent, immersed in their habitual enmity. He watched his dad as he examined the remaining souvenirs of his life, a museum curator carefully appraising the worth of some ancient artefacts. He picked up the boxing glove and, reaching inside pulled out a ribbon of white, stained fabric.

.......wet slippery flesh, rubbing, sweat lubricated. Rope scraping, burning back. Ref's arm sliding, squeezing in, pushing, separating. Noise: squeaking rubber on taut canvas, squeak squeak. Punches. Slap! Smack! Leather on taut skin. Breath. Gasping, panting. Fuck! That hurt! Focus, focus, focus......

'What's that?' Frank asked.

'The wrap. It's the wrap,' his dad said, winding the fabric strip around his hand in demonstration of its purpose.

'I never knew you boxed, dad. You've never said.' Like so many other things in your life, Frank thought.

'Yes, well you bloody well know now,' said his dad, with his customary curtness.

'Were you any good?'

His father stared blankly through the window, across the garden, Frank's question left hanging, unanswered. He had been good, too good.

.......squeak, squeak. Slap! Smack! Thwack! Squeak, squeak. Move, must keep moving my feet, keep focused. Clanging bell. Sitting, breathing, sucking in air, cigar smoke, sour beer. Sucking in the stench of humans. Soft caress of a sponge, cool water, rivulets down his bruised face, down his aching chest. Clanging bell. Tom's shrill voice shouting, focus, focus, focus....

In the silent void of the kitchen Frank thought, recalling his childhood, his teenage years; his dad's over reaction when he had been suspended from school for fighting. Clelland, the headmaster looking across his tidy desk; looking sympathetically at father and recalcitrant son. Why not enrol your son in the boxing club in the old cinema down

Kirk Lane? he had suggested in his reasonable mild voice. Channel his adolescent aggression he said. Dad had leapt to his feet, chair keeling over, shouting. Shouting. Spittle sparkling in the shaft of sunlight. 'No, no, no!' Mr Roberts, teaching maths next door had burst through the door and helped restrain his father. Helped escort him from the school. Pale faces watched from classroom windows. Later there was whispering in playground corners and looks from teachers. A strange event in the past. Frank loaded the boxes into the back seat of his car, loaded his dad into the front seat and folded the wheelchair into the boot. They were ready to go.

'I want to stop off on the way, see somebody like.'

'Who? What for dad? Said Frank, eyeing the time, patience stretched. 'We've a long way to go.'

'Won't take a lot of time son.'

They pulled into the car park, under the shade of a majestic chestnut tree, near the ornate wrought iron entrance gate. Frank hefted his father's wheelchair out of the boot and helped him out of the car, into the chair.

'What's all this about dad?' said Frank, impatience seeping into his voice.

'You'll see soon enough son,' said his dad. 'You'll understand, when you see.' Frank pushed his father along a path lined beech trees and rose beds, through the heavy scent of roses and cut grass.

'This is it son, we're here.'

They stopped and Frank spun the wheelchair to face a simple pale gravestone. 'Who's this dad, who's Kenneth Benson?' said Frank reading the inscription. There was no answer. Frank looked down at his father. He was staring at the gravestone.

.........smells; sweat, cigar smoke, sour beer. Noise; primeval baying, shouting. He's dropped his left. There, an opening! Quick! Red leather flashes through the air. Sharp slap! Impact jars the bones of my arm, Christ! His head snaps round. Sweat, a crescent arcing out, glittering in the flood lights. Body performs a graceful pirouette, then a slow fall to the canvas, bouncing. Noise; cheering, shouting. Ref slaps the canvas.

Slap! Slap! Counting, counting. But, he could go on counting forever and ever……..

Then in a voice choked with tears told his son the story, the only story of his life. 'Kenny was dead, son. I'd killed him,' said his father, wiping his face with his cuff. 'I think about it every day. About Kenny. The fight. I should have said something, spoken to somebody.'

Under the dome of the intense blue sky, watched by a small group of distant mourners, Frank fell to his knees, gripping his dad in an embrace. Father and son united in grief, two pugilists at the end of a long bruising contest that had lasted a lifetime.

STREET LIVES

Asgard Close

STREET LIVES

Michelle

by

Alex Williams

Harry's frail body used to drift along the path and up the steps to his door, his pickled egg eyes staring ahead. Now his wheelchair squeaks up a ramp, his face pinched, his yolks about to extrude.

A month ago, an ambulance screeched to a halt outside his house, and my cheeks bunched as I smiled behind my kitchen window. Was this it? Was this the end of him? Would my life finally start? I danced with my ecstatic feather duster while he was in hospital. With him out of the picture, I'd be able to have friends, get a boyfriend, even sell my bungalow. The woman in the mirror winked at me and I grinned back.

Three days later his son, Frank, stood by his front door with two builders. I hadn't seen sweet Frank for years, but I remember playing with him when we were kids. Perhaps he'd tidy up the place and move in?

'My dad had a stroke,' he said to me, 'he's okay, but he's in a wheelchair so I'm having a ramp installed.'

I handed him the get well soon card and pushed the sympathy card into my back pocket. My teeth bit together behind my smile.

'I hope he's okay,' I said, 'let me know if I can help.' Shit, he's alive, and a cheap mis-matched wooden ramp adds to the horror show. As If the overgrown hedge, the weeds and the random rubbish strewn around the front garden weren't enough. I'd never sell a house next door to such a hell hole.

Together Frank and I looked through Harry's filthy front window. Piles of newspapers, boxes and random crap were stacked up against the inside of the glass. Where would it end? Compression? His lounge becoming a sausage machine that would squeeze him out through the extractor fan? I'd actually like to see that.

'Are you going to clean up while he's in hospital?' I asked as I edged closer. Should I touch his arm? No.

'I'll try, but he's funny about his stuff.'

Did Frank remember what happened thirty years ago, when he was sixteen, and I was fifteen? He caught my eye over the garden fence and threw me a dazzling smile? The next day, he put a note in my school bag asking me out. My brother found it and took offence. There was a fight outside the science room. I'd ignored Frank from then on and acted like he didn't exist at all.

'I would have said yes you know, if it wasn't for my brother.' Our eyes locked for a moment and his cheeks flushed. He turned and scuttled into the messy house.

Sometime later, Harry's wheelchair squeaked up the ramp for the first time. Frank retreated back to his own home hundreds of miles away, and carers took his place. They never tidied up though, and I sit at my window, waiting for my life to begin.

Street Lives

19

ASGARD CLOSE

STREET LIVES

Looking After Your Own

By

Polly Smith

Faded floral wallpaper peels from my bedroom walls revealing glimpses of bare plaster. I gaze at the mucky windows with their chipped yellow frames. Canary yellow paintwork that matches the scuffed skirting board edging the dismal grey of my threadbare carpet. A Zimmer frame and commode collude to imprison me in the confined space. The limp décor matches the misery of my mood. I have no energy to venture from my room. Helpless and ashamed I am. To be sure, who'd be thinking this is my life ?

But whose to help me? All of ye, busy neighbours, noisy neighbours. Ye be strangers to me now. Don't you wonder where I am, what I be doing all day? Spare me ye'r time? Could ye not be calling round?

Twelve months ago our Michael turned up on me doorstep. Never thought I'd be seeing him again. I'd given up all hope. Overjoyed I was. A fine strong lad so he is. Got himself a good job too, works with computers. I was pleased when he moved in. He said he'd look after me. He does his best but life's tough. He's out a lot and my days seem endless and lonely.

I like to think on happier times; the good times with Mary and baby Michael. Over and over I relive the pain of leaving them. It's sixty years since I left them behind in Ireland. I came to England to find work. It was a chance to earn good money and set us up for a good life. But two years on with little chance to visit home, the marriage was over. Mary wanted to make a new start for herself and Michael in Ireland. Why didn't I try harder? I should have gone back and fought to keep them. I never got over losing them. My life was a blur after that. I stayed in

England and lost myself in work and drink. Yes I've had a few lasses over the years, but no one to compare to my Mary.

A key in the lock interrupts my thoughts. 'Will that be you Michael?' No reply suggests it is. Two minutes later the throb of rock music pounds through the bungalow. It's murder. I've told him, but he neither turns it down nor turns it off. With belly ache in my gut, I hope for something to eat soon. I stare beyond the grimy windows and try to imagine the view of the valley bottom. It's beauty long since obscured by a wilderness of overgrown weeds and bushes.

The bedroom door opens, the click of a switch and my room is bathed in harsh white electric light.

'Here you are Dad'. I squint, then blink trying to focus in the brightness. Michael puts a tray on the bed. Gratefully I chew on the dry cheese sandwich and take swigs of tea from a chipped pot mug. 'He's a good lad our Michael'.

'You got any cash Dad?' he asks as he draws the curtains. 'I'll see about a second-hand telly for you tonight.' I hand him £50.

'It's gonna be more than that Dad. How much've you got?'

I empty my wallet and he stuffs the cash in his pocket. 'Right I'll be off then.' He leaves me a tumbler of water with my tablets then walks away. He doesn't hear the disappointment in my voice as I bid him farewell.

Two minutes later the music stops and the front door slams, leaving a resounding silence. I pick up my dog-eared bible and remove the creased photograph from its cover. My gnarled fingers grip the image of my precious Mary cradling baby Michael. Quiet tears trickle down my hollowed cheeks as I dream of Mary and sunnier days.

Some hours later, loud music and raised voices break my sleep. Raucous laughter and the clink of bottles mean Michael's brought his tart back again. Vicky clatters into my bedroom in sky high stilettos. Her pale podgy face is smothered in thick makeup, smudged mascara and crimson lipstick. Tight black leggings and a flimsy leopard skin top cling to her shameless rolls of fat. She laughs, raises her glass and staggers out of my room. Since she came on the scene, my life's got worse. Michael moved me from the front to the back bedroom. Says I'm better off here because it's smaller and easier to heat.

STREET LIVES

'You'll be safer here Dad, you've less chance of falling. Stay in bed or your chair. I'll see to everything.'

He's thoughtful like that, wants to look after me. He's a good lad our Michael.

Mid-morning Michael brings me a mug of tea and toast. He's unshaven, pale and untidy. He has drink in him, so he does.

'You alright son?'

'Ah just tired Dad. Had a bad night.'

'You'll be late for work, so you will.'

'No I'll be fine. See you later.' With that he turns away and my heart sinks.

The front door bangs shut, but the clatter of high heels and the sound of the kettle whistling mean Vicky's still here.

Vicky's certainly wheedled her way into his life. She comes and goes as she pleases. To be sure, Michael can't know about the men that call. But I hear them alright. Panting, moaning, banging. Disgusting. I pray things will change. I want my home back, some peace. More time with Michael and chance to make up for all the years lost.

Not long after I hear knocking at the door, but Vicky ignores it. The knocking persists and a dog yaps. My heart lifts. Is this someone come to see me? But soon the knocking stops and my hopes fade.

Then someone taps on my bedroom window. I strain to make out a face, pressed up against the mucky pane.

'Are you there George? Are you alright?'

I recognise the voice. It's Sue Smith from up the street. She's known for talking a lot, but nevertheless it'd be nice to chat to someone.

I raise my arm and wave, beckoning her to come in. Her face disappears and a few minutes later I hear raised voices.

'Who the hell are you? What d'you think you're doing snooping around here? Fuck off! And take that bloody dog with you.'

Everything goes quiet, then Vicky barges into my room and screams hysterically in my face.

'What the fucking hell d'you think you're doing George, inviting that nosy cow in? You stupid bugger. Are you bloody mental? You're nowt but a silly old fool. It's time you went to the nuthouse. You wait till Michael hears about this. Just you fucking wait!'

STREET LIVES

She rants on and on. What can I do? She isn't interested in me or anything I try to say. Hopeless, I feel hopeless. Feebly I look down at the floor and withdraw into myself. There's nothing I can do. Eventually, red in the face and still raging she leaves my room. Not long after, I hear the front door slam. So I sit here in my familiar world of despair and isolation.

Daylight hours slowly drag into darkness before Michael comes home.

'Where's Vicky, Dad?' He asks.

'I don't know son. She went out this afternoon; didn't say where she was going.'

*

And that was the last time I saw her.

Michael asked after her. Sue Smith told him she'd seen her marching up the street towards Dr. Cullingworth's at number 11. He rang Vicky's mobile, but the line was dead.

So he went up to number 11. The Doctor told him Vicky had turned up at her practice ranting and raving. She'd complained about me and demanded she admit me to the 'nut house'. The Doctor refused to talk to her and 'sent her packing'. Vicky had stormed off in a huff. It seems that was the last time anyone saw her.

*

After that Michael changed. He blamed me for Vicky leaving and we argued a lot. A few weeks later a Health Visitor and Social Worker turned up at our house. Michael insisted we were fine and told them he was looking after me. But things got worse at home. Michael was drinking a lot and rarely spent any time with me. I struggled on, hoping things would change, but they didn't. Not long after, the Social worker called again and arranged for carers to visit me twice a day. I looked forward to their company. They made me meals and helped keep my room clean and tidy. But Michael resented the interference from 'the Social'. Some days he didn't come home at all. On pension day he'd get some food in, but never enough and I never saw any change. Then it turned out he'd not been paying the bills. That's not my way, I've never owed anyone a penny. We had terrible rows about the debts. In the end I dreaded him coming home. He left me heartbroken and penniless, so he did. The Social intervened then and arranged for me to move into Oakley Care Home. That was hard for me, but it was the only option.

*

Anyway, It's comfortable here. I've got used to it now. I don't go hungry, there's company when I want it and I get a weekly allowance. I save it up just in case Michael calls. It's not much, but he's lost his job you know, and he's not very well. You do what you can for your own, don't you?

Sue Smith visits every week and keeps me in touch with the local gossip. She says the Police have been doing some house to house enquiries. They're investigating reports of missing women in the area. The Police have been to Dr Cullingworth's several times. I suppose she'll have information about patients with odd behaviours or grudges towards women. The 'locals' think Vicky's disappearance might be connected somehow. Not that I care about that tart. She's got a lot to answer for.

ROWAN LODGE

Asgard Close

When Flowers Talk

by

Carrie Canning

Letters to Lilly-Fay.

Guilt paid for Rowan Lodge. I'll never leave here, not now, not in the next life, spirits remain in places they've loved. My Aunt, 'Spinster Gwen,' died seventeen years ago, leaving me her entire estate. She had her reasons. I live alone, though I'm not lonely, I have my cats Danu and Brigid and the spirit of my beloved dog, Merlin, is never far from my side.

Oakley is a quaint, semi-rural, market town. The older residents are a tight knit bunch, postulation knives at the ready to give new meaning to neighbourhood watch. It was Sue Smith who dared to pry.

'We worry about you Morgan-Fay, slight thing like you, rattling around that draughty old Lodge all alone. Why aren't you settling down? Having a family's not that easy once you're the wrong side of forty. Let's face it, you're hardly one of those women who choose a career over children, I mean you're only a florist.'

The thing is, I didn't choose to be childless, Lilly-Fay. You were taken from me in the cruellest of ways.

I should warn you, I court the unconventional; dreadlocks, piercings, body art. Our local tattoo artist, 'The Celtic Savage,' I know him as Carl, is very talented, also very discreet. I share his bed from time to time, nothing consequential, just sex. No tortuous romance or worthless words. Any love I had was spent far too young on your father, Patrick. I was just seventeen, Patrick two years older.

STREET LIVES

My parents, the aptly named Jones, Katherine and Ivan, were sober, reliable pillars of the community. Upright, respectable, committed to committees and the church roof. Brazen sham!

I loved my dad, as much as you can love a whittled, hollow, browbeaten sap. The sight of him pacifying my mother's convulsive temper made me sick. If he'd slapped her, hard, in the face, stood up to her, just once, then I might have felt more love than nausea.

Her failure to decipher the early signs, rendered my mother the sacrificial victim of an unwanted pregnancy. At the age of forty-two she gave birth, to her only child and a lifetime of resentment. A relentless woman, she piled on the agony until dad crumbled to nothing. I watched, little knowing that one day, the toxic, ruthless, bitch would demolish my life forever too.

I waited until my bulging tummy became impossible to hide, innocently believing my delicate condition would be my protection against her wrath. Instead her fury hit epic proportions. Dad swept up the shattered shards of an heirloom, his head cowed, evading the reality of my face. Smacked, mottled, red and blue and mother's final demand, 'I want her out!'

It was decided I was to stay with Spinster Gwen, until after the birth. I didn't protest, anything had to be easier than mother's acerbic mouth and withering glances. I liked Aunt Gwen, she was quirky. I remembered how at Granny's funeral six years before, she had arrived at the graveside shrouded in a floor length black, velvet hooded cloak and carrying a large wooden staff. One minute she was there, the next she was gone.

It was the 23rd of December. The 1.45 to Cardiff gathered speed past graffitied walls, housing estates and into the open countryside. Rivers of wintery rain trickled the grimy windows, the perfect camouflage for my tearful reflection. A reminder from a tiny fist deep inside, I dried my eyes and hugged my coat around me. I'm going to tell you what happened at Aunt Gwen's, Lilly-Fay, because I believe you'll understand.

The old cast iron letterbox lifted outwards in response to the knocker. 'What do you want? Hurry up, I'm feeding the cats.'

'It's me Aunt Gwen, Morgan-Fay.' The door opened a little way, I pushed it further and stepped inside. 'Aunt Gwen?' I slotted my umbrella into the hall stand amid several canes and the staff that I remembered from granny's funeral. I fingered the beautiful carvings, an Owl, Crow, Hare...'

'Don't loiter dear, tea's nice and hot, brewed just right for you knocking.'

The kitchen was lamp lit and cosy. My Aunt was sitting at an old wooden table, covered with a heavy, green, velvet cloth, then sheets of newspaper, littered with objects, some silver, some brass. The room smelled of coal fires and polish.

'The staff you were admiring Morgan-Fay, the carvings are my Spirit Animals, my Guides.'

'How did you know I was...?'

'I know things just like you know things, see things just like you see things.' Aunt Gwen huffed on the strange sickle shaped blade of an old bone handled knife. 'Now then Morgan-Fay, don't you go expecting any of that tinsel nonsense and Yule's been and gone so you've missed that.'

Despite her directness, her voice was gentle. 'Sit down dear, I've got a good blaze going.'

'That's an unusual knife Aunt Gwen.'

The old lady looked up, sweeping a rogue wisp of grey hair back from her serious silent features. 'It's a Boline.'

'What's it used for?'

'Chopping herbs, carving candles... it'll be yours one day.' Pulling one finger at a time, Aunt Gwen removed her polishing gloves. Several curious silver rings adorned her long, slender, fingers. She was taller than I remembered and slim, with a captivating youthful air.

'You said you were feeding the cats?' At last she smiled.

'Did I? Slip of the tongue my dear, they've all passed to spirit.' Aunt Gwen intertwined her fingers, resting her chin on her hands, her gaze intense, thoughtful. 'Then, you know all about the spirit world Morgan-Fay. That dog, he never leaves your side, Lurcher was he?'

'Merlin, you can see him!'

'We're very alike you and me Morgan-Fay.' Aunt Gwen slipped her cardigan from one arm. 'See this birth mark, you have the exact one.' I rolled up my sleeve and laid my arm next to hers. Identical deep red scars, like little maps. 'The mark of a Witch-Pricker, corrupt times my dear, should never be forgotten.' Aunt Gwen flexed her hand, fingering her rings affectionately. 'Silver has a unique beauty, a natural connection to the moon, to Luna Magic, makes it more precious to me than any gold or gems. She remained thoughtful. 'Do you like your name Morgan-Fay?'

'Well, it's different.'

'You won't remember Aunt Agnes, she died before you were born, leaving me all her jewellery. No use to me, all of it gold you see. Of course, your mother, Katherine, had her eye on it, so when I suggested they name you, Morgan-Fay, well, let's just say she was easily persuaded.'

'I never knew you had chosen my name Aunt Gwen.'

'Ugly woman, your mother, on the inside anyway, worst place for ugliness if you ask me.'

'Lots of people comment about it...my name I mean.'

Aunt Gwen smiled, 'You see other realms don't you?'

'I...well...yes...at first I didn't know the people I could see were dead.'

'Seeing beyond the veil and magic are the same really. Only there for those who see. The rest may mock. You must pay no heed and remember this. *'Ever mind the rule of three, what ye send out comes back to thee.'*

'That's weirdly familiar Aunt Gwen, is it a poem? Maybe I heard it at school.'

She laughed, nothing unladylike or boisterous, just a gentle, joyous trickle. 'Not unless you went to 'Hogwarts' my dear.' I giggled with her, though I wasn't sure why. Aunt Gwen gently patted my tummy. 'The Craft of the Wise, Morgan-Fay, spans many lives. She'll believe, just like we believe.'

'You think the baby's a girl?'

'Maiden for sure, she'll carry the mark too.'

'Aunt Gwen, this is all...peculiar, scary even, yet there's something...like when you know places you've never visited before, or when strangers are not strangers.'

'Nothing to be afraid of Morgan-Fay, Crow Nest Cottage is the perfect place for remembering.' Aunt Gwen fumbled with the cushions in her rocking chair. 'Now, there's bread and cheese in the larder and fruit cake. Make yourself at home, you can't mistake your room, I've hung a Rowan cross on the door, made it specially.'

My mind was struggling to process an unsettling wakefulness. Maybe Aunt Gwen was just loopy? Then I see dead people and she saw Merlin. I was confused and far too tired and hungry to think.

My parents visited once. Mother, glaring disdainfully at my pregnant belly, said there was news from Patrick's family. She told me that Patrick was going off to Uni, he wanted nothing to do with me or the baby. She insisted that, 'I shouldn't think of the child as mine, adoption was for the best.' I was warned that if I ignored her 'advice,' I'd be going it alone.

Lilly-Fay, my beautiful little Maiden, born at Beltane, the 1st of May, we share the same birthday and the same birthmark, just as Aunt Gwen said we would.

I was told to make separation easier, the nurses would take care of you. I rarely left your side, threw the tablets they gave me to stop my flow of milk down the toilet. I hoped that when my parents came, when they saw you, felt the weight of you in their arms they'd change their minds. They didn't hold you. Why would they? We were strangers, all of us. I buried my face in your tiny vest, breathing in your uniqueness. A nurse called Sarah, took a 'Polaroid.' I wrapped the photo in the vest and left the hospital alone.

Instruction was, I should stay at Aunt Gwen's until my clothes fitted me again. It didn't take long. I felt hollow, dead inside, like one of those old Yew trees that grow in graveyards.

Milk drenched my clothes. Aunt Gwen consulted her 'Medical Almanac, *cures and remedies for every season.*' She gave me Epsom salts daily and lined my bra with cold cabbage leaves to ease my sore, swollen, breasts. After five weeks I left the comforting refuge of Crow Nest Cottage with my gift of magic restored. My knowledge of the Craft and memories of past lives gently coaxed to the surface of my consciousness, filling a lifelong void. Yet my arms and my heart were agonizingly empty. Losing you triggered a primitive force to sluice through every vein, every sinew. I wanted to howl, run wild, search the wilderness, hunt you down, snatch you back, snarling at anyone who dared come near. Instead, futile tears fall onto a fading snapshot and a tiny vest soaks up my heartache. I knew then you would be my only child Lilly-Fay, any more would have been wrong.

I loved Aunt Gwen, though visiting would have dredged memories too painful, instead we wrote to each other often. We used a script known as the Runes of Honorios, no choice, when my prying bitch of a mother regularly rifled my stuff. Sadly, Aunt Gwen's last letter accompanied her will. This time there was no secrecy. Instruction was, my parents and I must all be present when the solicitor read it aloud.

Dearest Morgan-Fay,

Your mother insisted it was your choice to have the baby adopted. Yet your grief told a very different story. Too late, I have learned the shocking truth.
When I became ill, Ivan visited me. I voiced my concern that you may have been coerced into parting with Lilly-Fay. He confessed to a monstrous act, that I believe you should hear. Every truth, however painful, should triumph over deceit.
He and Katherine had manipulated, lied to everyone, told Patrick and his family the baby had died, and you wanted nothing more to do with him.
Take comfort, Morgan-Fay, Karma is a natural law.
I will be with you always.

Aunt Gwen.

There's no flight or fight from disbelief, instead my brain grappled desperately to comprehend. My parents had robbed me of my child, a theft beyond conception. Reflexively twitching away from my father's hand, my mother spoke, her eyes, cold and empty, 'I simply did what had to be done.' I have no shame in admitting, the satisfaction of smacking her square in the face, the image of blood gushing from her vile mouth, is a mild pain relief that I take often. I left as dad began bleating his apology to her. He died soon after; I didn't attend. The toxic venom of loathing had deadened my heart to them.

I moved into Aunt Gwen's cottage and lived there until it sold. In the cupboard where she kept her craft tools was note that read, *'From Crone to Mother, from Mother to Maiden, So Mote it Be!* I use her tools and robes often, though, one day, as the note says, they must pass to you Lilly-Fay.

Loss dogged my teenage years. Now I will tell you about my best friend Sabrina and Tom, the restless spirit of a World War One soldier.
    Sabrina Knox and I were inseparable, born just days apart. Neighbouring families, we played together, started school together. Then one day, she vanished. She was just fifteen years old.
    The 7th of June 1993 was sunny but not hot. I remember I wore my blazer. I had sprained my ankle playing netball that day, so I was sent home early from school. Amelia Carpenter claimed she and Sabrina walked part of the way home together. She said Sabrina left her to call into Potter's Newsagents for an ice cream. I thought that was weird, Sabrina didn't like cold things, said they gave her *'Brain Freeze.'* She adored her dog, Ruff, she would never have left him. Yet she was never seen again; she never did call to Potter's. Sabrina's disappearance left behind a deviant grief, an emotional wasteland. When I moved into Rowan Lodge, I planted a flower bed for her in the corner of the garden; Roses, Lavender and fragrant climbers. I tend the flowers, though the energy there is negative, draining. I'm certain my beautiful friend remains between the worlds, a discarnate, earthbound spirit, trapped by the trauma of her passing. I want to free her, to help her move on. If only she could reach me like Tom did.

I first encountered Tom on the day of the accident at the nearby students' house.
    An ambulance sped noisily down the street halting abruptly outside the students' lodgings. Blue lights flashing, two paramedics disappeared

into the house carrying a stretcher. I hurried down the street. One of the students, Amy, worked for me in the shop, I'd become really quite fond of her.

'Morgan-Fay.'

'Amy! What's happened?'

'Ben fell down the attic stairs. He's unconscious.'

Siren shrieking impatiently, the ambulance moved off, steadily gathering pace in the rain-washed streets. Josh thrust his hands into his jeans' pockets, casually kicking rogue pebbles into the road.

'Come on you two, I'll make us all a cuppa.'

The kitchen was large and littered with pizza boxes, beer cans and unwashed pots. Instantly I was aware of a presence. Standing in the corner of the room was the spirit of a young soldier. Amy sipped her tea, staring into her cup as though the words she needed were hidden there.

'Ben found letters, written by some World War One guy, he got obsessed with them, began acting really weird.'

'Where are the letters now Amy?'

'In his room I expect.'

'Can I see them?'

'Yeah sure, I'll get them.' Amy reappeared clutching a collection of letters. 'That room gives me the creeps.' She shuddered as she handed me the bundle.

'Why don't you join Josh in the sitting room? I'll take a look at these.' The spirit of the soldier remained, watchful.

'You must be Tom? Are these your letters?'

The soldier nodded. 'To my Maggie.'

'Why are you here Tom?'

'The boy Ben, it's my fault. I just need his mother, Anna, to forgive me. I murdered her Great Grandfather. It was wartime, but I killed him, in cold blood. I thought once Ben read the letters he'd understand. Instead he began living my memories, saw things, awful things, from the war. Now the yolad's lost his mind?'

'Because you're haunting him Tom, you must move on.'

'I can't, I'm in no man's land, it's what happens when you...kill someone...kill yourself.'

'Did you kill yourself Tom?'

'Yes, here in this house, in the attic, where the lad sleeps.'

'Why?'

'Let's just say to balance the books.'

'Taking your own life didn't balance the books Tom. The 'no man's land,' as you call it is your spirit hasn't passed over, remained earthbound, between the worlds.'

Tom smiled. 'Unfinished business.'

'No what's done is done. This world is for the living and you're dead Tom. Go, Maggie's waiting. Leave Ben in peace.'

'I can't, help me please.'

'OK Tom, if Anna is the only way…if I bring her here, you must promise me then you'll go to your Maggie.'

'Who you talking to?' I startled.

'No one Amy, just reading aloud. Listen we need to let Ben's mum know.'

'We can Skype.'

'OK Amy but let me do the talking. It's important she comes here first, before she goes to the hospital.'

Persuading Anna wasn't easy. She clearly thought I was a crank. Then as Aunt Gwen said; Clairvoyance, 'a gift or a curse?'

I thought that was the end Lilly-Fay. Then every ending is just another beginning.

I had been gone hours; the cats were in no mood to compromise. Feed them, then pour my wine. Dusk, the perfect time for a chilled glass of Sauvignon Blanc. Suitably sustained, Danu and Brigid joined me in the garden. I watched them preening contentedly, ears pricked, alert to the stirrings of nocturnal prey. An earlier shower had left the earthy petrichor of rain on dry soil, honeysuckle blossom providing a lighter note in the still evening air. Stretching the aching limbs of a very long day, I relaxed into the gentle curves of the wooden bench. Head tilted backwards, taking in the darkening sky and first twinkling stars. I concluded this might very well end up as a 'drain the bottle' kind of evening. I called to Danu and Brigid, but they were deaf to me, transfixed on a figure almost translucent in the twilight.

'Tom!'

He pointed towards Sabrina's flower bed. 'Come with me, I know about her.' His voice was barely a whisper, his journey from the earthly plane had begun. I followed, hurrying as his spirit grew weaker. 'Oakwell Manor Tom! Why here?' I watched through the rusty railings, as Tom, drifted towards The Temple Folly, his arm outstretched.

'Sabrina...is this where she is?'' The soldier was now little more than a mist. 'Tom! Please! Is this where her body is?' It may have been a trick of the light, or his one final effort but I was sure I saw him nod.

Standing amid a variety of lush greenery, Oakley Police Station, looks more like a hotel, small and quaint, with a central duck pond.

'Now then Morgan-Fay, we're not used to seeing you in here.'

The desk sergeant raised himself upright, silver buttons straddling his portly frame, his porky fingers clutching the desk. A frown furrowed his heavy forehead, jutting out above taut red pouches and porcine blue eyes. The only thing missing between Sergeant Roper and the jolly policeman was a personality.

'Sergeant Roper, I must talk to someone, I have new information about my friend, the girl who went missing. Sabrina Knox.'

'Well now, that's going back some time; sorry business, never did get solved.'

'Sergeant Roper, I know where she...her body's buried in the grounds of Oakwell Manor.'

'And where might you have got this *'vital information'* from?'

'I'm psychic, I see dead people. The other evening, Tom, a soldier from the First World War...'

'Oh so a ghost has told you the whereabouts of a body. See, we tend to take this kind of thing with a large pinch of salt, haven't the resources...' Sergeant Roper leant past me across the desk. 'Can I help you madam?'

A young blonde girl retracted the nib of a ballpoint with a swift click, slipping the pen and small pad into her bag.

'I'm Nancy Ballinger, I'm here about the demonstration, the sit-in, to save the old Willow...'

Sergeant Roper peered over half-moon specs, 'Aren't you the reporter from the Examiner?'

I stepped to one side, 'I'm going, this is bloody pointless.' The blonde girl followed me to the door.

'Actually, forget it, I'll call back later.'

'If you want to get out ladies, I have to press this button, here, under my desk.'

'Then press it!' The blonde girl snapped. Outside the reporter held her identity card in front of me. 'Hi, I couldn't help overhearing...'

AIREBOROUGH Chronicle

PSYCHIC CLAIMS TO KNOW WHEREABOUTS OF A BODY

A 'psychic' who believes she knows the location of the body of a girl missing for 25 years has said police are refusing to act on her information.
Local florist, Morgan-Fay Jones who claims to possess psychic abilities, says she received a message from beyond the grave revealing the exact whereabouts of the body of Sabrina Knox, who went missing on the 7th of June 1993. Miss Jones says she has told police the body of the missing girl is in the grounds of Oakley Manor.
The 15-year-old was last seen walking home from school. Her body has never been found.
Miss Jones, who owns Gaia's Garden florist shop in Oakley, said the police refused to take her seriously.
She said: 'I'm distraught; Sabrina and I were like sisters.'
The loss of their daughter devastated Mr and Mrs Knox, who have since died.
Oakley Police refused to comment.

The day was hot and humid, a short fat woman shuffled into the shop, wiping her face with a crumpled handkerchief. Arm fat swinging like putty, she lifted tangled mass of gold chains and dabbed her neck. 'Are you that psychic? I need you to talk to someone. Old sod, left me bugger all, after everything I did... '

'I'm sorry, no, I'm not that kind of psychic.'

'Well according to the paper this morning you got it right about... ' The pungent smell of stale sweat was grounds enough to be rude.

'Do you intend to buy anything because if not?' Amy held the door wafting her hand as the woman passed.

'Here, Morgan-Fay look at this.'

AIREBOROUGH Chronicle

CASE OF MISSING SCHOOL GIRL RE-OPENED

The investigation into the disappearance of a schoolgirl *25 years ago took a new twist today.*
Oakley Police have released a statement saying they have received more information about missing Sabrina Knox, who was last seen walking home from school.
Today police said: 'As a result of significant new information regarding the disappearance of Sabrina Knox on June 7, 1993. The case has now been re-opened, and the grounds of Oakley Manor cordoned off. Though the police have no further comment at this stage.'

'I don't get it Amy, they wouldn't listen to me. So who's come forward and why now?'

Oakley Manor had been sealed off for several days, so it was only a matter of time. Sue Smith, ever the triumphant harbinger of bad news, laid a newspaper on the counter. Clapping her hands together in prayer position she pressed her fingers to her lips.

AIREBOROUGH Chronicle

BODY DISCOVERED AT OAKLEY MANOR

Police investigating the disappearance of missing schoolgirl Sabrina Knox have found a body.
Officers have been searching the grounds of Oakley Manor, since announcing the 25-year-old case had been re-opened.
A spokesperson for Oakley Police said: 'Sadly we can confirm a body has been discovered at the site of the search. The remains have not yet been identified. A post mortem examination is due to take place later today.'

'So then Morgan-Fay, a body, just like you said, murdered I bet.'
  'Sue please, I....'

'I bet it's that Sabrina girl, been laying there all this time and not a few hundred yards from Rowan Lodge.'

'Sue, Sabrina was my friend.'

'Just imagine we could have a murderer, right here, on our doorstep and... '

'Sue for fuck's sake!' I thrust the newspaper into her hands. 'Just fucking leave it!'

Amy surfaced from the back of the shop cradling a large bouquet. 'Has she gone? Bloody hell that's the first time I've heard you drop an 'F' bomb Morgan-Fay.

'Amy, they've found a body.'

'Where?'

'Oakley Manor, somewhere in the grounds.'

'Shit! So this psychic stuff, is it for real then?'

'Let's just say there's a lot you don't know about me Amy.'

Amy smiled. 'Oh yeah, I forgot, while you were at the bank some woman rang. Sounded Welsh I think, said she was trying to trace a Morgan-Fay Jones.'

'What did you say? Did you tell her to ring back?'

'Yeah I told her best to ring back Tuesday...'

'Tuesday! Why Tuesday?'

'Well you said you didn't want any more distractions, on account of all the wedding flowers for Saturday, then it's Sunday, Monday's bank holiday...'

'Did it not occur to you that this might just be important?' I grabbed the receiver, cringing under the scrutiny of Amy's bewildered gaze.

'Look, I'm sorry Amy, this whole Sabrina thing...take the rest of the day off, I'll pay you.'

'I'm sorry Morgan-Fay... '

'Forget it sweetie, turn the sign for me would you.'

I paced to the back room, frantically thumbing the phone, 'number withheld.' Short of breath, my fingers tingling, I clenched my fists pressing my thumbs to my lips, my nails gouging painfully into my palms. 'I know it was you Lilly-Fay, please, please, ring back.' Stifling a scream of frustration a sob punched through my chest. I filled a glass with water trying to sip past the thicket of anxiety lodged in my throat. 'Please, Lilly-Fay you've found me.'

There's one certainty in my life and that's a well-stocked wine rack. It had been a hell of a day, Tuesday seemed so far away. The uncertainly of you ringing back felt unbearable. Quaffing a large swig of Chenin Blanc, I raised my glass, 'to you Dionysus!' Slumping, exhausted to the table, I took another hefty gulp. Suddenly, Danu launched herself onto the kitchen windowsill, her back arched. A thin, fly like man with greased back hair, hands cupped around plus powered spectacles was peering through the window. Brigid joined Danu, both cats hissing their fury.

'What the hell...!'

'Miss Jones, 'Mike Styslow, Oakley Examiner. It's been confirmed that the body found at the Manor is that of Sabrina Knox. Do you have a comment?'

'You bet I do! You've got sixty seconds to get the hell out of my garden.' Following the reporter down the path, I shoved him the last few feet and out of the gate. Calming the cats, I poured more wine, taking the glass with me I wandered to Sabrina's flower bed.

'Sabrina, you poor love, I can't imagine what evil you endured. Your bitterness and anger has made this such a sad place, now it's over, you've been found. You're free, go Sabrina, there are people waiting, people who love you.'

'Goodbye Morgan-Fay.' The merest whisper on a gentle breeze, the area was bathed in light. Pungent floral scents filled the air, like never before. To my joy, Sabrina had at last found peace.

Next morning the headline was on every stand.

AIREBOROUGH Chronicle

REMAINS OF MISSING SCHOOLGIRL FOUND IN GROUNDS OF OAKLEY MANOR

A murder inquiry has been launched after a post mortem revealed the body discovered at the bottom of a disused well in Oakley Manor is that of missing schoolgirl Sabrina Knox.

STREET LIVES

A police spokesman said: 'Sadly, we can confirm the human remains found in a disused shaft in the grounds of Oakley Manor were those of Miss Knox.....'

I stared until the print merged to a grey blur, grief slowly infiltrating the wasteland in my mind. A sharp tap at the door gathered my wits. 'I'm closed.' A very freckled man with pink rimmed eyes held an I.D. card to the glass.

'Miss Jones, Sergeant Bristow, Oakley Police, may I have a word?' The sergeant brought with him a toxic blend of coffee and cigarettes. 'We need to speak to you in connection with the recent discovery of a body now known to be that of Sabrina Knox.'

'We were best friends... '

'Not here, Miss Jones, down at the station.'

'What, why?'

'We need to discuss in more depth how you appear to have known the whereabouts of the body.'

'I'm a bloody psychic! Why is that so hard to believe? Look Sergeant, please, not today.'

'We'll try not to take too much of your time Miss Jones, if you'd like to come with me.'

Interview room three was sparsely furnished with just a table, chairs and an oversized wall clock.'

'You take a seat Miss Jones; our new DCI will be with you shortly. Can I offer you a drink? We have a new coffee machine'

'Only if it dispenses Gin.'

The sun streamed in through the rectangle of frosted glass like a glitzy guest at a dull party. As the minutes ticked loudly by, I considered easing the boredom by adding my own graffiti to the already heavily etched table. Never one to be kept waiting, I concluded thirty-five minutes was half an hour too long. Shoving the chair back I grabbed my bag just as the DCI entered the room.

'Hello Morgan-Fay.'

'Patrick!'

The sound of laughter, that only one of us could hear, filled the room, nothing unladylike or boisterous, just a gentle joyous trickle.

Colonial Gossip

by

Peter Lewis

AIREBOROUGH Chronicle

Street Lives

Local historian George Broadbent is continuing his series where he looks at the history of streets in our beautiful town of Oakley.

***

Last week a local roof insulation contractor contacted me about letters he had discovered in the loft of Rowan Lodge. The letters are an interesting addendum to my article about Asgard Close. They are from a Dot Matheson to her parents who lived at Rowan Lodge during the nineteen forties. Dot lived in the North West Province of India and are a small window into Colonial life and events during the Second World War.

*

10th December 1941

Dear parents

Still feeling well though a little disturbed by the news from Malaya. Stewart has now been promoted to naval attaché at HQ C-in-C Far East and is therefore spending more and more time in Delhi, though when is home he always brings lovely treats and is very attentive to his pregnant wife. According to him, the Japanese have little chance of success, especially now the United States has entered the war. You might also have read that two of the Royal Navy's finest battleships have been sent north from Singapore to oppose the landings in Malaysia. Even so it's not quite as peaceful here as it has been, not least because many of the locals here are serving with the Indian III corps and hence are heavily involved in repulsing the Japanese.

The weather, however, remains a very pleasant 70 degrees and of course in December there is relatively little rain. Yesterday we went over to the officers' club and spent a very pleasant afternoon drinking tea while watching the bowls. Thinking of you both in wet cold Somerset.

Your loving daughter
Dot

*

12 December 1941

Dear Parents

We are still composing ourselves after receiving the horrific news about the two battleships, Repulse and Prince of Wales, which, as you will know were sunk by Japanese bombers on the same day that I wrote you my last letter. Stewart does not understand how the Japanese pilots were allowed to attack as both ships were within range of our airbase at Tengah. You may remember that he was based there when he got back from Britain last year, undertaking a review of the flying training on behalf of the Fleet Air arm. Although the Japs have had some initial success against the Indian III Army, he is confident that it will be a different story when they meet the British and Australian troops, which will be any day now. Meanwhile we have had some wonderful sunsets and yesterday was so warm (30degrees) that I was able to wear that lovely white dress that you bought me for my birthday.

Your affectionate daughter
Dot

*

STREET LIVES

15 February 1942

Dear Parents

You have no idea how shaken up we all about the news from Singapore. While Malaya is still a long, long way away, it is still a worry. Stewart reckons that over 80,000 British troops have surrendered, in addition to the 50,000 Indians and Australians taken prisoner by the Japs on their march down through Singapore.

I am now starting to look enceinte but am still in good form health wise and getting some very complimentary comments from both the officers and ladies at the club on how well I look. Even the Commodore said I looked "blooming". No real signs of morning sickness yet, thank goodness.

Stewart is off to Southern India tomorrow on one of his regular inspection tours of the port facilities in the South. It's a bit of a bore but he's cleverly managed to find a very nice place to base himself, away from the winds and heat but convenient for the coast. Somewhere called the Honnametti Estate.

Your loving daughter
Dot

Otley Writers

Martin P Fuller
A law enforcement officer for nearly thirty-five years Martin started writing five years ago when he joined Otley Writers creative writing group. His preferred genres are comedy or dark twisted tales that cause unease before midnight. Martin lives in Menston

Mari Phillips
Although Mari has lived and worked in Yorkshire for 37 years she still considers herself born and bred Welsh. She hadn't written anything since school and joining Otley Writers rekindled her love of poetry and she discovered a talent for writing short stories, flash fiction and memoirs. Her work has been published in CafeLit and the Otley Writers anthologies.

Carrie Canning
Otley born writer Carrie lives in her hometown in the beautiful Wharfe Valley. As a Druid the natural and supernatural worlds provide inspiration for her writing. Her work appears in the Otley Writers anthologies. She is working on her first book, a dark collection of tales of twisted lives and twisted minds.

Alyson Faye

Alyson is tutor/freelance editor and horror writer. She lives in Bingley with her household of rescue animals. Her hobbies include swimming, eating, old movies, singing and walking her dog doing her Heathcliff impersonation on the moors. Her latest flash fiction collection is out on Amazon. Her blog is www.alysonfaye.wordpress.com

Pamela Line

When Pamela was a child she realised she didn't want to grow up, being an adult seemed like hard work, so she didn't. Writing short stories is one way of showing and telling how she feels. Every tale has an element of truth, of an experience that has shaped her. Sharing memories is part of how we see ourselves and how others see us.

Christine Nolan

Christine's interests in Social History, Woman's Issues and Education influence her writing. Born in Leeds she grew up in a working-class home and left school without any qualifications. During her adult life she has gained a BA (Hons) degree and been involved in many social organisations. Widowed and retired she is a Bereavement Counsellor.

Sandy Wilson

Sandy writes memoirs, fiction and sometimes poetry. His book *Memory Spill* is a memoir of his childhood in Scotland. His work appears in the anthologies *The Pulse of Everything* and *The Darkening Season* and he has contributed to *The Drabble*. He has had two poems included in Indra's Net, an international poetry anthology. Sandy lives in Leeds..
www.alexanderwilsonwriter.wordpress.com

STREET LIVES

Serena Russell
Serena has deep convictions and for a number of years has felt her writings are spiritually guided. She gathered these messages and has published them in a book *Fragments of the Beyond*.
Although she has written short stories her main interest lies in poetry. Serena lives in Otley and is a member of Otley Writers.

Cynthia Richardson
After a successful career in further education, Cynthia retired from her role as Bradford and District Learning Partnership Manager in 2012. A friend encouraged her to take up writing as 'she always has a good tale to tell'. Gathering on her varied life experiences, Cynthia has a passion for writing short stories.

Alex Williams
Alex has a 'why not?' philosophy when writing. Could a shadow think for itself? Could a mushroom be a ghost? Could a man live inside a shell? The answer to all these questions has been a resounding 'why not?' She is currently working on a flash fiction collection of quirky stories and run a children's book business called 'Half Man Half Octopus.' Find out more at halfmanhalfoctopus.co.uk

Hannah Silcock
For over three hundred years Hannah and her ancestors have come from the wild lawless spaces of Northumberland. Her writing is inspired by this history. Ideas and thoughts also come from her Druid life; observing, listening, understanding, learning to interact, honouring and connecting with nature, then their stories are told.
The seasons turn and she turns with them.

Pauline Harrowell

Pauline started writing about seven years ago. Poetry is her default setting, but since joining Otley Writers she has also tried her hand at short stories and flash fiction. Pauline found being part of a group exposed her to new writing formats. She has had poems published in websites and magazines. Her work also appears in the Otley Writers anthologies.

Polly Smith

Two years ago I decided to explore the world of creative writing with the 'Otley Writers'. The humour, talent and support from the Group has inspired me to keep going. To date writing has become a favourite pastime that triggers interest in all manner of topics.

Kelly McCarthy

Kelly McCarthy has been a professional art doodler for many years, producing moving doodles for the BBC and ITV and static doodles for Royal Doulton and Boots and painterly doodles for various galleries. She is now doodling with words.

Jo Campbell

Jo writes flash fiction and short stories with a passion for supernatural horror and dark tales. She has work published on Horrortree.com *Trembling with Fear* and in Otley Writers anthologies *The Pulse of Everything* and *The Darkening Season*. She has performed her work at Leeds Art Gallery and Ilkley Literature Festival. Jo blogs as : Jocampbellcreepycreations.wordpress.com

Russell Lloyd

Former husband, Army Officer, solicitor, invigilator, postman, TV extra, life class model, taxi despatcher, pollster, mystery shopper, medicine evaluator, interviewer, warehouseman, clerk, waiter, Charity Secretary, Quaker warden.

Russell writes for the joy and flare of ink among the lines to unwhitened the page within and without.

John Ellis

John has lived in Yorkshire for most of his life and has spent many years exploring Yorkshire's diverse landscapes, history, language and communities. He recently retired after a career in teaching. In addition to the Yorkshire Murder Mystery series he writes poetry, ghost stories and biography. He is currently working on his memoirs of growing up in a working-class area of Huddersfield in the 1950s and 1960s.

www.jrellisyorkshirewriter.com

Acknowledgements

Otley Writers creative writing group would like to thank

Chris Canning who designed the book cover and the illustrations.

Sandy Wilson who formatted and published the book.

John Ellis for proof reading.

Otley Writers Publications

Writers write to be read, or what is the purpose of it all. This sounds like something I may have read somewhere, but it is what I truly believe. This innate need to be read led our creative writing group Otley Writers to publish our own works.

Street Lives is an ambitious anthology of fictional stories about the inhabitants of an imaginary street, Asgard Close. Astonishingly for such a small group, many members too have published their own books in a wide range of genres from crime fiction to horror and children's stories to memoir. Information about these exciting publications can be found on the next few pages.

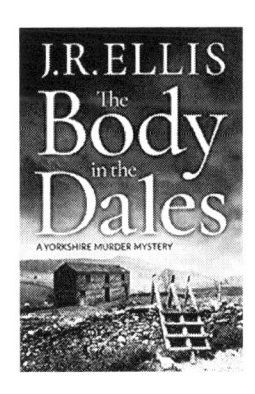

The Body in the Dales is a murder mystery that introduces Detective Chief Inspector Oldroyd. A local man is found murdered in a cave system in strange circumstances. The case proves to be a perplexing investigation for Jim Oldroyd with no shortage of suspects. Set in the Yorkshire Dales the book reflects author John Ellis's love of the region and Yorkshire culture.

The Quartet Murders the second Chief Inspector Oldroyd murder mystery is set in Halifax in Yorkshire where a violin player is murdered during a performance attended by Jim Oldroyd. The resulting criminal investigation involves a priceless violin, the ruthless world of wealthy instrument collectors and the theft of valuable artefacts by the Nazis during the Second World War.

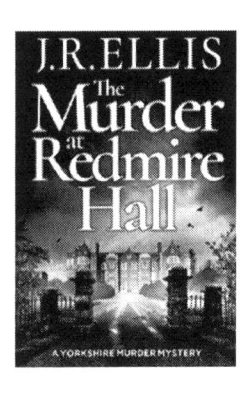

The Murder at Redmire Hall is the third Chief Inspector Oldroyd murder mystery.
An impossible murder takes place behind a locked door during a spectacular illusion.
DCI Jim Oldroyd and his team investigate this Agatha Christie-esque crime.

STREET LIVES

Memory Spill by Sandy Wilson is a humorous and at times poignant account of his childhood in Scotland. The memoir begins in 1953 and spans almost two decades. It is a time when life was uncomplicated. At Lasswade Primary School an inappropriate film is screened, a railway station mysterious burns down and children dance with the devil...........

Bad Lands by Alyson Faye is a collection of flash fiction pieces, from drabbles of 100 words to longer pieces up to 1000 words. Written over the last three years my short shorts reflect my interest in ghost stories, history, old movies, real life issues such as homelessness and just the 'what if' factor when a seemingly normal situation starts to tilt off centre, leading to dangerous waters.

The Runaway Umbrella is a book with illustrations for children aged with illustrations. Izzy buys a penguin umbrella from the Rainy Days shop, when a wind gets up the umbrella takes flight. Izzy sets off on a chase helped by various people, but there is something magical about it. Will she ever catch it?

STREET LIVES

In a **Bench for Billie Holiday** James Nash tenderly retraces seventy years of life through seventy new sonnets. Whether lightly sketching moments of truth or revisiting his younger self with the benefits of insight and experience, he imbues each fourteen-line fragment with wit, wisdom and wonder.

Maggie Moore's hilarious adventures over one school year. She gets the worst part in the school play, her world record attempt goes disastrously wrong and as for her act in the talent show, well let's just say she didn't expect underpants to fly out of her trumpet and land on the judge's face. Still at least she has three best friends and this, her diary.
Alex L Williams writes as Firna Rex Shaw.

Meet Eric Trum, the stick man with a big bum. This is another children's character from the inventive mind of Alex L Williams writing as Jonny Staples. Find out how things don't always run smoothly for the little stick man. If it's not his large bottom getting in the way, it's his neighbour Jeremy Mothballs, trying to spoil his fun. How will he cope?

STREET LIVES

Chris Moran's poetry is eclectic and entertaining, even whimsical, spiritual and philosophical, deeply personal and relatable. The book charts her recovery from alcoholism and the depths of despair and subsequent multiple sclerosis diagnosis. Her poetry documents her life with courageous honesty and unexpected humour. Profits from this book go to the Multiple Sclerosis Trust.

With these endlessly inventive and marvellous poems Glenda Kerney Brown explores the things that she values, the things she cleaves to, and the underlying tragedy of our human experience, which is that we inevitably lose the things we love. With an artist's palette Glenda commemorates the past, celebrates the present and contemplates the future in honest and beautiful poetry.

Serena Russell believes we all carry the seed of enlightenment within us. The messages in this book are a small collection of those received by her over the years.
Beautiful poetic writing of a profound religious experience.

OTLEY WRITERS

Printed in Great
Britain
by Amazon